The Last Remnants

VISION

K.P. Merriweather

MAJESTIK MULTIMEDIA • ST. LOUIS

The Last Remnants
Volume 1: VISION
Published by Majestik Multimedia
A subsidiary of Create Space Independent Publishing Platform
Copyright © 2009 Kimberly Merriweather

First Edition

This book is set in Lora Type Text with some portions set in Andalus Type.

Printed in the United States of America

First Edition: August 2016
First Printing: August 2016

ISBN-13: 978-0692550694
ISBN-10: 0692550690

For more awesomeness, visit *Majestik Multimedia*!
www.majestikmultimedia.com

CHAPTER ONE

Pained wailing startled Joni Warren awake in total darkness. She laid frozen by indescribable terror as the nightmarish sound of the hollow agonized cries reverberated around her. Joni *knew* if she didn't get up, the monster would torture her next.

It was always the same: at first it was *nothing*, just gloomy shades swirling in the distance. The shadowy haze grew from the edge, transforming into not an animal, or human, or article, or even an amalgam of all three, but into some faceless monstrous creature with numerous arms and legs and sharp jagged teeth. It never had eyes. Those pools of void would *rob* her soul - sealing her away *forever*.

The monster brought with it insurmountable feelings of dread and horror nearly driving Joni to the brink. The *powerlessness* against the violence it wrought... she hated since she couldn't combat *it* directly. No manner of spells, martial skill, or weapons of monster-creature-hunting-slaying-destroyer-power worked against the beast – the incantations were weak or reflected or negated or simply didn't turn *on* and the enchanted weapons *always* broke or exploded or fizzled against it – yet this faceless monster always screamed at her, hating her, loathing her, wanting her, needing her, desiring *her*...

Willing herself to move, Joni sat up, then struggled to her feet. She reached out blindly in the darkness and grasped a knob then turned it, opening a door. Joni cried out when bright light blinded her.

Once her eyes adjusted, she saw the exit revealed bright sun glistening on newly fallen snow. Joni drew a shallow breath and stepped out onto the meadow. The view of unspoiled beauty transformed into a valley in spring surrounded by fields of wildflowers with a small cabin in the distance. Turning back, the door behind her faded into smoke, leaving her in the grasslands.

"I know I'm dreaming," Joni said to no one in particular. Yet when she tried willing herself awake, she never left from where she stood. She reached up and felt the chain around her neck, holding the amethyst pendant she cherished. "This can't be real!" Blowing a heavy sigh, Joni started walking for the cabin, hoping if she found someone there, they would be kind.

She soon approached the cabin surrounded by overgrown shrubbery. Joni noticed as she came closer, the wooden planks were old and worn and the place appeared abandoned. She peered into the dusty windows, unable to make out if anyone lived inside. Joni grunted when the rusted handle refused to turn once she tried the front door.

Stomping for the rear porch, the cabin's side door abruptly opened and Joni came to a full stop when a tall, tanned broad-shouldered young man with shoulder-length dark hair stepped outside. He wore a navy overcoat, black gloves, dark brown slacks, black boots and smoky glasses donned his face. Joni gasped when she sensed faint pangs of recognition course through her, yet she couldn't call to mind who he was.

"What are you doing here?" demanded the mysterious young man.

Joni suddenly found it hard to speak as he took long strides, immediately closing the gap between them. He grabbed her by the waist, pulling her near and gazed intently into Joni's eyes. She shoved the young man away and socked him across the jaw, forcing him staggering rearwards.

"Get your hands off me!" Joni shouted. The stranger chortled and Joni shuddered, disgusted. She jumped, punching him a second time and knocked him to the ground. "Who do you think you are feeling me up like that?" she spat over him, clenching her busted hand while the young man at her feet held a hand to his mouth.

"I was just feeling you out," the stranger murmured.

"You're not real!" Joni turned away. "I'm dreaming and you don't exist!"

"This is real," he said softly. "Look at me."

"Just tell me how to get out of here."

"Do you really believe I'm just a figment of your imagination?"

Joni groaned and ran a hand through her hair. "*My dreams tend to be lucid,*" she thought. "*There's no way to tell!*" Joni heard him stand and dust himself off. Turning, she stared back at him thoughtfully.

"What makes you think I'm only a dream to you?" implored the stranger.

"You *have* to be a dream," Joni declared. "Things like this don't happen to me – guys like you don't notice me."

The young man smirked and shrugged his shoulders. "What can I say?" he replied.

"Tell me, why am I here?"

"It's difficult to explain," the stranger answered, "but just know I'm not going to hurt you. I'm here to help you, okay?"

"What are you going on about, *helping* me?" Joni scoffed. "I don't need your help!"

"You *will* and you *do*." Joni pushed past him, marching for the cabin's rear porch. "Well, I guess I'll see you later."

Joni glowered back at him. "Yeah, right!" she grumbled. The stranger waved at her then stalked off, heading for the woods.

Joni, left behind, glared at his back in shock. "*Why didn't he say anything?*" she wondered. "*Why are you being so weird to me?*" Before she could take off after him, a haunting voice called her name.

"Who's calling me?" Joni answered, searching around.

The door to the cabin creaked open and she whirled around, grasping her pendant. Finding no one on the other side, Joni relaxed slightly and cautiously made her way inside. The chill, dank atmosphere nearly suffocated Joni and the cold dampness wove around her limbs as she searched for the source of the voice.

"Joni..."

Joni entered more rooms, heading farther into the rear until coming across the final door. She hesitated as a clammy sensation enveloped her body and her palms grew moist with perspiration.

Joni's lungs constricted - her heart fluttered in her chest like a panic-stricken bird - and she grew sick with fear, utterly terrified of what may be on the other side. She forcibly took in a deep breath in an effort to calm herself and shut her eyes for a long moment before releasing them as she exhaled, then opened the door.

Her eyes widened in terror and she screamed, *horrified* at what she saw. Despite the dim lighting, she saw clearly the crumpled bloodied heap at her feet: a young man with a deep gash around his neck with the split open wound traveling down his chest.

Contents from his body spewed in every direction, with gobs of crimson and black gelled guts staining the walls and floor, streaming in a pool beneath his mutilated form. His head, sickeningly twisted in an unnatural manner, exposed flayed skin and sinewy tendons from the mortal wound.

Joni recognized his ghastly pallid face and his blank, glassy, haunted brown eyes staring sightlessly wide into dead space. His mouth, frozen open in a silent scream, had his tongue hanging grotesquely to the side.

Joni tried in vain shutting her mind to the cruel realization of the cold execution, her thoughts descending into gibbering madness when it came to the surface full force. She refused to believe such an innocent soul could meet such a grisly end. Joni's knees buckled and she dropped onto the ground in despair. She gingerly ran her

hands through his sticky hair, caressing his skin that was ice cold to her touch. Her mind shut down at once, marking out her world.

Joni roused when a firm hand shook her by the shoulder.

"Joni, can you hear me?" called a gentle voice.

Opening her eyes, she gasped when she saw a middle-aged man with short graying sandy hair and tired green eyes wearing a pale blue suit kneeling next to her.

"Dad!" Joni cried and sat up, frightened and relieved all at once. "What are you doing here?" She threw her arms around him and started sobbing. "I'm scared... I can't do it alone."

Her father rubbed at her back. "You're plenty strong," he murmured in her ear. "Please believe it."

"It's trying to kill me! Please help me."

Pulling away once her tears subsided, Joni's father took her hands in his, squeezing them gently. "I'm sorry," he said softly. "I can't..."

"Then why did you come back?" Joni wailed.

He looked away, his face shadowed by pain. "I came to apologize," he muttered.

"About what?" Joni shook her head. "You did what you thought was right."

"No, I was careless and let my ego get out of control."

"What are you saying?"

"It's a tragic mistake, the whole thing..."

"I don't understand..."

"I probably can't stop it from happening, but please, don't follow in my footsteps." Joni took his face in her hands, forcing him to look at her. He gave a sad smile, looking directly into her eyes. "Live your own life."

"What are you trying to warn me about?" Joni asked as he removed her hands and rose to his feet. "Dad, please tell me!" He walked past her, heading for the dark door. Joni scrambled to her feet and hurried after him, grabbing him by the arm before he grasped the handle. "Please, don't go in there," she pleaded. "It'll kill us both!"

"You can't run from it forever," he replied and slipped out of her grasp. Opening the door, he instantly faded into mist.

On the other side, the monster stirred. Joni backed away, shaking. It was going to catch her and torture her again if she didn't find a hiding place. Even after waking up, always screaming and thrashing, it would happen *again* the next night when she closed her eyes.

The monster *always* waited for her, lurking under her bed, hiding behind her closet. It followed her daily, wherever she went – to the park, to school, to the store – even lurking around her family when she visited them with great reluctance. Yet no matter where she ran, the monster continually found her and took its time, savoring her pain as it pulled her apart with demented glee.

Joni *knew* how to pretend – she was a skilled actress. Though it pained her inside to lie constantly, Joni understood she had to give up everything if she accepted the monster into her life. Her life would cease to exist if she allowed *it* to surface.

The monster mocked her, laughing at her from its hiding place. It beckoned to her and Joni refused as usual.

This time it'll be different from before, she kept telling herself.

It used to happen in the background without her being present – but *this* time, the monster was going out into the open. It wore her down until she was too tired to stop it.

The monster swore, in no uncertain terms, that it was going to destroy *everything* she ever loved. Joni was too frightened to speak, afraid to say the names that it might use to mark them for death, yet deep down she accepted Death already had them listed. It was just *waiting...*

It was going to happen, this time in her presence, and this time involving her *directly*. Joni didn't know how soon – though it was soon enough – and she was going to *suffer*.

Joni screamed.

There was no denying it, no evading it, no *destroying* it even. She tried mightily tracking its source and stop it *by all means* – but it was always impossible and she accepted she had *no* chance.

Though by now *doomed*, Joni tried putting on a brave front and fought skillfully at her best, yet she lost *every time*. The beast devoured her, forcing her to become part of that lurking shadow threatening to stop her heart once she acknowledged it lived.

It happened *again*.

The monster advanced anyway, ascending and descending and making its way from the edge of the shadowy depths, finally catching up to where it cornered her, nailing her to the wall of swirling pitch below.

The constant pain, *tearing* at every manner of fiber in her being, happened here and elsewhere and far away, always hot and cold, prickly and burning, numb and throbbing, but always here as well, in the place she always *thought* it was safe.

The monster jammed its sharp claws and jagged teeth into Joni's soft flesh, slashing her to shreds as it ripped her apart piece by piece, mightily rending her to ribbons of tendon and bone.

It was always then she woke up screaming.

CHAPTER TWO

Joni stepped off the school bus with haste and raced down the street. She had to cover two miles before getting home and figured with her middling speed, she would most likely miss the phone call she foresaw.

"*It's only true if I make it true!*" Joni thought. "*Give me ten more minutes!*"

A sudden roar spooked her and she turned around, spotting a motorcyclist barreling down the road. Joni jumped back as the tall lean helmeted rider approached, stopping nearby.

The cyclist appeared ominous wearing all black: a motor jacket with zippers and chains, tough denim jeans and stiff leather boots. The sleek black helmet came off, revealing a pale-faced young man with silvery bobbed hair, bright violet eyes and a beaming wide-toothed smile.

"Hey Joni," the motorcyclist said pleasantly. "Want a lift?"

"I ought to smack you, Signe!" Joni screeched and hit Signe on the shoulder with her backpack, forcing him dropping his helmet. "Don't scare me like that!"

"I wasn't trying to," Signe complained.

"Well, don't do that again!"

Joni scooped up the helmet before it rolled away and tossed it to him. Signe caught it and placed the helmet on his head as Joni slipped her backpack over her shoulders.

Getting behind him on the cycle, she placed her arms firmly around his waist. Signe nodded, flipped down the visor and revved the engine, then took off with purpose.

Joni thought about her day and the earlier week as Signe darted through traffic, heading for her house. Glad that Friday finally came, Joni relished her weekend recovering from surviving her hectic week after as a junior in high school. Looking forward to the first football game later that evening, Joni couldn't wait to go cheer for her alma mater, Nortiniry High.

Nortiniry was notorious for having a losing football team, the Knights. The mid-sized town's school district - built on a pyramid system with four elementary schools, two middle schools and one high school - couldn't compete against other districts with more schools. Most people around town blamed the small school's constant pool of poor talent on the coaches.

Joni found it hilarious when the district brought in a professional coach to help the team become successful. In the end, it was a miserable failure: when the Knights played against all the other schools, they still got beaten badly each time.

Joni found joy in watching the team playing for the hope of one win, though it never came. The Knights lost each game the year before and with the best seniors gone from last season, the new players were assumed even worse.

Joni couldn't wait to get to the stands and heckle the opposing fans as well as chide the other players. All while she cheered for her favorite team that made playing badly seem like an art form.

She wanted something to cheer for to escape, putting herself fully into a demanding exercise to get her away from the reality that pushed her close to the edge. Though high school football was a means to get out the house and away from it all, Joni also put herself into any sports she could manage getting into.

Joni was quick to protest when the coaches complained about her playing sports deemed exceptionally dangerous for girls. She made them eat their words with the intensity she approached each

game. Joni was proud of her accomplishments in playing with the boys on her team – especially football and hockey – even if only used in practice as a fill-in.

Joni constantly pestered the other teams, threatening them with her yet untested skill. It wasn't that she could play very well, since she couldn't throw any farther than arm's length, or strike the puck any farther than from crease to the offside line; it was due to owning supernatural talents that no other people had.

Accused of being a witch many times before, Joni didn't think of herself as such. She didn't ride a broom since she had no idea how to fly, let alone levitate and she completely, almost passionately, hated cats. Joni had no warts on her face, though she had one on her wrist that kept coming back with a vengeance.

However, she possessed abilities few seventeen-year-old girls had: casting simple spells and healing those who had minor injuries. Joni could even see what was happening in places far from her home. There was even a time she caught a glimpse of the future.

Joni thought about the day she had a dream about a phone call several months ago. It seemed to come from a future version of herself, warning about a death of someone close to her.

First she worried it was about her older sister who was attending college a few states over. The matter didn't improve after getting a strange letter from Kacey detailing her distress of trying to earn her degree and dealing with their father's illness.

Joni didn't believe it at first, not wanting to will the matter coming true. She was utterly devastated when her father passed over the summer, occurring on the day school let out for the annual three-month vacation. Joni still wasn't over it, even after getting the vision. For three months, she fell into a deep depression her mother found difficult bringing her out of.

When the relationship became too strained, Joni stayed with her grandparents who welcomed her in. They grew concerned with her increasing isolation and refusing to speak to them, closing herself off in her father's old room where he grew up.

After sending Joni to live with her uncle and aunt, the only excuse she had was the hustle and bustle of the city life became too much. Joni had no problems with them, yet felt ignored by their indifference, as they focused more on their demanding jobs. Frustrated with other people in general, Joni returned to the lake house, closing herself off totally for the rest of the season.

Her thoughts returned to her father, a powerful magician named Terrell. He was one of the few people who helped Joni understand her magical abilities and never hesitated helping others with them, even to the point of using his restoration skill selflessly.

Still upset and angered that he fell easily to an inexplicable illness of indeterminate origin, she found it difficult accepting knowing he had a strong healing skill. Joni hated the world after his refusal to heal himself from whatever it was, helpless and unable to save him when she watched him fall asleep and never wake again.

Joni increased her grip around Signe, burying her face into his shoulder as the warm late summer winds blew through her wavy red hair.

"I shouldn't be bitter," she mused, "but I hate that I'm around nobody else who'd understand anything about Magic!"

Joni secretly wished she could let the pain and hatred go, but it was her only connection to her memories. She felt if she did, they would fade like ash into water, never to surface again.

Signe pulled onto the lone dirt road and approached the driveway leading to a small stone cottage. He cut off the engine as Joni hopped off and hurried up the steps, slipping her pack off her back.

"What's the rush?" Signe asked, taking off his helmet. He walked behind her while she searched frantically for her keys. Joni dropped her pack once she retrieved the keys and unlocked the door.

"I'm expecting a phone call," Joni declared once the door came open. Dashing inside, the telephone rang once before she could approach. Quickly diving for it, Joni struck the button that activated its speaker. She grunted after hitting the floor with a hard thump and cringed in pain.

"Hey, Greta!" Joni greeted breathlessly from her place on the floor.

"How'd you know it was me?" Greta yelped in surprise from the other end of the line.

"Call it a good feeling," Joni said, grimacing as she got up. Signe entered the parlor with the helmet tucked under his arm moments later and chuckled at the sight of her. Drawing closer, Signe held out his free hand to Joni and she pushed him away, shaking her fist at him. "So, are you going to the football game tonight?"

"Yeah, of course we're going!" Greta retorted. "I've got to cheer on Ryan, remember?"

"We're just going to lose anyway," Signe drawled, rolling his eyes. "I can't believe you're going regardless! You should just forget about it and make better use of your time." Joni glared at him, her face immediately flushed red. She kicked his shin and Signe broke into a fit of laughter. He dropped his helmet and doubled over, clutching his sides as he guffawed. "You're so cute when you're pissed!" Signe crowed. "You should see your face!"

"You're not saying what I think you're saying!" Joni snapped.

"Is that Signe Blanco?" Greta asked.

"Unfortunately, yes," Joni griped.

Signe calmed and stood upright, tousling Joni's hair. "I mean it," he said, "the Nortiniry Knights lose to the TriCity Titans every year!"

"Damn Joni, why is it that you're always taking the cute ones?" Greta complained. "You don't even *date* them!"

"I don't know," Joni protested. "The good-looking ones just want my attention."

Signe grinned wolfishly. "It's not our fault us men are attracted to pretty redheads," he said and leaned over, kissing Joni on the head. "I'm off helping Mister Arcendo in the shop. Tell Greta and Ryan I'll see them at the game."

"Which Arcendo?" Greta cut in. "Dad Arcendo or Uncle Arcendo?"

"His uncle Howard," Signe clarified as he picked up his helmet.

"I thought it wasn't worth your time, Signe," Joni retorted.

"Laters," Signe called, waving a hand over his head.

"You'd better make it your time," Greta grumbled. "I thought you swore to come see Ryan kick TriCity's ass tonight!"

Halfway across the floor before he neared the front door, Signe halted and whirled around, stunned. "I didn't say that!" he fussed.

"Oh my God, he's picking up a knife!" Greta cried in mock horror. "Signe, you'd better come or he'll slash his wrists! I'm serious; Ryan's sharpening it right now! What kind of person are you?"

Signe snorted and shook his head. "You got me," he said with a wry smile. "I'll come! Just stop pulling my arm, okay?"

"Besides that, Joni," Greta continued, "I want Signe to meet my new boyfriend, Slake."

"Is he there right now?" Joni asked as she got up off the floor.

"No, he's not here. Is he there at your house?"

"Yes, Greta," Joni teased, rolling her eyes. "He's hiding under my bed as we speak."

Ryan laughed out loud from the other end of the line.

"Shut up, Ryan!" Greta screeched.

"Stop stealing her boyfriends," Signe ragged and approached Joni, punching her playfully on her shoulder. "Come on and date me, will you? I'm horny as hell and I'll turn gay if you don't go out with me!"

Joni punched Signe's arm in return. "Go home!" she spat. Signe laughed again and put on his helmet.

"He's got a point you know," Ryan replied.

Signe waved Joni goodbye and stepped out, shutting the door behind him.

"So, Greta," Joni said as she leaned against the table, "is Ryan finally playing the *big position?*"

"Ryan thinks Coach Oran is nuts putting him in as quarterback," Greta answered. "He's too skinny and too lame to throw the ball." Joni giggled when she heard Greta suddenly squeal and yell 'owch!' "I'm killing you, Ryan!" she squawked.

"Tell him good luck for me, okay?" Joni said as laughter and rushed footsteps filled the line.

"We'll pick you up later," Ryan's voice called from far away.

"Tackle her good, Ryan!" Joni jeered. "I promise; I'll be at the door this time." She shut off the speakerphone function and let out a heavy sigh.

It was an inside joke among her friends that Joni always stole Greta's boyfriends. Joni thought her magnetic personality attracted them and they always wanted to call her, asking her all sorts of questions and hoping for a date.

Joni preferred they talked to Greta as her runs with boys never seemed to work out after a month or so. Though Joni turned down all offers, she still felt guilty about Greta unable to find the love she craved.

"*I hope this new boyfriend of the moment leaves me alone!*" Joni thought as she left the parlor. "*As long as I have these freaky Powers, dating's so out of the question!*"

CHAPTER THREE

Heading into the kitchen, Joni's thoughts wandered on this mystifying person named Slake while she browsed her pantry for an afternoon snack. Joni paused in front of her refrigerator, realizing she never even heard of such a boy, let alone know if he was even in any of her classes.

"Maybe if I check the lake for answers," Joni murmured as the sound of thunder rumbled softly in the distance. "It's not like I'm able to ask Signe or anyone else right now..."

She kicked shut her refrigerator and scooped up her spare key on the nearby counter then headed out the back door through her kitchen, exiting into fresh air.

Joni shielded her eyes from the harsh afternoon sunlight filtering through the trees. She stopped short at a squirrel on her porch frozen in place, spooked by her sudden appearance. Breaking out in cold sweat, Joni carefully walked by and the bold squirrel eyed her closely as it refused to leave the path.

Picking up a nearby rock, Joni chucked it, forcing the squirrel sprinting out of sight. "Damn yard rat!" she fussed as the rodent scrambled up the tree, chattering at her.

Joni shuddered and hurried down the steps and onto the walkpath. Once waking to find such a squirrel on her chest after a morning nap on the back porch, she now feared rodents of any type – including gerbils, hamsters and guinea pigs. However, squirrels drew most of Joni's ire and she'd antagonize them every chance she got.

Joni ambled through the narrow path under the shade of sky-reaching maples and tall pines as she ventured into the woods behind her house, going toward a small pond away from the cottage. The melodies of various songbirds assaulted her ears as she walked in near-seclusion, drowning out her thoughts about her father who had the cottage built on the land after saving for years and purchasing the materials.

The house seemed out of place with the other homes in the area, crafted mainly of stonework and brick. The environmentally friendly cottage had a small windmill on the far rear of the home's boundary, solar panels on the roof, and rainwater catch for power conversion.

Joni quickened her pace once she drew closer to the pond. She shivered slightly, despite wearing a heavy sweater against the chilly air surrounding her. Though she usually enjoyed the wind against her, Joni knew she didn't have time to waste, already regretting her promise to wait on her friends.

The unaltered woodlands in the rear of her home brought back the strongest memories of her father. Joni felt more at ease from the nature enveloping her and happy memories began to surface. Passing by a patch of flowers and herbs used for various teas, slowly, the bitterness returned.

Recalling Terrell growing steadily ill from an unknown sickness that even the doctors couldn't understand, Joni used her best healing skill in crafting various teas for him, given the plants and resources.

"There's nothing anyone can do, Jelly Bean," Terrell told her one day, "not even the gods."

"I nearly knocked myself out making this," Joni complained. "Why don't you just make yourself better from whatever it is?"

"It's my time to go." Terrell gave a faint smile and ran a weak hand through her hair.

"But you're in your prime!" Joni protested. "You're not even forty-nine yet! So, why now?"

"The good die young, you see," Terrell said dryly and Joni winced.

"Then why should I waste my time making all these teas for you?"

"Because you love me... At least I hope you do."

"Argh, Dad," Joni snapped, "don't say stuff like that!" She punched him on his arm and Terrell chuckled in response. Joni blushed, immediately growing embarrassed.

"Then keep making teas for me," he said. "Stay with me, will you?"

Joni nodded and continued to do as requested; making teas and listening to the stories he had to tell.

As the weeks progressed, Joni grew increasingly troubled. She knew Terrell had other abilities – ones he would always fail to elaborate on – but the main ability that gave her the most worry was his power to heal others with a mere touch.

Joni voiced her concerns about his getting similar symptoms after healing someone, afraid he would grow too physically sick due to the constant strain, and eventually kill himself.

"You're not a god, Dad!" Joni complained after another discussion. "Why do you do keep doing this? You're not supposed to do this."

"I help others," Terrell said simply. "I do it so nobody else would have to feel pain. The world is so full of it..."

"But isn't that the part of living? Isn't pain supposed to help us remember the good times?"

"If I can take it away for a while, it makes me happy that these people are better, at least for longer," Terrell explained. "They can finish what they need to do in order to die in peace."

"But what about you?"

"I'll be fine, Jelly Bean."

"What about me?"

"You're not strong enough to do what I do," Terrell told her sternly. "I don't want you to do what I do."

"Why not? I've gotten better – I can heal minor scrapes and aches even!"

Terrell waved her away. "You don't need to use up your will helping those who come to you. So don't take their illness head on... Give it to the earth and let Her take care of it."

"How do I do that?"

Terrell shook his head. "You can't save me with that technique... I've got too many years of taking away too many symptoms." He took her hand and gave it a firm squeeze. "It's too much for you to handle, even the earth. I would just poison it."

Joni said nothing, having run out of any more excuses to get her father to change his mind. She later had her suspicions when an unknown stranger called the house and mistook Joni's voice for her mother's.

The grateful caller told Joni about Terrell's treatments which were helping him getting better from an incurable illness. Joni promised to send his thanks while looking in on her father who was white as the sheets. Later, Joni worried what was to become of Terrell once he began declining the teas and chose to stay in bed more often, opting to look outside to the woods.

One afternoon, Joni tried prying answers from Terrell to no avail. "Dad, what did you try to heal that guy from?" she asked.

"Whatever do you mean, Jelly Bean?" Terrell quipped.

"Come on, Dad!" Joni complained. "Don't play around! Somebody called a few days ago, telling me how great you were in helping them overcome some illness the doctors said he had no chance to recover from!" Terrell tensed and looked away, avoiding her gaze. "Dad, what is it you took a part of? Why can't they find it in you?"

"Don't worry about it," Terrell grumbled.

Joni grabbed him by the shoulders, holding him firmly. "You have to let it go!"

"I can't," Terrell said simply. "I... I just can't." Joni clenched her teeth as Terrell gently pried off her fingers. "There's something I want you to take..."

"What is it?"

"First, this." Terrell reached around the back of his neck and unclasped his silver chain he wore of an amethyst pendant shaped into a heart. "My lucky charm."

"It's not so lucky now, is it?" Joni cracked.

Terrell chortled and handed it over to Joni. "Also, there's something else... it's in the basement. Take it after I leave."

"I'll do that," Joni murmured and took the necklace from his outstretched hand.

Terrell gave her hands a gentle squeeze and let go, averting his gaze to the window. Joni stood there for several moments, powerless and without anything else to say. After several long moments of silence, Terrell spoke again.

"I know you like to use the future sight when the sun is out on the water," he started.

"I don't travel too far," Joni admitted.

"Don't get lost." Joni nodded. "Also, remember; never look into moonlit water, understand?"

"I promise."

Joni sighed and looked out the window as well. She stiffened at the sight of a faint apparition standing there, waiting. It vanished quickly into mist before she could say anything.

The next day, Terrell was dead.

Approaching the pristine true-blue waters, Joni looked down at its glassy surface, sparkling from the afternoon sun. She found it odd the water's surface was eerily still despite the breeze blowing around her. Kneeling down, Joni stared back at her crisp reflection.

"I want to go where Greta and Ryan are," she said softly and touched the frigid water, forming ripples across its surface.

Her reflection wavered and the cool breeze picked up, throwing about dust and leaves. Joni sat on the edge, waiting for the image to clear as the background of the woods and the afternoon sunlight and her mirrored copy faded.

The broken scenery quickly stabilized, turning into a sunny afternoon kitchen inside Greta's house. Ryan sat at the table, one hand in a bowl of popcorn while the other flipped through a teen magazine. Greta sat across from him, feet on his lap while she ran an emery board across her long fingernails.

"I wish I was strong enough to hear them as well as see," Joni complained, watching the two talking soundlessly. Greta looked up suddenly, pausing in mid-stroke. She nudged Ryan and he ignored her, stuffing a handful of popcorn into his mouth. "Does she notice me?" Greta set down the emery board and got to her feet, suddenly nervous. "Okay, I won't watch you anymore!" Greta seemed relieved and the image slowly faded.

The cold winds began to subside and Joni gasped, noticing the afternoon sun had furthered from the sky and the pinks and violets of sunset turned into the blues and grays of dusk. Remembering her promise to her friends, Joni quickly stood.

"They're probably at my doorstep, banging and hollering for me!" Joni thought and took a step away. Before she headed back to the path, she recalled her reasons for coming out. "That's right, Greta's new boyfriend... I wanted to know if he'll be a keeper." Glancing back at the pond, Joni grew uneasy looking down at the evening sky filling it. "Dad warned me not to look into the water when the moon's out... But it's not out."

Returning to the edge, she knelt down, touching its surface and gasped when no ripples formed. "What the--?" Joni cried when her fingers appeared to touch glass. "That can't be right!"

The clouds moved from the sky, revealing a ray of moonlight. Joni pulled her hand away, watching in shock and awe as silver threads formed from the droplets of water. The clouds continued to pass and the full light of the moon came into view, strengthening the silvery threads and holding down her hand. Joni pulled hard, trying to break them.

"*I can't stay here!*" she thought frantically. "*Dad warned me about looking into the water with the moon... I just can't deal with that right now!*"

Joni gave a firm yank, only to have a great force pull her forward. She pulled away and tumbled back, striking hard on the ground. She cried out in terror, watching her body slump backwards.

"What's going on?" Joni murmured, looking down at her pale hands. "Why am I separated from my body? Am I dead?" She looked back at the pond of moonlit water and the exterior wavered, as if static filled it. Joni touched it and the silvery surface changed into dark mist. "What's this?"

The image cleared, showing a darkened room. Before Joni could study more closely, the room faded and many scattered images sped by, eventually slowing to focus in on a tiled room with hardwood flooring.

"*That's the school gymnasium,*" Joni noted and tensed when she saw a middle-aged man with a short spiky white hair wearing a dark trench coat pacing outside the door. He banged at the door with the flat of his hand and pointed a shotgun in her direction.

Joni gasped and the view flickered out, changing and shifting to show a tall young man with tortoise-green horn-rimmed glasses and feathered shoulder-length orange hair wielding a glowing long sword, charging toward her.

Joni shielded her face as he leaped at her, only to vanish. The pond's surface gained many cracks on its face and standing in his place was a short young man with waist-length greasy blond hair.

He wore dark clothing similar to Signe's cycling outfit, surrounded by shadows.

Joni withdrew, noticing the young man held a mystical hardened weapon glimmering in cold pale light. He beckoned to Joni and she shook her head, stepping away. The blond's face darkened in rage and he slashed down, releasing the sound of shattered glass. Joni ducked as shards flew in her direction.

Once the fog faded, Joni watched in horror as dark red began filling the pool. Touching the water, she found her hand easily went through and scooped the liquid in her cupped hand.

Joni realized in horror that she held not dyed water, but blood. Suddenly bubbles appeared on the surface. Without thought, Joni reached in and touched slight warmth. She grasped onto the mystifying object and yanked out the collar of a pure white sport coat.

Intrigued and disturbed, Joni ignored the voice of reason yelling at her to leave the matter alone. She pulled with all her might, even getting on her haunches and reaching in with both hands. Giving a final pull with what strength she had left, the heavy object released from its binds and Joni fell back with a hard thud, stunned when she revealed a tall slender young man covered in tacky crimson.

"What are you doing in there?" Joni cried and climbed forward, grabbing him before he sank back into the reddened deep.

Holding the mysterious stranger in her arms, Joni brushed his sticky feathered blond hair from his face, sensing his shallow breathing slowly thin as the heat from his body turned cold. She sucked in a breath, noticing that his pure white sport coat slowly turned red from absorbing the bloody water.

"Who are you?" Joni inquired. "Why are you dying?"

The young man looked up at her, his deep blue eyes displaying sadness and pain. Joni stroked his thin, delicate face and he took her hand. A spark generated between them and he instantly faded into white light.

Too stunned to move, Joni watched in silence as the darkness enveloped her, eventually fading into a dark cloudy sky. When the cold winds picked up again, Joni realized where she was and staggered to her feet, brushing herself off.

Joni gave one final look at the body of water reflecting the dark sky. Hearing footsteps crunching across the vegetation, she took off for home, too intimidated to further investigate.

CHAPTER FOUR

Joni came to her front door, finding a sheet of notebook paper taped there.

"*You suck major,*" the note read in flowery handwriting. "*Come to the game so we won't kick your ass like TriCity's doing to Nortiniry!*"

Joni blew a short sigh and ripped the message from the door. "*I stayed out there too long,*" she thought with disgust and headed along the walkway. "*How am I getting to school now? I'm four miles out... that's at least an hour's walk!*"

Hearing a mechanical roar, Joni let out a yelp and looked up the road, spotting a lone headlight coming her way. Swallowing her fear, she waited until the cycle stopped and the helmet's visor flipped up, revealing a familiar gentle face.

"Looks like you need a lift," Signe said, grinning.

"Why is it that you always seem to come when I need you?" Joni asked.

Signe shrugged. "Um, is it because I'm just awesome like that?"

"Argh, shut up!" Joni got on behind Signe and he turned down the visor. "I swear, you must be stalking me."

"Maybe."

Signe revved the engine and peeled out, making a tight U-turn then raced ahead to their intended destination.

Signe entered the school's parking lot and idled the engine as Joni stepped off. In the background, the school band played to a hyper, excited crowd, their music nearly drowned out by the noisy cheers.

"What, no hug?" Signe complained.

"Not tonight, buckethead." Joni leaned forward and flipped up his visor. "How are we doing?"

"Do you sincerely want an update?" Signe chuckled. "Whatever you did to Ryan's essentially paying off. We even scored a touchdown tonight!"

Joni gasped, her eyes widening in shock. "That's straight crazy!"

"What's with that look?" Signe laughed harder when Joni blew a raspberry at him. "Yes, *one* touchdown! They switched up their game once to stop him throwing and now we're stuck running it in!"

Joni giggled. "Just a touchdown... I don't believe it!" She pumped her fists. "How awesome is that?"

"Hey, I was about to find a pay phone and call you!" Greta's voice called. "Come on, we're at halftime!"

"Have fun, okay?" Signe said gently.

Joni turned around and waved at Greta as she approached. Glancing back to Signe who continued staring longingly at her, Joni rolled her eyes. "If I hug you," she snapped, "will you leave?"

Signe grinned broadly in response. "Yes," he drawled. "Please, just this once?" he pleaded, batting his eyes.

Joni blew an annoyed sigh. "Fine, if you'll stop begging and everything." Reaching over, Joni put her arms around him and Signe pinched her rear in response. Joni squealed and punched his back as he laughed. "Argh, get out!" Joni waved him off and ran over to Greta, meeting with her.

"Why don't you just date Signe and stop the madness?" Greta teased over the roar of Signe's motorcycle speeding away as Joni walked in step with her. "He'll chase you forever, you know!"

"That's the fun part for him, I think," Joni replied. "It's the thrill of the chase... How else he'd get his jollies?"

Greta scrunched up her face and shook her head. "Total horror show!"

Joni rolled her eyes. "I'm not worried about it." She nudged her friend with her elbow. "So, is it true with what he said, about how Ryan's running from TriCity to score?"

"If our weak defensive line can make them fumble, then we have a sure shot of winning for a change!"

Joni put up her hands in mock surrender. "Maybe I'm good luck if I'm *away* from the game!"

Greta blew a raspberry and waved Joni away. "Nah, just good luck in pissing off Ryan!"

Joni chortled in response. "I'm not *that* bad, Greta!"

"Right, you can't be bad as TriCity's Number Eighty-Two... That slab of beef's got a vendetta on him for sure with the way that guy's been pulverizing Ryan all night!"

Approaching the bleachers, Joni paused in step at the sight of a tall slender young man with feathered canary blond hair wearing a dark navy blazer, white dress shirt and gray slacks waving at her.

"Who's that waving at us in the stands?" Joni asked and waved back hesitantly.

"Huh?"

"The guy with the East Nortiniry blazer." Joni pointed ahead. "Why is he at a Nortiniry game? Are the rich kids from East Nortiniry betting *for* us for a change?"

"No, you dummy!" Greta fussed. "That's Slake, my boyfriend I was telling you about! Besides, he transferred out and you know East Nortiniry's got nothing but uniforms!"

"Oh, you got you a rich doctor-in-training, huh?" Joni said wryly. Greta pushed Joni playfully.

"Shut up!"

"Hey, I'm not saying anything's wrong with it! You *need* to branch out!"

"*You'd* better not branch out to them!"

Upon approach, Joni noticed the young man had a thin face, high cheekbones and deep, clear blue eyes. She swallowed hard, watching Slake greet Greta warmly, embracing her gently.

"He's the guy from that crazy vision!" Joni realized, stunned.

"Hey, this is my friend Joni Warren," Greta said, gesturing toward Joni. "Joni, this is my boyfriend Slake Corbitt. Don't steal him away, please?"

"I promise to go butch for you, alright?" Joni numbly stuck out a hand. "Hey, Slake," she grumbled. Slake smiled and shook her hand. Sudden warmth rushed through her and Joni immediately grew dizzy.

"Hey, are you alright?" Greta called as Joni wavered. Slake caught her before she fell.

"I just feel faint," Joni murmured. "Don't worry."

"Damn, Joni, aren't you red!" Greta put up her hands. "Don't get sick on me, okay?"

"Doesn't your boyfriend talk much?" Joni asked as Slake led her to a nearby bleacher. Joni sank into her seat, slouching forward.

"Why say something when you don't have anything to say?" Greta spat, rolling her eyes. "Besides, I like it when my boyfriends are pretty and just smile and nod."

"What, you'd rather have an insanely good-looking 'yes dear' robot?" Greta glared at Joni, and then turned away, huffing.

After the band dispersed, the players returned to the field, resuming the second half. Joni watched with disinterest while the TriCity Titans refused to let the Knights move an inch and continuously clobbered Ryan and the other players. After several fumbles and interceptions on both sides, when the Titans regained possession, the crowd around them suddenly roared and cheered.

"Joni, look!" Greta shouted, shaking her friend by the arm. "Ryan intercepted and found an opening!"

Joni looked up, watching Ryan sprinting across the field with the football tucked in his arm, trailed by several opposing players charging after him.

"That's straight crazy!" Joni shouted, quickly rising to her feet. "He's running ninety-nine yards; he's going in to beat TriCity!" She jumped up and down in joy, cheering. "Go Ryan!" Joni screamed at the top of her lungs. "Take it all the way!"

Ryan jumped over two large TriCity Titans linesmen closing in and hurtled around them, slamming hard into the ground. A referee walked over, spotting Ryan's hand gripping the ball over the goal line. The referee threw up his hands.

"It's good; it's in!" Greta whooped.

"We're actually going to beat them!" Joni cheered.

The offensive line reassembled in the Titan's two-yard zone. Joni grabbed Greta's sleeve, shaking her.

"Are they nuts?" she cried. "They're not even kicking it in!"

"They must feel pretty confident to try a two-point conversion!" Greta replied.

The crowd cheered louder when the quarterback took the snap and stormed through the defenders, throwing elbows before reaching the end zone.

"Yes!" Joni screeched. "Just hold out one more quarter!"

"I doubt it!" Greta spat. "Before that, both our Running Backs got creamed out there - Laig's out with a major concussion and Fullerton's with a busted leg!"

"I think they'll make it!"

Cringing when the Titans blazed through with another touchdown and a successful field goal kick, Joni bit her nails watching the clobbering the Knights received during the last quarter.

"They just got lucky out there," Greta said once the Knights missed another chance at a touchdown. "The defense is so bad, they'll get nervous and not even move!"

"Hey, who's that straw going out there for the kick?" Joni asked as a short slender player walked confidently out onto the field. "How is he going to make it from sixty-five yards away? That's impossible!"

"No way, I don't believe it!" Greta howled. "They're finally putting out that Randy Alister!"

"Who is he?"

"He's that kid with the uncle from the comic book store... He can't play any sports, but he was in football for credits. Might as well get it over and done with, right?" Greta snorted. "He's been getting trampled since freshman year, but they finally found that this guy can kick and *never miss*! He's our only secret weapon!"

"How can he get it in with three seconds left on the clock?" Joni spat.

"It's possible!"

"It's not like they can fumble and stop the clock!"

"Miracles happened on less."

Joni smirked. "Go, Randy!" she called out. "Kick ass!"

Ryan set down the ball and Randy stepped back, surveying the field. Joni felt the odd chill blow through her again and shivered slightly. Turning toward Slake who sat nearby, she noticed he watched the game with great interest. Slake became aware of Joni staring at him and blushed slightly in return as his smile turned nervous.

"*Does he sense something weird too?*" Joni wondered. Slake patted her knee gently and turned his attentions back to the game.

Joni looked back to the field, watching Randy rush forward and gear up for the kick. Giving a swift boot, the pigskin sailed over the goalpost with ease and a deafening roar of Nortiniry fans ripped through the stands as the buzzer sounded, signaling endgame.

"We won!" Joni screeched. "We finally won by two friggin' points! Alright!" She jumped upright and grabbed Greta's hands, pulling her to her feet. "We did it; we finally beat TriCity's Titans!"

"Yeah, at seventeen to fifteen!" Greta said, yanking out of her grip. "Big deal!"

"It *is* a big deal!"

"Only because TriCity's kicker sprained his ankle on the conversion and after our best defensive lineman got knocked out in the second quarter, our team got turned into dog meat out there first before even getting it done with!" Greta pushed Joni away. "That was a whole hour of pure hell!"

"Why are you so sour?" demanded Joni.

"Forget it," Greta grumbled and stormed off.

"Wait!" Joni reached out for Greta and let out a mild cry when intercepted by a nearby student who grabbed for her, dancing around. "Hey!" Joni shoved the dancer away and pushed through the crowd of rowdy students, searching for Greta. "Come back! What's going on?"

"Hey, Joni!" a familiar voice called. Joni looked back over her shoulder, spotting Ryan waving to her from the field below. She ran down the bleachers, passing other students and hurried up to Ryan, hugging him tightly. "Owch..."

"Sorry!" Joni said sheepishly. "So, how does it feel to finally win a game?"

"Painful!" Ryan leaned against her, sighing heavily. "Joni, I know you're a big fan and all, even getting scary out there on the field during practice, but promise me one thing, okay?"

"Sure!"

"Whatever you do, don't hit me low! I've been through enough punishment with those sacks of beef tonight, especially that huge Number Eighty-Two fella!"

Joni giggled. "I won't, promise." She draped his free arm over her shoulders as they headed off the field together. "You guys kicked ass out there tonight!" she said excitedly. "What made you work so hard?"

Ryan shrugged. "No idea... I guess we finally clicked and everything just worked out."

"Why didn't you sit out during the second half?"

"I didn't get banged up *until* the second half!"

"So, how's about recovering at my house? They're sure rioting like nobody's business tonight!"

"I know it!" Ryan limped along Joni's side while she walked with him toward the crowded parking lots.

"Aren't you going to change out of your uniform?" Joni asked.

"I just want to get home," Ryan complained. "I've had a rough night."

"It couldn't be that bad!"

"Man, did you see that Randy's kick? I thought my eyes were playing tricks on me!"

"What do you mean?"

"When he wound up to kick, for a minute there, he seemed to pause, like on tape or something... then at the last minute: bam! He kicked that ball into space!"

"What do you mean; something like stop-motion or whatever?"

"Yeah."

"Is your ride here?"

Ryan nodded. "It's near the front... I figured if I was going to play quarterback, I need to be close to some wheels to get my broken body home!"

"You're just a little worse for wear, Ryan; bruised but not broken, right?"

Ryan laughed heartily before grabbing his side, grimacing. "Right," he groaned.

"*Still, that's weird*," reasoned Joni as she helped Ryan to his pickup truck. "*To stop for a split second before kicking a ball...*"

"Joni...!" Ryan cried and collapsed to his knees.

Joni quickly grabbed a hold of his arm, watching in terror as the color quickly drained from his face. "Ryan!" she pressed, "what's wrong?"

"I think that last sack..." Ryan began coughing furiously, vomiting blood.

"Somebody!" Joni wailed. "Help! Somebody, help! He's dying!" Growing frustrated as the excited commotion of the crowds and players drowned out her pleas for aid, Joni laid Ryan on his side, trying to remain calm. "Don't worry, somebody's coming!" she promised. Joni blew a hard sigh as beads of cold sweat broke out over her forehead and neck.

"*Can I heal him from this?*" Joni considered, wiping at her eyes that began welling with tears. "*Dad said not to take on a little like he did, but to take it out and give it to the earth. How can I do that since he never told me how?*" She put her hands on Ryan's chest. "*Let me see what's wrong with him!*" His body began turning transparent and inside she could see muscles and bone. Looking deeper, she noticed his ruptured kidney and darkness quickly filling the void. "*I can't fix that!*" Joni shook her head, clearing her vision back to normal.

"Joni..." Ryan groaned.

"I'm making sure you'll get to the hospital!" Joni said and scrambled to her feet. Noticing Slake approaching, she ran up to him, grasping him by the sleeve. "Slake, he needs help now – it's really serious!" He nodded and waved at her to stand back. "Make sure he doesn't go into shock, okay? I'm calling for an ambulance!" Joni let go and hurried across the commons, reaching for the cluster of pay phones situated there.

After dialing for emergency, once connected to the switchboard operator, Joni let him know what details he needed. Growing extremely chilled again, after hanging up the receiver, she turned and noticed swirling shadows nearby.

"*What is that?*" Joni wondered and reached out to touch it. A firm hand abruptly pulled back her arm and she yanked free from the grip then whirled around.

A young man with shaggy ebony hair, wearing a gray hooded pullover sweatshirt, jogging pants and black high-top sneakers stood in front of Joni. On his sallow face, he wore wide dark sunglasses with silver reflective lenses.

"Hey," Joni remarked, "why are you wearing sunglasses at night?"

"Because I'm cool like that," answered the shady student. "Like, did you know ruptured kidneys are really, really serious? He can die from blood poisoning, you know!"

"I know," Joni answered and grew tense. "Hey, wait... how did *you* know?"

The young man grinned brightly. "I know what you know," he answered vaguely.

Joni pushed him away and took a hesitant step back as he leaned against a nearby pay phone, fingering the various bands of etched silver on his hand. "How much do you know?" she demanded. "What you've been up to; spying on me or something?"

"I'm not a perv," the hooded young man replied and chortled. "I'm concerned for Ryan too you know! We're good friends."

"I want a name!"

"There's no point knowing me yet... I have to make sure things fall into place first!"

"What are you talking about?"

Blaring sirens wailed in the distance and Joni left the phones, watching the ambulance approaching the lot. Slake waved them down as they came to a stop nearby and the emergency technicians exited, immediately attending to Ryan.

"You'd better be extra careful in the coming months," the young man warned from behind. "It won't be easy!"

"Why do you say that?" Joni replied warily.

"Well... Let's just say that what you do affects a lot of things around here!"

"I--!" At a loss for words, Joni watched the young man walk away, whistling a tune. She clenched her hands and ground her teeth, fuming.

"*I can't obsess over that weirdo right now,*" Joni mused and hurried for Ryan's truck. Approaching Slake, she touched him by the arm, gaining his attention.

"Slake; I'm taking Ryan's truck back to his house," she said. "Will you tell his parents for me what happened?" Slake nodded. "Want a lift home?" He shook his head and Joni walked for the pickup. A strong hand gently grabbed her by the arm and Joni turned, noticing Slake holding a set of keys in his hand. "Yeah, I'd need that, won't I?" Joni murmured as he set the keys in her palm. Slake smiled gently. "Take care, okay?"

Slake backed away as Joni entered the truck and gave it a start. Switching on the high beams, she idled, watching Slake walk away. After he left her line of sight, Joni drove the truck back to Ryan's house, gripping the steering wheel with tense hands.

CHAPTER FIVE

Pulling into the darkened driveway, Joni cut the engine and leaned on the steering wheel, breaking down into tears.

"I can't tell the Arcendos this," she moaned. "I just can't do it... I hope Slake will do this for me!"

Regaining her composure and wiping her eyes with the back of her hands, Joni withdrew the keys and stepped out the truck. Hurrying up the steps of the darkened house, she heard footsteps coming at a hurried pace down the sidewalk. Joni turned toward the sound, gripping the keys firmly as the footfalls came nearer.

"Who's there?" Joni called. "Say something!" The heavy clouds moved away, showering moonlight on the darkened streets. She blew a relived sigh as Slake appeared from the darkness and approached the stoop. "Thanks, Slake!" Joni said gratefully. "You're one in a million!" He smiled and blushed slightly. "Here, give the keys to them and lock the door for me, okay?" She handed him the keys and hurried for home before he had a chance to answer.

Once Joni entered her house, her phone rang.

"*Who could be calling this late?*" she wondered as she rushed over and picked up the receiver.

"Joni," a woman's voice said over the line. "Are you alright?"

"Missus Arcendo!" Joni said, surprised. "I'm hanging in there, I guess..." She twirled the cord around her finger. "How's Ryan; will he get better?"

Joni cringed when she heard Ryan's mother break down in tears. The phone changed hands and she heard Ryan's father's voice instead.

"I know you're good friends with my son," he said. "We called to let you know he's slipped into a coma due to the serious infection he gained."

"How terrible..." Joni murmured. She sank to the floor on her knees, overwhelmed. "I wish there was something I can do..."

"Please keep him in your prayers."

The call disconnected and dial tone flooded Joni's ear. She dropped the receiver and it swung off the table as she sat on the floor in the darkness, too stunned to move.

Over the next several weeks, Joni found concentrating on her classes difficult since her thoughts and worries centered on her continuing nightmares, aggravated by her overwhelming apprehension about her friend.

She called Ryan's parents every day, only to hear his condition unchanged. The guilt and fear hit Joni hard and she spent most nights practicing her healing technique whenever she could on herself and her barely live potted plant she kept on her desk.

After enduring another day of classes, Joni pulled into her dark violet wool coat and grabbed her backpack full of books, slinging it over her shoulder. She raced out the classroom, hurrying down the hall and expertly maneuvered around the other students who exited their rooms.

Bolting outdoors into the frigid autumn air, soft flurries of snow swirled down around Joni as she searched for her bus. She easily spotted Greta standing at the curb, wearing a bright pink parka with a fur-lined hood, a pleated lavender skirt, black tights and brown suede boots.

"Hey, Greta!" Joni called, waving at her. Greta ignored her, approaching a football player who had the standard-issued Nortiniry High's blue and silver varsity athlete jacket. Joni puffed a sigh and turned away.

The bus pulled to the curb and Joni boarded, taking a seat near the back. Dropping her backpack on the floor, she groaned and ran her hands through her hair.

"*I bet Greta's pissed at me,*" Joni thought as she looked out the window, catching sight of the driver stepping off the bus and withdrawing a pack of cigarettes with lighter. "*She's been ignoring me since that Slake guy stopped talking to her after that wild game.*"

"Hey," a familiar voice called to Joni moments later, "did you do your Geometry assignments?"

Looking up, Joni noticed the shaggy haired young man with the silver sunglasses and gray hooded sweatshirt. He grinned and sat in the seat before her, resting an elbow against the edge as he leaned toward her.

"Who are you?" Joni snapped. "Are you *even* in my class?"

The young man chuckled. "Why else would I ask?" he answered.

"Why do you care?" Joni waved him away. "Besides, you're not cheating off me. Do your own assignments, okay?"

"Just don't move your fist more than you move that pretty mouth of yours." Joni reached up to slap him and he pulled back, smiling widely. "Whoa, with that kind of hand, you can really work me over!"

"Shut up and leave me alone, okay?" Joni sank back into her seat, folding her arms across her chest.

"Hey, Ryan'll get better," the young man said. "I'm visiting him later."

"Really?"

"We're good friends, him and I."

"Do you play on the team?"

"Sometimes."

"Are you that Randy Alister guy everyone's buzzing about?"

"With the kick that never miss?" The young man's face flushed slightly in response. "Yeah, that's me."

"Where did you learn to kick like that?"

"The other football."

Joni raised an eyebrow at him. "What?"

Other students filed onto the bus, filling the vehicle with idle chatter. Moments later, the driver stepped inside and closed the door, then started the bus. Greta walked past Joni and Randy, taking a seat in the far back as the bus pulled away and started its route.

"Hey, Greta," Randy called. "Why're you sitting next to that weirdo?"

"Shut up, shit-for-brains," Greta grumbled.

"That's a hell of a response!"

"Why do you care?"

"Ooh, someone's in a bad mood!"

"What weirdo are you talking about?" Joni asked, slightly intrigued. "Besides, you don't choose which seats to take. You just grab what's free anyway." Turning in her seat, she spotted Slake sitting in the far rear with his dark indigo overcoat draped over his lap while he faced the window. Joni snorted and rolled her eyes. "That's her former boyfriend, Slake," she replied, "and he's not weird, just a good listener!"

Randy scoffed. "Then why is he known as Mister Stoneface in class?" he retorted.

"Maybe he doesn't have much to talk about!" Joni snapped, facing Randy. "Or maybe with Ryan being sick and all, he's depressed about it too!"

"Oh, what would he know?" Greta spat. "He doesn't know Ryan at all! Hell, he showed up in town four months ago."

"You mean to say he's a summer fling?" Randy jeered. "Whoo, Greta, good going! You really know how to pick them!"

Slake's pale face flushed scarlet in response, darkening the slight freckles dotting his gaunt cheeks and sharply defined nose. He folded his arms across his chest, growing tense.

"What'd you know about that?" accused Greta.

"I know you're not getting any – that's why you're in total bitch-face mode today!"

"Shut up!" Greta threw her backpack at Randy and he ducked as it landed in the seat next to him.

"Right, and good luck getting a word out of Mister Stoneface about it," Randy said and laughed harder. "Kiss and don't tell, is that it?"

"Stop messing with Slake, okay?" Joni protested, glaring back at Randy. "You're being mean for no reason!"

Randy got on his knees and turned to Joni, draping his arms over the seat's top. "You see how big he is compared to me?" he said. "Look at those huge hands! I mean, *really* look! If he played basketball – and he's tall enough I'm sure – they'd call him 'The Flyswatter'!"

Joni leaned over and looked back at Slake, noticing his elongated fingers on his large thin hands. "*Randy does have a point*," she mused. "*Randy's only a few inches taller than me and Slake towers him! If I stood next to that giant, he'd squash me!*"

"Hey Greta, sit in my seat," Randy called. "I want to feel you up." He grinned slyly as he picked up her bag and slipped it over his shoulder. "You'll feel better if you let me. I'll even carry your books home and everything!"

"Oh gawd," Greta griped. "I have between a horn dog and an ex-boyfriend to sit with."

Randy pat at his seat. "Come on," he crooned, "I promise not to feel up your skirt. Just your blouse."

"I so have anti-static in my bag." Greta snapped as she immediately rose to her feet. "This shit blinds you forever!"

"I hope you're not friends with Signe," Joni said and scooped up her backpack. She touched Greta on the shoulder once Greta sat in front of her in Randy's seat. "Hey, what happened between you two?" she inquired. "I thought this was a sure thing this time!"

"*You* happened, as usual," Greta grumbled, brushing off her hand. "You're toxic, Joni. I don't want to talk to you anymore." Joni gasped and clenched her teeth, stunned. "All he did was ask about you!" Greta went on. "I couldn't take it anymore and kicked his ass to the curb."

Joni scoffed, finally finding her voice. "And you're pissed at *me* about that?" She shook her head. "I don't know what your deal is. I'm not dating anyone anyway!"

"Don't worry," Randy said to Greta, draping his arm over her shoulders. "I'll be your rebound if you want." He then glanced up and waved at Joni. "Laters," he teased.

"Argh," Joni snapped, "both of you suck!"

"Not as hard as you!" Randy gibed and Greta snorted.

Stomping toward bus's rear, Joni approached Slake and smiled faintly at him. He looked up in her direction, giving a slight nod in acknowledgment.

"So I guess it's me and you again, huh?" Joni quipped. Slake looked away, gazing out the window. "I don't find your hands freakishly large or anything," she continued. "You're a tall guy. It can't be helped." Slake grunted and dug through his coat pocket, withdrawing black leather driving gloves.

"*Such smooth moves,*" Joni reprimanded herself as Slake put the gloves on his hands and let out a short sigh, folding his arms across his chest. "*You're embarrassing him further!*" She sighed and sat next to him, setting her backpack in her lap.

"So, I guess it's true that East Nortiniry has nothing but uniforms," Joni said in a vain attempt at conversation. "Doesn't that crimp your style?" Slake didn't answer and Joni grunted.

"Yeah, keep digging that hole," Randy hooted. "You'll really catch his attention gabbing about nothing."

Joni glowered back at him and he stuck out his tongue. "You keep messing with me," she warned and shook her fist at him in return, "and I'll knock that snide grin off your face!"

"I like 'em aggressive!"

"Argh, you're disgusting!" Joni returned her attention to Slake. "You hear about how much face-time that dork's getting from the papers? I don't think I can handle getting hassled like that all the time."

"I don't mind a free ride," Randy called back. "It's easier than having to think and wouldn't he know? I bet he's hiding out probably wanking in some locker dreaming of you."

Joni glared back at Randy who giggled with Greta. "I'll break your legs!" she spat then blew an annoyed sigh. Slake smirked and Joni smiled slightly. "So how come I hardly see you in my classes these days?" she asked. "You just disappeared after the first football game of the season... you know, with Ryan and all..." A paper ball suddenly bounced off Slake's face and Joni clenched her hands, growing incensed. "Hey, who threw that?"

She scowled at where Randy and Greta were sitting, spotting Greta with a notebook in her lap, ripping out a sheet.

"Hey, he didn't even flinch!" Greta declared as she crushed the paper. She turned, tossing another paper ball and it bounced off Slake's head, falling into his lap.

"Don't throw stuff at him!" Joni complained. "What is this, 'pick on Slake' day?"

"Look, he didn't even blink!" Greta tore out another page, mashed it into a ball and threw it. The crumpled paper hit Slake's nose and fell in his lap. "Yes! Three points!"

"Wait until we play floor hockey," Joni huffed, "then we'll see how you like having stuff thrown at you!"

"Oh, get off," Greta teased. "You suck at floor hockey; you can't even play the goalie position right!"

"Try one over your shoulder," Randy rallied, "and see if it hits!"

"Don't egg her on!" Joni protested. Another paper ball came at Slake and he caught it, tossing it behind his seat. Joni turned to him, surprised. His expression stayed neutral. "I bet Slake's really good at hockey!" Joni went on. "With reflexes like that, he'd cream you guys!"

Greta snorted. "Yeah, right! He never plays team sports; he's just a lame spectator!"

"He's the only guy I know who's willingly getting an 'F' in Gym," Randy interjected.

"He probably doesn't play because he can smoke you out the water!" Joni retorted.

"You hear that?" Randy called, then both he and Greta burst out laughing. "He's so lame, even that blind kid Mahoney can kick his ass!"

"He's so lame, he's banned from sports to protect his family's honor!" Greta chimed in.

Joni growled under her breath. "You two suck major!" Greta and Randy continued laughing. "Look, Slake, don't worry about her," Joni said, turning toward Slake. "She's all mouth and Randy too. I bet you're really good at sports!" Slake said nothing as he continued staring at the passing scenery. "What sports do you play? Do you like the Winter or the Spring sports? What about the Summer and Fall ones?" Joni grunted when she received no answer. "Well, you know outside of Football, in Nortiniry there's Floor and Field Hockey, Volleyball, Basketball, Baseball and Softball, Tennis, Soccer and Lacrosse. I think that's all the sports we have..." Slake's face twitched slightly. "So you like Lacrosse?"

"Alright blabbermouth, get off the bus," Greta called. "Unless you're planning on walking home in the snow!"

Joni slung her backpack over her shoulder and stood. "Where's your book bag?" she questioned. "Did you forget your homework or

something?" Slake avoided her as he grabbed his coat and silently rose upright, looking straight ahead.

Greta huffed and stomped over to Joni, grabbing her by the arm.

"Hey!" Joni protested as Greta led her off the bus.

"You sure are talkative today!" Greta complained, dragging Joni away. "Why are you so interested in Mister Stoneface?"

"When did he become Mister Stoneface, you poseur!" Joni snapped and pulled out of Greta's grip once they stepped off. "Besides, I'm just being friendly!"

"Yeah, right!" Greta exclaimed as the bus rumbled away. "You're such a user!"

"No, I'm not!"

"Don't be a complete dummy and fall for him," Randy interjected. Joni turned around and smacked him with her backpack. He laughed, putting up his hands. "Owch, lady!"

"Why are you in my face?" Joni shouted. "You're really working my nerves!"

"You know nothing about that Slake Corbitt guy!" Randy objected. "He keeps to himself in class and doesn't say much. I mean, you know what they say about those silent types: one wrong word and boom! Everyone's history!"

"Oh, come off it you two!" Joni griped. "Slake's not crazy – he could be insanely smart and *choose* not to waste his breath on people like you!"

"You got the *insane* part right," Randy said and quickly jumped out the way of another swing.

"Yeah, if he's so *smart*," Greta snapped, "he'd say something by now!"

"Yeah, *something*!"

"What, are you Greta's parrot now?" Joni grumbled. "You stupid nut job." She shook her fist at Greta. "You thought it was cute when he didn't say anything at first!"

"Yeah, at first!" Greta spat back. "Now, it's creepy!"

"But then you said he wouldn't shut up about me!"

"When he wasn't saying anything, all he did was ask about you!" Greta complained. "He's obsessed and I wasn't in for that."

"You must be a total freak if you like creepy guys like that!" Randy accused. "I'd leave you alone too if you're into dealing with total whackos!"

"Whatever!" Joni huffed and stomped away toward home. "Just leave me alone!"

CHAPTER SIX

The next day, Joni entered her mathematics class and took her assigned seat. The teacher came in moments later and greeted them dryly before instructing them to turn in their homework assignments. Joni sighed and opened her backpack, rummaging through the myriad of books and papers. She felt a light tap and looked up, spotting several papers held before her. Joni took it out of hand and scanned it.

"*Who still uses manual typewriters?*" she wondered at one report that had extensive strikeouts and liberal use of correction fluid, then peeked at the next paper, noticing it had printer wheel tabs on the side and dot matrix text. "*They could've at least made the text darker... Kacey told me about some NLQ setting or whatever.*" Turning to the last sheet, she found Slake's name written in classical handwriting style at the top. "*This is Slake's paper,*" she realized and turned in her seat, finding the young man writing in a notebook, oblivious to everything else around him. On the back of his chair lay his dark overcoat with his leather gloves hanging from the pockets. "*I don't see why Greta and that Randy guy barking about Slake acting strange these days. He's probably just as upset as I am about Ryan!*"

Joni passed the paper ahead then took out her Geometry book, giving the matter no further thought as she focused on finishing her forgotten mathematics homework.

After class, Joni received the papers of her row and looked down at Slake's assignment. "*He's got an A-plus,*" she mused and turned toward Slake who continued writing in his notebook. "*...all questions* *completed and correct!*" Joni tapped him gently on the arm and he looked up.

"Hey Slake," she said, "would you tutor me in Math sometime? I'm really starting to flunk out you know." Slake said nothing as he took his paper from her and tucked it into his notebook. "Look, I'm not going to copy your work. You're insanely smart and I just need some help. I know I should study more but I just don't have time. Without a calculator, I'm sunk." Slake ignored her, passing the remaining papers behind him then returned to writing in his notebook. "What are you writing about?"

Slake shut the notebook and rose from his seat. Joni grit her teeth and turned away, watching him leave with the other students who filtered into the hall, heading to their next class.

While shoving her own books and papers into her backpack, she heard the teacher call for Randy. Joni looked up, watching him stomp to the front of the class, grumbling under his breath.

"Man, this totally sucks!" he complained. "Look Missus Meyers, why you're making this stuff half our grade? I know I totally bombed that test this time and my homework was turned in half-assed but..."

"Enough, Mister Alister," Meyers objected. "You're getting a tutor or you're flunking. Which is it?"

"I guess I'll flunk it out."

"I suggest that you not flunk out. If you just memorize the formulas you use to get to the answer, then you wouldn't fail as often."

"I don't have time to study!" Randy griped. "With practice and volunteer work and all--!"

"Nortiniry High depends on that kicking leg of yours," Meyers snapped, cutting him off. "And I'm sure so do your college prospects."

Randy paled behind his silver-reflective sunglasses. "But--!"

"If you ruin the school's chance at a winning season, I will make sure you don't pass junior year *at all!*"

"Alright, I get it!" Randy groaned. "Who's my tutor?"

"Mister Corbitt."

"What?" Randy squawked. "Mister Stoneface's my tutor?"

"Ha, Randy, that's what you get!" Joni called, scooping up her pack and slinging it over her shoulder. "Don't talk about people you don't know well!"

"Shut up, will you?" Randy snapped back.

"You're the one to talk, motormouth!"

"I know you're a very smart young man," Meyers interjected, "but why do you let your work go to waste? What you do on the tests could be applied to the homework!"

"Why do you make it that homework is half our grade?" Randy objected. "If I do well on the test, then you should give me some credit!"

"I do – half."

Randy clenched his teeth and stormed out the classroom as Joni also headed for the congested hallways. Leaving the door, she bumped into a young man and he shoved her back in return.

"Watch it!" he growled.

"Hey," Joni retorted, "you should watch where you're going, you greasy blond!"

The young man glared at her, shifting his long bleached hair out of his gray eyes. He wore all black: jeans with tears at the knee, T-shirt with the sleeves ripped off at the shoulder and leather boots with heavy chains around the ankles. Joni quickly felt her blood freezing in her veins as he sneered at her.

"This can't be just coincidence; that's the guy I saw in the pool!" she thought in horror. *"He's going to be trouble..."*

"Watch yourself," he snarled and stormed away.

"Am I supposed to be afraid of that?" Joni called after him. Turning away, she bumped into another person and fell back, stunned. "Owch!" Looking up, Joni faced Slake who stood over her.

He held out a hand and she took it, getting pulled to her feet. "Is it true you were asking about me?" Joni asked.

Slake blanched and motioned with his hands for her to move out the way. Perturbed, she stepped aside, watching him walk down the hall.

"It *must be true*," Joni mused and followed him. "*He looked like he was about to hurl because of my asking!*" She approached his side, walking in step.

"Why don't you ever say anything?" Joni inquired. "Why do you always keep to yourself? I just want to be friends, you know!"

Slake headed for a nearby locker, turning the lock. Opening the metal door, he placed his worksheet-laden notebook inside then held out a hand to Joni standing behind him.

She looked at him blankly, bewildered and he gestured again, growing annoyed. Joni then slipped off her bag, handing it over and he grabbed the pack, stuffing it into the locker. Closing it shut with a firm bang, Slake continued his way down the hall.

"Well, think about it!" Joni called after him. "At least I don't call you Mister Stoneface!"

The bell rang and the students in the hall scattered. Joni raced after Slake as others pushed and shoved him aside while he calmly walked down the packed corridor. Joni caught up, standing before the men's restroom. After making a quick check for anyone watching nearby, Joni opened the door and stepped inside. Her arm suddenly grabbed in a firm hold, she turned out and stood at the ready to defend with her fists up.

"Oh, it's you!" Joni said in relief and relaxed her stance, facing Slake. He grunted and folded his arms across his chest, glaring down at Joni with a strong look of disapproval. "Well, I didn't want you caught in hall sweeps, you know!" His face flushed red then he pointed ahead angrily. "Hey, I'm not trying to be weird or anything but I'm not leaving until you talk to me!" Slake repeated the gesture

again. "Well, you can forget it!" He blew a hard frustrated sigh and stormed past her, only to freeze. "What's wrong?" Slake backed away and grabbed Joni by the arm. Joni staggered when pulled and both hurried into a nearby stall. Slake quickly shut the door and locked it. "Slake--!"

Slake put a finger to his lips and Joni nodded as the restroom door opened. Slake stood on the toilet, lending Joni a hand and she took it, also getting lifted. She braced herself against the wall, standing precariously on the seat's edge.

Joni held her breath, listening to the monitor's shuffling footfalls pattering softly against the tiles every few moments as he bent down, glancing underneath the stall door before heading for the next. The stall at the end opened and clicked shut and Slake stepped down softly, waving at Joni to follow.

Quickly stepping off the seat once Slake unlocked the door, both silently crossed the room. Joni looked back as they sneaked for the door, noticing the end stall in use and the monitor's pants were down. Before they could reach the door, Slake suddenly sneezed.

"Who's in here?" the monitor bellowed.

Joni grabbed for Slake by the hand and both raced out the restroom. Exiting into the hallway and approaching a classroom door, she tried the handle, finding it locked. Slake pulled at Joni's hand and pointed ahead.

"Look, we're not cutting class!" Joni snapped. "The best we can do is hide out in Study Hall until everything's clear!"

The restroom door banged open and the monitor stormed out, adjusting his belt. "There you are!" he shouted.

"He's spotted us!" Joni yelped, pulling at Slake's hand. "Let's get out of here!" Slake sprinted ahead, taking Joni with him.

"You two are getting a month's detention!" The monitor thundered after them.

"Hold on!" Joni cried. "You're too fast!" She stumbled ahead as they both turned the corner and approached a set of steps. Joni let go, hurrying down the flight as Slake raced up. He stopped, looking over the banister when he realized Joni was no longer by his side. "I'll catch up; just get going!" Slake nodded then continued running and Joni ran into the school's bowels.

Growing tense at hearing another set of footsteps following once she entered an area with little-used classrooms, Joni looked around her surroundings, taking in the scene of an area she hardly ever entered. The walls were in dire need of new paint, while cracked plaster that repaired the weakened ceiling from rainwater fell in chunks from above. Joni approached a door at random and opened it, entering the darkness.

"Hey, you bring the smokes?" a voice inquired from the shadows.

"What?" Joni yelped. The door swung shut behind her and she turned around, searching for the disembodied voice.

"Hey, that ain't Cameron!"

"What are you guys doing down here in the dark?" Joni asked, searching for the walls. Her hand struck leather and she quickly recoiled.

"Ah, not so fast," sneered the familiar voice. Joni pulled away when a firm grip grabbed her hand.

"Hey, Kipper," replied the same nervous voice, "what are you doing with her?"

"I might have a bit of fun," Kipper answered and chortled. "You joining in?"

"And get kicked out for raping some chick?" retorted Kipper's companion. "You're nuts!"

Joni struggled out of Kipper's grasp and Kipper socked Joni in the back, forcing a cry out of her. "Come on, Lacroix," he complained, "nobody's knowing a thing unless she squeals!" Joni kicked at Kipper and he grabbed her leg, throwing her down onto the floor. Kipper pounced atop Joni, holding her arms above her head.

"Get off me!" Joni screeched.

"At the rate she's going, she might!" Lacroix protested. "I'm out!"

"Then get the hell out and take Cameron with you, you bunch of sissy-assed punks!"

"Where's the door?" Lacroix grumbled.

"To your left." Dim light wafted in from the hall as the shadow of a bulky young man in a varsity athlete jacket and jeans exited. The door swung shut, killing the source of light. "Now it's you and me!"

"Get off, you pervert!" Joni yelled. Kipper chuckled, nuzzling her neck and she worked a hand free, yanking at his long hair. "Someone'll hear and you're so getting your butt in major trouble!"

"No one ever comes down here!" Kipper snapped and grabbed her wrist, slamming it to the floor. He pressed harder against Joni and licked the side of her neck. "Now if you play nice," he muttered in her ear, "it'll be over quick."

"Slake!" Joni screamed.

Kipper sat up and scoffed. "Seriously?" he spat. "I can't believe you're calling on that stone-faced idiot!" Joni wrenched her wrist free and Kipper grabbed her hand, crushing back her fingers. Joni yowled in pain and Kipper leaned in. "He can't save you!" he hissed. "That son of a bitch can't touch me; he won't do a thing!" Kipper nibbled on Joni's ear and Joni dug her nails into his hands, scratching as hard as she could. He chuckled darkly and tightened his grip. "You like that, yeah?" he murmured.

Moments later, the door opened, letting in light from the corridor. Kipper looked up and Joni screamed.

"Shut up!" Kipper shouted and punched Joni's chest. Joni gasped for breath, seeing stars. "Did Lacroix tell you to get lost, Cameron?" he snarled. "I'm trying to have some fun here!"

Hearing heavy footsteps approach, Joni tensed, fearing the worst. Kipper suddenly let out a surprised yelp when yanked back with force and tossed across the room. Joni scrambled to her feet, shaking in fear.

"It's *so dark in here!*" Joni thought as Kipper roared and fought back against his silent enemy, clearly enraged. "*I can't see anything!*"

"Oh, so you're trying to show how tough you are, eh?" Kipper sneered. "I can see in the dark as clear as day!"

Bright light abruptly flashed, illuminating the room for a brief moment. Joni gasped, catching sight of Slake holding a golden broadsword that suddenly appeared in his hands.

"Slake, be careful!" Joni called as Kipper charged forward and Slake slashed down, knocking him back against the wall. Slake stood over Kipper with the dimly glimmering broadsword as Kipper struck the floor, stunned.

"Better be careful you fool," Kipper growled, "she's watching!" Slake drew the blade and Kipper kicked him in the groin, forcing Slake faltering.

"Slake!" Joni screeched as Slake slipped to his knees. He jammed the blade into the floor, leaning against it for support.

"I guess we're playing that game, eh?" Kipper crowed. Indigo electricity cackled around his hands and a black steel saber formed, glowing in pale navy light. "Then feel the pain from the Kuroiken!"

Slake beckoned to Kipper and the young man advanced with a forward slash. Slake turned out the way and Joni screamed when Kipper riposted with an over-the-shoulder pierce, jamming his blade into Slake's side.

Joni ran away once the duel intensified, frantically searching for the exit. "*I need to get out of here before it gets really ugly!*" she thought, feeling along the wall with her hands. Her hands met cold metal and Joni turned the handle, opening the door. She stumbled out into the hall, then turned and screamed.

"So I find you," said the hall monitor, grinning maliciously. A shout came from inside the enclosed room and he tensed. "What's going on in there?"

"Slake and Kipper are fighting," Joni explained. "Please, don't punish Slake; he's trying to protect me!"

"All of you are going straight to Detention!" The hall monitor pushed Joni out the way and yanked open the door then stormed into the room, switching on the light. "What's this here?" he bellowed.

Joni peeked from behind the monitor's large frame, spotting Slake gasping hard for breath on his knees in the empty room that had desks and chairs piled up against the walls. Around him, heavy smoke filled the air. He pushed up the sleeves of his white button-down shirt and grabbed for his navy suit coat nearby on the floor.

"Where's Kipper?" Joni demanded. "He was just in here!"

"You two were up to something!" the monitor spat. "I don't know and I can only guess..."

"It's nothing like that!" Joni protested.

"I *will* find out and you two *will* get suspended!"

Joni pushed past the monitor and knelt beside Slake. "Are you sure you'll be okay?" she asked.

Slake nodded and stood unsteadily to his feet. Slinging the blazer over his shoulder, Slake walked back for the door. Immediately pausing in step, he turned to face Joni and she stood. Slake waved at her to come over and she hurried to his side.

"Thanks," Joni whispered to Slake as they walked past the monitor. Slake smiled faintly in response.

CHAPTER SEVEN

Joni entered her History classroom silently with Slake trailing behind her. She took a seat closest to the door as he slipped his sports coat on the back of the chair and sat in the seat next to her. Placing his head on the desk, Slake closed his eyes.

Joni blew a disconcerted sigh, half-listening to the instructor. "*Where did Slake get that weapon he beat on Kipper with?*" she thought, grasping her necklace with trembling hands. "*How can he carry around something like that if it's not even in his pockets?*" Joni glanced at Slake and shuddered. "*I hope he's not a magician! Dad warned me about others ... some want only power, others like hurting people with spells.*" Joni folded her arms across her chest and leaned forward in her seat, disgusted. "*Which one are you?*"

A knock resonated on the classroom door moments later, scattering Joni's thoughts. She looked up as the teacher opened it and Signe entered with motorcycle jacket and helmet in his arms. He approached the desk behind Joni and draped his jacket on the chair's back and set the helmet under the desk.

"Why were *you* running late, Mister Cyclist?" Joni asked, turning to Signe as he took his seat. He ran a thin hand through his bobbed hair, sighing heavily.

"Well, I had some errands to run," Signe explained. "It took longer than I thought."

"You're all dressed up." Joni said, giving him a once-over. "What's with the fancy polyester? Going to a roller disco contest later?"

Signe chuckled, blushing slightly. "Because I can't afford silk and yes, I'm going out dancing tonight." He leaned forward and ran a hand through her hair, grinning. "Are you coming with me? After we get done with all that dancing, we can hang out. I even got condoms and lube."

Joni smacked his hand away. "You're sick, Signe!"

Signe laughed heartily. "You know you want me!"

"Go hump a chair."

Signe tapped Slake's shoulder and he roused, yawning softly. Slake leaned back as Signe leaned forward, whispering in his ear and Slake nodded with eyes half closed.

Joni stiffened when Slake's eyes suddenly snapped open and he turned in his seat, focusing keenly on her. Joni blushed slightly as Slake's jaw tightened and he faced forward, his back rigid.

Signe grunted and left his seat, taking one unoccupied near Slake. He then cupped a hand to his face, smiling dreamily at Joni. Joni's flush turned darker in response and she turned away.

"You're so pretty," Signe murmured.

"Shut up, Signe," Joni retorted, "and tell it to somebody else."

"You know I'm harmless."

"I'm Joni and how do you do?" she quipped.

Signe snorted. "What a sense of humor!"

The teacher walked about the room, passing assignments and Joni took her paper. Looking at the work, she grimaced. "A group project?" Joni griped. "Argh..."

"Do you want to be my partner?" Signe asked. "Then afterwards we can go skinny-dipping in Tahiti..."

"Are you really that good?" Signe nodded, smiling wolfishly. "I mean, in History, you horn dog!" Signe laughed robustly. "Alright, Harmless, if we get a collective 'F', know you're personally getting a knuckle sandwich!"

"I love my women feisty!"

Joni shook her fist at him. "Remember, 'F' is for 'fist'!"

Signe grinned. "I'll keep that in mind." He moved his desk closer to Joni's. "Let's answer the questions we know first and then help out on the ones that we don't know."

"I think you're going to be helping *me* out more than me helping you!"

"Well, hey, the teacher might be a stickler for details!"

Joni nodded and Signe reached over Slake's desk, taking two pencils from his jacket pocket. He handed one to Joni and both started on their worksheets. While Signe worked, Joni glanced at Slake, spotting him fuming in anger. She nudged his ankle with her foot.

"Come out of that storm cloud, huh?" Joni said softly and Slake smiled faintly. "You feel like putting a dunce cap on me when it comes to History?" Joni waved at him. "I'm not a big fan of it, since it's ancient and all but hey, you can join the party if you want!"

Slake moved his seat closer between Signe and Joni.

"Let's have a threesome later," Signe piped. "How's that sound, huh?"

Joni kicked Signe in response and Slake laughed.

"See there," Joni declared, "I figured a smile would crack that mask one of these days!"

Signe groaned and rubbed his shin. "Yeah," he mewed, "at my expense!"

As the three worked on the work assigned, a sensation of doom clouded over Joni. She glanced up and cringed when she spotted Kipper peering into the classroom's doorway. He grinned sardonically at her once their gazes met and she turned away, swallowing back the acrid burning in her throat.

"Hey, are you alright?" Signe asked, touching Joni's arm. She flinched and he immediately withdrew, appearing concerned. "You look ready to hurl!"

"I don't know," murmured Joni. "I think breakfast isn't agreeing with me!"

"You'd better hurry and not chuck on us!"

Joni nodded and left her desk, successfully walking past the teacher's desk without notice and slipped quietly out the classroom. Making her way down the corridor, she looked around, searching for Kipper. The sensation worsened, forcing her coming to a pause.

"Alright, Kipper," Joni called, balling her hands into tight fists, "what do you want with me?"

"What I want," Kipper answered, "is to know how well you see!"

Joni searched for a form to place with his voice, only finding he remained bodily nonexistent. "I see perfectly fine, thank you!" she snapped. "Now come out of hiding so I can kick your greasy butt!"

"Can you see this?"

Joni swiftly ducked out the way when black steel unexpectedly lashed down at her, striking the concrete wall. Kipper formed before Joni, grinning madly. She immediately stepped back, her eyes widening when her sight fell upon the thin darkened steel saber.

"That's the weapon he had in the vision!" Joni thought. *"This is insane!"*

Kipper held his blade at ready. "You like what you see?" he teased and changed his stance, forcing the blade glowing in pale violet light. "It'll be the last thing once I get done with you!"

"What're you doing with a *sword* in school no less?" Joni demanded.

"Nobody else can see it but you and me!"

"What do you mean?"

"I mean, I can get rid of you and nobody would suspect a thing!"

Joni jumped away as the saber hummed when Kipper swung, slicing at the air near her. "That *thing* had better not connect with me!" she yowled.

"That's what I'm going for!"

"Why are you trying to kill me?"

"I don't need to explain to you!" Kipper placed his hand on the flat of the blade. "Kuroiken, summon the darkness!"

The blade glowed brightly and shadows sprang up around them, rushing toward where they stood.

"The hell you don't!" Joni yelped and bumped into the wall, her hand reaching wildly searching for something to counter the weapon. She grabbed onto a lever and pulled it down, causing a loud buzzer resonating through the halls. The reaching shadows dissipated and the classroom doors suddenly opened.

"Damn you!" Kipper screeched and plowed past Joni, racing down the corridor. Moments later, Slake and Signe pushed through the crowd, running up to her.

"Are you okay?" Signe asked as Slake glared ahead, seething.

"Yeah," Joni replied, "just a little scared out of my skin, is all..."

"Let's get out of here..."

Signe walked Joni down the hall with Slake following silently.

The group came outside into the cold, following other students who filtered outdoors mostly in a haze of confusion. Joni spotted Greta and waved at her. Greta looked up and rolled her eyes.

"Hey, Greta," Joni called, "come on over!" Greta blew a frosty sigh and approached, stuffing her hands into her parka. "Where's your buddy Randy? I got a new boyfriend for him."

"Hey!" Signe squawked and punched Joni playfully on the shoulder.

Greta snorted, trying not to laugh. "Where's the fire?" she asked instead.

"Kipper tripped the alarm," Joni lied. "I guess he didn't want to be in class any longer!"

"Well, Principal Faber is so killing him once she finds out!"

Randy approached, hands in the pockets of his hooded sweatshirt. "Hey, there's a siren!" he exclaimed as alarming wails resounded in the distance.

"Why do you wear those sunglasses all the time?" Joni asked. "Don't you get yelled at by the teachers?"

"It's because I'm forever cool," Randy said, grinning, "Also, they're prescription. Because of my rare condition, any kind of bright lights will forever blind me."

"That's terrible," Signe replied and Randy nodded.

"You're full of shit," Joni remarked.

Randy snorted, smirking. "And so are you."

"I bet those firefighters are probably really ticked off since it's close to lunch," Greta murmured. "Answering a false alarm, no less!"

Joni nodded in response, then half-listened to Greta and Randy chattering away to each other.

Moments later, Signe left Joni's side and stood next to Slake, speaking to him out of earshot. Joni watched them standing from afar, while Signe rubbed at his exposed arms from the cold and Slake paced, clearly enraged. Moments later, a tanned young man with hazel eyes and sandy hair pulled back with a red band approached Signe and Slake from offside, holding on a white short jacket. Joni tapped Randy on the shoulder.

"Huh?" he answered, turning to her.

"Who is that guy?" Joni asked, pointing ahead. "I never saw him in our classes."

"Who are you talking about?" Greta asked, looking in their line of sight. She shrugged. "Isn't that Signe's brother Martel?"

"I think so," Randy replied.

"Did he go somewhere over the summer?" Joni questioned. "Otherwise, I'd never thought they'd be related!"

"What kind of question is that?" Greta scoffed. "Obviously he did, because compared to Signe, Martel's burnt toast!"

"Yeah?" Randy guffawed. "You think you can't have a relative who's ambiguously brown?" He doubled over, laughing harder. "You racist!"

"Argh, shut it!" Joni snapped, shaking her fist at him.

Greta giggled and Joni ignored them both as they resumed their conversation. She watched Signe smile as he received the jacket, then gave Martel mock jabs in return and they both laughed. Slake shook his head before storming away. Martel looked up and waved at Joni. She blushed and hesitantly waved back.

"Does Martel know you?" Randy asked.

"What?" Joni answered.

"He's waving as if he's known you for a while."

"I never met Martel." Joni shrugged her shoulders. "I think Signe's mentioned him before though..."

"He's probably transferred from another school. You don't get looks like that living in Iowa!"

"Ha, it's called getting over a summer tan, Genius," Greta drawled.

"It's already October!" Randy squawked. "He must've burned like three layers for that tan!"

Joni rolled her eyes, then shivered in her sweater and ran her hands over her arms. "I can't stand being out here in the cold," she griped. "I don't see how Martel can hang out without a coat on!"

"Yeah," Greta cracked, "thin as you are, you'll turn into a virtual iced lolly in a minute!"

"Whatever..." Joni grumbled.

"I think you left your coat in Math class," Randy remarked.

Joni rolled her eyes. "Thanks for the tip," she said dryly.

"I can always warm you."

Joni's face flushed red and she kicked at Randy who pulled away, laughing. "Argh, beat it!" she huffed over his laughter.

"Look at you all heated!" Greta teased. "He's done his job for the day - you can't be cold now."

Joni internally debated whether or not to return inside the school while Greta and Randy fell into another round of giggles. She weighed how cold she was versus her ill feelings caused by her already bad day.

"*At this rate, I might start drinking to forget,*" Joni thought as she ignored conscious reason and left the two, racing back for the doors.

CHAPTER EIGHT

Finding the exit doors unlocked, Joni pushed them open and walked down the corridors. She cringed when she heard haunting laughter. "Who's there?" Joni demanded. "It better not be you messing with me, you grease ball!"

"You'll find out soon, Baby," a voice Joni didn't recognize answered. "I'm watching you..."

"Like I need more creeps in my face!" Joni grumbled and shuddered in disgust.

Growing chilled within the heated building, she hurried to the empty classroom and picked up her coat. Joni pulled into it and suddenly grew warm then turned around, finding Slake standing before her, smiling faintly.

"Hey, Slake," Joni greeted, "were you checking in on me?" He nodded. "Well, I'm okay now, thanks." She stepped past him and he took her gently by the arm. "I guess you can come with me." The two exited the classroom and entered the hall. While they walked, Joni sensed Slake grow tense. Looking around, she gasped when she noticed the shadows moving along the wall. "Did you see that?" Joni whispered. Slake said nothing in response. "Well, we're almost at the entrance – then we can get out of here and things can get back to normal!"

"Things will never be normal!" Kipper's voice hissed. Slake stopped walking and stood before Joni, shielding her from attack. "You are something special – something I want, something I need..."

"Well, this *something* is going to kick your butt in a minute!" Joni called.

"Heh, as if." Kipper materialized in the corridor as the lights dimmed around them. "If I'm correct, then you have no idea what you're getting yourself into; too bad that stone-faced fool hadn't the guts to tell you!"

"What are you talking about?" Joni demanded.

"Take a look at him. I totally kicked his ass and yet, he hasn't anything to show for it!"

Joni turned Slake around and he forced her away. "Slake, is he telling the truth?" she demanded, grabbing his arm. "Face me, please?" Slake glared at her and she withered under his harsh gaze.

"Not a single cut or bruise, you punk," Kipper crowed as Joni held fast to Slake's arm, studying his flawless face. "Yet he sliced me good and he's paying for it!"

Slake grabbed Joni by the arm and pulled her forcibly aside. She whirled around, facing Kipper who stood before them with a manic look in his wild gray eyes. Slake tightened his hold around Joni, stepping away and she stumbled back, trying to keep up.

"See my face?" Kipper thundered. "See what he did to it?" He stormed over and grabbed Joni's hand, forcing her fingers touching the raised blood-encrusted scars across his nose and cheeks. "I might go slicer-dicer on him and see what comes up... or what doesn't!"

"There's a considerable difference in skill obviously!" Joni yelped when Kipper let go. "You probably couldn't touch him; that's why he isn't cut up!"

"Watch me!" Kipper reached over Joni, grabbing Slake by the shirtfront. Slake grunted and twisted Kipper's wrist, releasing his grip.

Kipper pulled away and threw a sucker punch with his other hand, cutting Slake across the cheek with a bladed molded knuckle around his fist. He laughed hysterically as Slake loosened his hold on Joni and staggered back, clutching his face.

Joni kicked Kipper away and turned to Slake, finding instead of red blood oozing from the deep cut, it was sticky violet. Slake growled under his breath, glaring hatefully back at Kipper as he clenched his hands.

"Take a good look," said Kipper as he wiped off the bloodied blade on his jeans. "They're healing right up!" Kipper placed his bladed hand on his hip while the other ran through his long bleached hair. "He's not even normal, let alone human because humans don't have *purple blood!* "

"So...!" Joni watched the dark red line etched into Slake's skin slowly disappear, awed by the sight. "You're right!" She turned toward Kipper. "Still, you shouldn't be beating him up to get your kicks!"

"I'm shocked!" Kipper said, grinning mockingly. "How would you like it if I beat on *you* for kicks?"

"Get lost!"

Kipper lurched forward and Slake jumped before Joni with fists raised, ready to fight.

"Again with the protecting, eh?" Kipper snorted. "I went easy on you the first time... this time, I'll show no mercy!" Kipper snapped his fingers and a black leather jacket with many silver buckles and zippers appeared on his body. He reached inside the pockets, withdrawing a small black staff. "Moon Staff, reveal to me!" Black light surrounded his hand and the small staff grew larger, becoming eight feet long with a crescent shaped head.

"You'd better not touch us with that!" Joni spat as Kipper pointed the scythe ahead.

"Yeah," Kipper smirked, "unless you got something to counter this, I'm coming for you!"

Before Kipper advanced, he suddenly stiffened and arched in pain, crying out in agony. Kipper dropped his polearm and collapsed forward onto his knees. Joni cringed, noticing a ring with a sharpened outer rim lodged in Kipper's back, glowing dimly in silver light.

"*Aye*," a voice grumbled in her mind, "*take that!*"

"Who threw that?" Joni cried. "Who said that?" Slake took Joni by the arm and rushed her toward the school doors before she could initiate a search for the thrown weapon's source. "They nearly sliced that creep in half! Don't be an idiot and stick around in there!" Slake yanked open the door shoved Joni outside, forcing her stumbling forward. Whirling around after hearing the tumblers turn, Joni slapped a palm against the glass, watching Slake run through the dimly lit corridor. "Slake, come back! Don't fight them; they might kill you!" She tried the door, finding it locked then banged on the glass as the shadows increased, blocking her view.

"Hey, Joni," Randy called, "what are you doing?"

Joni turned around, blushing slightly. "Don't tell me you're checking on me!"

"Okay, I won't." Randy shrugged his shoulders. "Something wrong though? You look worried about something."

"Slake forgot something and went back to get it," Joni hedged. "But the door locked after him!"

"Well, he'll be alright; it's not like he can't take care of himself." Randy walked ahead and Joni followed him. "Anyway, we'll be going back in a few minutes..." He blew a disconcerted sigh. "So much for my lunch; I totally missed it!"

Joni put on the best smile she could muster. "Well, they'll probably let us go home early or something," she said in false cheer.

"I hope so; I'm starving!"

"Students, please enter the gymnasium via the athletic field," stated the voice of Principal Faber over the public announcement system, "and file by order of homeroom."

The large student body took their time, congregating toward the frost-covered track area.

Following Randy, he continued talking about trivial matters and Joni nodded, listening halfheartedly while lost in her own thoughts.

"*I hope Slake's okay against that crazy blond!*" she thought. "*There's also that weirdo who tried to whack the fool. I don't know who to trust...*" Joni gazed worriedly at the sparse cloudy skies. "*I don't think I can handle all these creepy guys in my face. I should just drop out and take my exit exams...*" Joni glanced back over her shoulder at the school exit doors. "*If Slake ever gets out of there, he's got a lot of explaining to do!*"

Later Joni boarded the bus and frowned when she saw Slake wasn't in his usual spot. Sitting in the empty seat, Joni stared out the window.

"*Despite his Magic, could Kipper seriously hurt him?*" she wondered. "*I'd never thought that dangerous nut would have Magic too!*" Joni grasped the amethyst pendant she wore. "*I shouldn't get involved. Dad told me that magicians who fight with Battle Magic are dangerous against healers! That greasy blond's the definition of a Battle Mage and I definitely don't want to be around that loose screw!*"

"That was really something!" Greta's voice cut in, scattering Joni's thoughts.

"I know, right?" Randy answered.

Joni let go of her necklace and glanced up, watching Greta board the bus with Randy, speaking animatedly while he nodded in interest.

"Principal Faber had to dismiss everybody because the fire department found out some parts of the school were major fire hazards," Greta went on, "and need a bunch of work done!"

"I think *everyone* knows *that!*" Randy replied, snorting. "That's common knowledge!"

"Who'd they pay off to keep it open that long anyway?" Joni asked.

Greta took a seat near the middle of the bus, facing the window and Randy sat across from her in the next seat.

"It's not like there's much of a point," said Greta, "since the school's been unaccredited for the last three years."

Joni grinned. "Right, and that means your diploma isn't worth shit, Mister Football star!"

"Hey, I got a Plan B," Randy retorted, looking back at her.

"What's that?"

Randy stuck out his tongue at her. "Ain't telling."

"Dork," Joni groused and Randy snorted.

"I bet it was that uppity Clarence Schroeder who tripped it, the nosy bum! He's not even from around here - he transferred out from TriCity and is already giving everyone grief, claiming he wants this to be a better place to learn!"

"Nortiniry's the wrong place to do it then," Joni said and laughed. "He's wasting his time."

"I heard his parents couldn't keep the ritzy house out in Garden Place," said another student near Randy. "They had to move back to the ghetto since the recession."

"This isn't the ghetto, dummy!" said a student across from Joni. "North Side is pretty descent." Joni glanced toward the olive-skinned young woman wearing navy horn-rimmed glasses, a bright green bulky padded coat, big floppy hat resembling a wolf's head complete with ears and dark jeans. Joni's heart skipped a beat when she noticed the agate-leaf designed bracelet she wore on her right wrist, glimmering dimly.

"What about the Pleasant Valley area?" Greta continued. "Now *that's* ghetto!"

"Hey, you live near the Pleasant Valley area," Joni protested, returning her attention to Greta. "It's not that bad!"

Greta turned in her seat, giving Joni a wary look. "What do you know about Pleasant Valley?" she retorted. "You moved back to Lakeview, remember?"

"I heard that Mister Stoneface lives right down in the worst part of Pleasant Valley: Hillside District!" Randy interjected. "That's the worst block in the county!"

"No, it's not!" Joni countered. "The worst block is in... um, Great Acres, or Idylewilde!"

Greta laughed. "Idylewilde? Really? That's the best part of town you can come up with?"

Joni glanced toward the young woman who held a thick book in her hands, reading its contents. "Some help?" she asked helplessly.

"Hillside's crime has gone up recently," the young woman replied without looking at Joni. "After the shopping center closed down, a lot of people left."

Joni huffed and left her seat in the rear, taking the empty one behind Greta.

"Don't kid yourself," Randy drawled. "I wouldn't be surprised if Mister Stoneface has to sell out to get extra spending money!" He left his seat and sat next to Greta, nudging her side with his elbow. "Did you see the clothes he wears?"

Greta slapped Randy's hand and Randy grinned.

"You know he dresses that nice all the time!" Joni retorted and poked Greta's shoulder, making her look up. "Ask Greta yourself. She dated him for a while."

"I don't know..." Greta murmured, turning away. "Didn't Signe say that with threads like that you'll have to work a side hustle at Super Value Mart or something?"

Randy burst out laughing. "He's a sell *out!*" he crowed. "Looks like that aren't cheap!"

"You're so disgusting!" Joni snapped, glaring at him.

Randy put up his hands in mock surrender. "Hey, I'm telling the truth!"

"Where do you hear this stuff from?"

Randy waved Joni away. "Around... You know I hear stuff."

"It's probably that motormouth Bobby Milian," Greta said and Randy nodded. They both started giggling when Joni's face turned red in extreme irritation.

"What are you talking about?" Joni snapped. "How would you know him, Randy? He left the 'hood years ago!"

Randy shrugged. "Like I said, I hear stuff."

"Then how are you even talking to that crackpot crank?"

"What are you getting so mad for, Joni?" Greta teased. "You hated Bobby's guts."

"I still hate him because he talks too much, always starting rumors and whatever!" Joni sat back in her seat, folding her arms across her chest. "He was always spouting crazy far-out stuff."

"I heard he got out some days ago," Randy answered.

Joni's eyes widened. "Got out from where?" She leaned forward and grabbed Randy's sleeve. "Tell me!"

"Didn't he serve time for that bomb threat a few years ago?" Greta inquired.

Randy nodded and pried off Joni's fingers. "He called me up and said he's waiting for his paperwork to clear."

"How close are you to that lamer?" Joni inquired.

"That lamer makes pretty good business at my uncle's store," Randy said. "So it's my business to be nice to the dude."

Joni flashed Greta a shrewd grin. "Hey, Greta, you can tag him," she joked. "I heard those prison guys beef up big time!"

"Shut up!" Greta snapped, rolling her eyes.

"I mean it! Besides, as much as I want to punch Bobby in the neck, he hates my guts too!" Joni punched her free hand into her palm. "I used to trash him in primary school, the doofus crank!"

"Now he can trash *you!*" Randy quipped. Joni flicked her hand at Randy's hood-covered head, revealing a shaggy mullet underneath and a small gold hoop in his left ear. "Watch the hair!" he complained and ran a hand through his disheveled locks.

Joni snickered and tugged at his other ear. "Cut that mullet, will you, dork?" she gibed. "I think you lost the other earring from all that hair!"

"I'm still rockin' the '85, okay?" Randy bat her off. "Party up front, business in the back!

"Isn't that supposed to be the reverse, idiot?"

"Bobby's pretty smart," Greta interjected. "He took advanced science courses... something you'd never wrap your head around."

Joni glared at Greta. "Hey," she spat, "I'm no idiot."

"Yeah," Greta shot back, "you are."

"There's a difference between stupidity and not studying," Joni clarified. "I'm more of the latter than the former."

"Right," Greta drawled. "Sure." Both she and Randy fell into a fit of giggles as Joni growled under her breath, growing irritated.

"I don't see how the doofus crank even kept up with school," she griped, "with his mom's special brownies and that banana cake she always had baking..."

"You were always about Magic and mutants and conspiracy theories and special ESP Powers and stuff," Greta retorted.

"Hey, I like to read, okay? Everything else is a snoozefest!"

"No wonder your grades suck!"

Joni ground her teeth and sat back, unable to say anything else.

"Maybe you need to try out those special brownies and the banana cake," Randy murmured. "Get your mind open about science and math, two subjects you suck major in!"

Greta suddenly bawled in laughter. "It won't make you any smarter!" she heckled. "Just admit it Joni, that red hair took all your smarts!"

"Stop picking on me," Joni groused. "I'm not an idiot."

"Don't worry about Joni," Randy said smugly and shook his head. "It's too late for her!"

Joni shook her fist at Randy. "It'll be too late for you if you keep bugging to copy my homework!" she growled. "I mustn't be too stupid if you keep hassling me about that!"

Randy waved her off. "I didn't ask you this time because we didn't get any homework tonight, Genius!"

Joni grew increasingly annoyed when Randy razzed her. "Argh, you're so damn annoying!" She shook both fists at him.

"Argh!" Randy mocked. "You sound like a pirate!"

"Hey, let's see if he's still in the neighborhood," Greta suddenly piped as Joni immediately stood.

"I'm so going to snap on you!" Joni said through gritted teeth.

"I love it when you get hot," Randy jeered, fanning himself with his free hand. "It's such a turn-on!"

"Joni, cool it!" Greta said and pushed Joni by her shoulder back into her seat. "He's just pushing your buttons; don't get so bitchy!"

Joni groaned and slumped back. "I don't want to bother that crackpot crank," she complained. "He's nothing but a bad memory I'd rather shake!"

"It'll be fun!" Randy turned to Joni, grinning. "Hey, he might have some of that space cake to make you smarter!"

Joni narrowed her eyes at Randy. "I'll pass Math class on my own, thank you!" she said sourly.

"Also History and Geography and..."

"Oh, shut up!" Joni pushed Randy and he giggled.

"Save that for later when I'm really bad!"

"Ugh, you disgust me!"

CHAPTER NINE

Joni later exited onto the frost-covered street corner with Randy and Greta following. She looked around as the bus rumbled away.

"Hey, what did you do with your backpack?" Greta asked. "You had it this morning."

"I put it in Slake's locker," Joni answered.

"You're so getting an 'F' on your homework tomorrow if he's gone another day!"

"Whatever. So where's Bobby's house?"

"That's what I'm trying to remember." Greta started walking ahead. "I think it's down this way..."

"No, if I remember correctly," Randy said, grabbing Greta by the arm, "he lives somewhere this way."

"Yeah right," Greta scoffed. "You didn't grow up around here!"

"I did and I'll show you!"

"Argh, you guys, why don't we split up?" Joni grumbled. "Greta, you cover the side street, Randy will cover the east end and I'll cover the west end. Then we'll come back to this three-way stop and tell each other our finds."

"Good idea," Greta said and hurried down her assigned street.

"For a ditzy girl, you sure have brains!" Randy teased.

"This coming from some dead metal-head?" Joni chided. "You're the one needing my help!"

Randy laughed and waved her away before taking off down the street.

Joni shuddered from the frigid rush blowing around her and tightened her wool coat. "*That same freezing wind I felt,*" she thought.

"It's *not normal at all!*" Joni looked up at the house facing the three-way street corner. "*Is it coming from there?*" The large gray and black two-storey home, with dark shutters covering the windows, seemed out of place with the other brightly colored houses on the block. Joni looked down the street, spotting her aunt's compact sedan in the driveway. "*Well, I'm about seven or eight houses away from Aunt Renee's and I remember Bobby lived here when I used to visit.*" Walking up the frosted walkway, she stomped up the steps before the shaded sunporch. "*If I get into trouble from Bobby, I can make a break for it.*" Joni tried the screen door and it opened with a metallic groan. She approached the front door, pressing the nearby buzzer.

"Hey, Joni!" Greta's voice called, "found anything yet?"

Joni turned around as Greta jogged up the street. "Not yet," she called, "I'm checking out this one."

"I'm going down on this end, okay?"

Joni waved her friend away and turned around. She gasped at the sight of a tall semi-muscular young man wearing smoke-tinted horn-rimmed glasses, silver hoops in his right ear and had short reddish-orange hair with the front spiked up. He was dressed in a sleeveless red athletic shirt that showed off his muscular arms, tight stonewashed jeans and white high-top sneakers.

"Hey," the young man said brightly. "Don't I know you from somewhere...?"

"*Now I know this isn't coincidence at all – he also appeared in my vision!*" Joni thought, amazed. "*This can't be good...*"

"Can't you talk?" When Joni said nothing, the young man chuckled. "I guess you're so wowed by my handsomeness that you've lost your voice?"

Joni grunted. "Um... hi," she said sheepishly.

The young man leaned against the doorframe, grinning. "Need something?"

"I'm looking for this guy named Bobby Milian," Joni explained. "Does he live here?"

The young man nodded. "You got it, Baby."

Joni waved him away. "No way," she said, incredulous. "You can't be that fat crazy kid with the sandals!"

Bobby chortled and adjusted the glasses on his face. "Times change, huh?" he murmured. "What a wonder hardcore training can do!" He opened the door wider. "Want to come in?"

Joni put up her hands. "Not really..."

"So why are you wasting my time?" Bobby continued to smile despite the hardness in his eyes. "Did you come here on a dare or something?"

"No, that's not it." Joni took a step away. "I was talking to Randy about some old classmates and..."

"Oh, right, that pasty jerk with the aviators." Bobby smirked. "I remember him. Doesn't he play on the team with that country boy with the crooked teeth?"

"You mean Ryan Arcendo?"

"Yeah." Bobby snapped his fingers. "Yeah, and that Ryan guy hung out with that cute brown-haired girl and she hung out with that dummy redhead..."

"Hey!" Joni yelled, clenching her hands. "I'm no dummy!"

"Oh!" Bobby laughed aloud. "So *you're* that dummy redhead!" He reached forward and ran his fingers through a lock of Joni's hair. "Your hair... about time you grew it out. It's good to see you've grown up from being a tomboy to somebody mighty fine, huh?"

Joni slapped Bobby's hand away. "Don't even start with me!" she snapped and shook her fist at him.

"Whatever happened to that ghetto sister of yours?" Bobby put his hands on his hips. "She's still going into County for fighting at the Rose Bar or what?"

"Or what?" Joni spat. "She's goes to Missouri University."

"Majoring in what, Chemical Studies?" Bobby scoffed. "She's a bigger pothead than my parents!"

"Kacey never did drugs!" Joni protested. "It was her friends she always bailed that did!" She threw up her hands. "Argh, why do I bother?"

"I know deep down you like me; you can't resist me." Bobby laughed as Joni stormed away, slamming open the sunporch door. "Hey," he called after her, "if you see that cute friend of yours, tell her I'm looking for her!"

"Talk to her yourself!" Joni called over her shoulder. The door shut after her and Joni came down the steps as Randy came up the walk.

"Hey, what's wrong?" Greta asked once she approached from the other street. "Who pissed you off now?"

"Bobby worked my last nerve!" Joni grumbled, picking up a fistful of snow from the porch and began packing it down. "He thinks he's so cool and can talk about anybody he wants!"

"You say Bobby lives in that house?" Randy asked, astonished. "That's like, the best house on this block!"

"But it's so creepy and dreary looking," Greta complained. Joni grunted and scooped up more snow to pack. "Come on, gray and black? Gross..."

"At least the other houses are more colorful!"

"Eat this, Milian!" Joni snapped, hurling the handful of snow at the house. It crashed through the sunporch's window, landing on the planks.

"The hell?" Bobby's voice shouted from inside.

"Let's get out of here!" Greta yelped and all three scattered in various directions.

Joni entered her house and slammed the door behind her, panting hard for breath. She came out of her coat and chucked it aside on the couch then headed for her kitchen.

Entering the side door leading to the basement, Joni switched on the overhead light, revealing the finished room of stone and concrete. It housed many cardboard boxes covered in a light film of dust jammed along the walls and shelves built to accommodate tools, creating narrow aisles. She groaned at the sight.

"*It'll take hours going through them all!*" Joni thought in dismay and made her way down the stairs, approaching several tucked under the stairway. "*I don't know why it's so important finding what Dad left behind. It's been awhile since he moved on.*" Joni started her search in one box, rummaging through its contents. "*I really didn't want to go through his old things, but with that vision and now all the people I'm running into, I know it's not just coincidence after all!*"

Finding nothing but old papers of various reports, Joni closed the box and took several others down from its place, setting them on the floor and nearby chair. She sat beside the collection and began unpacking, sifting through what they contained.

"*I hope whatever it is can help me since more and more people are showing up with Magic these days... And with the vision starting to come true, I need to find out as much as possible!*"

Finding art supplies in one box, Joni opened the next unmarked box, discovering old books and used fountain pens with empty inkwells. Setting them aside, she pulled out a large black wooden book with metal hinges.

"What's this?" Joni murmured, noticing that it had nothing written on its front. Opening the book, she revealed an old weathered page titled *The Book of Legions*. "Why would Dad keep this?"

Running a hand across the page, it glowed dully in pale violet light. Joni heard rattling and stiffened, fearing the worst. When she heard no footsteps, Joni set aside the book and sifted through the box's remainder, withdrawing more papers with chemical formulae and a paperback about Magic Traditions.

Finally reaching the bottom, she found two dimly glowing clear vials. Pulling them out for closer examination in the yellow-orange light, Joni realized they held colored dust inside, with one red and the other light blue.

"*Is this ink powder?*" Joni wondered and pulled against the stopper on the blue vial. The cork shimmered in bright gold.

"*Owch!*" a voice cried faintly.

Joni froze and glanced around for the voice's source, finding none. "I must be stressed out if I'm hearing stuff..." she muttered and pulled the stopper again.

"*Hey!*" the voice wailed and the small bottle shivered then slipped from her hand, rolling away.

Joni gasped and scrambled to her feet. "Who said that?" she demanded.

"*Take your sweaty hands off me!*" a harsh tinny voice squawked. Joni let out a cry, dropping the red vial and it struck the floor with a dull clink. "*Hey, watch it!*"

Joni stepped toward the hazily glittering vials, overcome with fear and confusion. She poked them with her toe.

"Hmph, I'm just hearing stuff," Joni grumbled. "There's nothing inside those things!" She returned to her boxes, placing what she took out.

"*What did she say?*" the calm voice asked.

"*She called us nothing!*" the minute harsh voice screeched. "*I ought to teach her a lesson!*"

"*Calm down; it's no good getting angry!*"

Joni turned around, finding the red vial shivering on the floor. "Wah!" she yelped and jumped on the chair. "It's moving by itself!"

"*Let me out of here,*" the voice continued to yell, "*and I'll show you what nothing is!*"

"Yeah, right!" Joni cried and picked up the paperback. "I'm not letting you out!" She tossed it down, striking the vials.

"*That hurt!*" the other voice wailed and the voice from the red vial began spewing curses.

Joni got off the chair and ran back upstairs, seeking shelter in her father's room. "*Did those things ever talk when Dad owned them?*" she thought. "*Argh, I must be losing my mind!*"

Once she caught her breath, Joni realized nothing chased her and she returned to the basement, grabbing the heavy hardbound, then sneaked into the kitchen.

Opening the black book and turning the page, she frowned when she came across one page she could read, while the remainder in a written language she never saw before.

"This looks so strange," Joni murmured. "The writing's just some weird shapes and symbols..." She glanced back at the single page that made her feel uneasy.

"Do not lose this Remnant," Joni read. "*Do learn to control the Remnant's massive power. Don't trust anyone. Do anything to keep the Remnants from landing in the wrong hands. These Remnants must not be broken and their powers scattered or disaster will befall this world.*"

"It's even come with rules, seriously?" Joni grumbled and shut the book. She crept toward the stairs, peeping over the banister. The red vial continued shuddering while the blue vial remained still.

"*Please, let us out of here,*" called the calm smooth voice. "*We've been cramped in here for a long, long time.*"

"What about the other one?" Joni spat. "I'm not letting out just *anything* that wants to hurt me!"

"*My brother won't do anything to you as long as I'm around!*"

"He'd better not!" Joni approached both vials. "I'm not so sure about this..." She picked them up and headed back upstairs, setting them on the table. "What are you? How come I can hear you?" She received no answer. "Well?" Joni grunted and opened the book once again. "Why would Dad write this in a secret language?" After getting no response, Joni blew a hard sigh. "Well, I'm keeping you out here where there's some light out that box. Once you two tell me what's going on, then maybe I'll free you!"

Hearing a knock at her back door, Joni flinched, startled.

"Who's there?" she called tentatively.

"Who else?" Randy's voice called from the other side. Joni turned around, spotting Randy waving at her from the back porch window. "Are you letting me in?" Joni left the table and unlocked the door, opening it wide. Randy glanced over her shoulder. "So who are you talking to?" he asked.

"Nobody!" Joni answered, her face flushing scarlet. "Why would you care?"

Randy smirked. "For real? Last I talked to him; he was crying his eyes out, 'cause everyone keeps blaming him for stuff!"

Joni giggled. "Alright, Randy; what is it?"

"Are you inviting me in?"

"And have you rape me?" Joni waved him away. "No, thanks, you vampire!"

"Hey, I don't do the raping thing." Randy put up his hands. "I should be more scared of *you*. You can easily take me on with that broom there and give me one hell of a prostate exam!"

Joni laughed harder, shaking her head. "You're straight crazy, you know that?"

"So, get any news about Bobby Milian?"

"Yeah, that's his house and he's got eyes for Greta." Joni snorted. "Do you think her record will break this time?"

"Only if Bobby finds you revolting," Randy said, shrugging his shoulders.

"Let's hope he's gay. She can't blame me for that!"

Randy shook his head, smiling. "Alright, thanks for the alert." He waved her off and left down the steps, returning to the woods.

Joni faced the vials on the table. "A warning would've been nice!" she hissed as she shut the door.

"*He couldn't hear us anyway,*" answered the calm voice. "*Only you can.*"

"Argh, so I'm crazy now too?"

"*I feel something about him...*" grumbled the tinny harsh voice. "*I think he may have hidden mystic powers that when unleashed will affect you...*"

"What?" Joni snatched up the faintly pulsing red vial. "Look, you tell me what it is and straight up too!" The light died and she grabbed the vials, marching into her father's room. Throwing open the bottom desk drawer, she dropped them into the dark space. "In you go!" she snapped.

"*Wait!*" cried the voice from the blue vial.

"*Hey!*" shouted the harsh voice from the red vial. "*Not again!*"

"I don't want to hear neither one of you until I figure out what you are!"

"*We are Legions, silly girl!*"

"Well, tough cookies; I can't read that heavy old thing anyway! Besides, you could be lying!"

"*Wait!*"

Joni shut the drawer, cringing at the sounds of muffled yelling and rattling resounding from within.

CHAPTER TEN

A slight chill passed through Joni and she shuddered. Approaching the bedroom window, she peered outside and found nothing unordinary in the woods. She then headed for the parlor, drawing the main window's heavy curtains closed.

When the sense of unease refused to leave, she peeked again from a corner and noticed a shadowy figure walking the somberly lit road. Once he came closer to her line of sight, Joni noticed a tall young man strolling in the darkness of the autumn evening, with frosty puffs of breath floating over his head.

The young man then came to a stop in front of the Warren residence and Joni recognized the delicate features from the glow of the porch light.

Leaving her window, she approached her door and unlocked it, throwing it open. Spotting Slake standing several feet away from the driveway, hands stuffed into his coat pockets, Joni waved at him.

"Are you okay?" she called. Slake said nothing in response. "Well, what do you want?" Slake shook his head, smiling slightly. "Aren't you going to say anything?" When Slake gave no response, Joni blew a short sigh and grabbed her coat she left draped on the couch then jogged down the steps, making her way over to him as she pulled into the garment. Slake stepped back, slightly nervous once she approached and shook his head, turning away.

"Wait, don't leave!" Joni grabbed his arm and he paused in step. "Why come all the way out here and just stand there? What are you doing out here, spying on me like some pervert?"

Slake turned to her, his blue eyes giving her a hard glare and Joni bit her hand, taking a step away. Slake's eyes softened somewhat in return and he looked down at the ground with sagging shoulders. Joni reached out and he gently grabbed her wrist, buttoning the cuff of her coat for her. Joni blushed slightly in response, pulling away.

"I want to know what made you come out here since I live two miles away from everyone else!" Slake blew a short sigh and Joni buttoned the other cuff to her coat. "If it's to show me you're not dead from giving Kipper a well-deserved beatdown, thanks."

Slake put out a hand and Joni timidly took it, getting led down the street. Joni looked around her surroundings, taking note of the direction he was going while she hurried to keep up with his long strides. After several moments, they approached the street's end that had markers near them.

"*He's taking me beyond the dead end,*" Joni thought. "*There's nothing but a large field out here where the guys would play football and soccer and baseball...*"

The street lantern's glow became dimmer as they left the street and went further into the fields, coming across dense woodlands.

Happening upon a small path, Slake let go of her hand as the track became more difficult with tall weeds and low-hanging branches. Joni followed close behind, trying to keep him in her sights when he seemingly blended into the night.

Approaching a crumbling brick wall standing six feet high, a nearby street lamp buzzed and flickered on the other side, casting dim light over them. Slake climbed the wall with ease while Joni searched around for something to use as leverage.

Coming across a crate, Joni stood on it, jumping upwards. Grabbing at the brick's top layer, she tried pulling herself up, only to lose her grip. Joni jumped down on the crate and moments later, a rope came over the edge. She grabbed it and climbed over, coming to the top and turned, easing down.

Once Joni jumped down near his side, Slake withdrew the rope and wrapped it around his arm, then gestured ahead. Turning, she saw a looming three-storey house with a darkened interior facing the brick wall, surrounded by dilapidated buildings. Inside, the house had no evidence of life and Joni wondered who would ever squat there.

"Do you live next to those condemned houses?" Joni inquired. Slake walked ahead and she jogged after him. "What street are we on?" Slake stomped up the old wooden steps and dropped the rope near the door, trying the handle. The door groaned open and Joni peered inside. "Hello?" she called.

Slake entered and maneuvered in the dark easily while Joni stayed on the other side, hesitant. Later, he returned with a small candlelit lantern, giving his face a warm glow. Slake held out a hand and Joni took it, entering with him. The door creaked shut behind her.

"Do you live here alone?" Joni asked as she accompanied him, getting led around the house. "This must've been some great place to stay, despite the old furniture and not having any lights!"

Slake approached a fireplace, placing the lantern on the mantle. Joni noticed a framed photograph of a young man with narrow light blue eyes, fine features and long curly blond hair.

"Is that your brother?" she questioned and Slake nodded. "You guys look almost alike, except your eyes are darker than his."

Slake smiled warmly and grabbed the lantern, continuing the first flight of stairs with Joni at his heels. The two entered room after room housed with various articles carefully placed, representing a certain period of time. Amazed, Joni asked Slake numerous questions and he would smile and stay silent, letting Joni touch all she wanted.

Finally coming to the third floor, Joni entered the room first, wandering around and checking the items occupying the interior. Slake came in moments later, placing the lantern on the nearby desk.

Leaving across the room, Joni happened on a chest and knelt down, opening it. Inside she found many silk dresses with matching hairpieces. Pulling out a striped blue silk dress, Joni held it up for Slake to see.

"What do you think of this one?" she called. Slake nodded in approval. "Want me to try it on?" He flushed and turned away. "I'll be extra careful with it," Joni promised. "I won't ruin it, I swear!" Getting to her feet, she approached a freestanding mirror nearby and wiped away the dust with her coat sleeve. Holding the dress in front of her, she gave her reflection a critical look. "This one is really pretty. I wonder where someone got this," she murmured. "I've never seen anything like it before!"

Slake coughed and Joni turned, noticing he stood with his hands in his pockets, looking down at the floor. His cheeks and ears burned bright red as he shifted nervously on his feet.

"Oh, you're waiting for me to put this on, you perv!" Joni teased and giggled when his face turned from scarlet to tomato red. Slipping out of her coat, she let it fall to the floor and set the dress aside, pulling out of her sweater. "Do you think I'll look weird being flat chested?" Joni asked. "It might look good if I was a B-cup or something, right?"

Chucking the sweater atop the coat, she picked up the dress and undid the buttons, then slipped it over her head. Pulling her arms into the sleeves, she frowned when she found the buttons were in the back.

"Hey, Slake," she called, "would you lend me a hand?"

Slake silently approached and pulled out of his leather gloves, placing them in his overcoat pockets. Joni looked at herself in the mirror under the lantern's glow as Slake started the task of buttoning the dress.

"Do you think this looks okay on me?" she probed.

Slake smiled tentatively and turned away, rummaging through the chest. He withdrew a hair comb, placing it in her hair then leaned back, giving her a long once-over. Blowing a satisfied sigh, Slake turned away, folding his arms across his chest.

Joni turned to face him and undid the buttons to his coat. Slake knocked her hands away, grunting. "I just want you to stand next to me, that's all!" she protested. "I want to see how we look!" Slake sighed as he came out of his coat and set it on the floor, then stood next to Joni as she faced the mirror. "Smile, Slake; don't look so sad!" Joni leaned against him, studying their reflections in the mirror.

"You look so handsome, like some captain of a yacht or something," Joni remarked, "and I'm like this beautiful princess of some foreign land, ready to be swept off my feet!" Slake chuckled. "Well, can you come up with one better?" Slake wrapped an arm around her shoulders and stood straighter, smiling brightly. "That's it; there you go!"

Slake took Joni's small hands into his slender ones, clasping his elongated fingers around her own. He pulled back and placed Joni's free hand around his arm as he placed his hand to her hip, then led the way, waltzing to a silent tune. Joni giggled as she stepped in time.

"So we're on your ship, huh?" she teased. "You're entertaining a bunch of high-class people and there's wine and music and everyone's dancing and having fun..."

Slake grinned as Joni continued making up the story of their alter egos and their adventure together while they danced. She laughed when her silent partner clearly appeared to be enjoying himself.

While they waltzed, the moon slowly came into view from behind the clouds and cold light filtered in, casting faint shadows into the room. While dancing near the window, Joni fell silent when he pulled her closer, overwhelmed with guilt.

"*I'm not supposed to be with him,*" she thought. "*In my vision, he gets seriously hurt and dies in my arms! I don't even know who he* really is... *why is he even bothered with me?*" Joni looked up into his eyes and Slake looked down at her, smiling warmly. He brushed a hand across her cheek, and then gently ran a hand through her hair. "*Please don't fall in love!*" Joni prayed as he leaned in closer. "*I can't do this...*"

A loud creak resonated downstairs and Slake suddenly let go, causing Joni stumbling back and striking the floor on her rear. He quickly pulled her up and placed a finger to his lips. Joni nodded and Slake returned to the desk, blowing out the lantern, casting the room back into darkness.

Slake crept into the hall, searching for the intruder. Joni ran to the window, looking out at the dark street below. She immediately spotted a motorcycle parked out front and grew uneasy when she realized she didn't hear it approach earlier.

Exiting the room, Joni spotted Slake descending the staircase and hurried after him. They crept down the steps and Slake suddenly held up an arm, holding Joni back when they heard someone rummaging through the room. He pushed her away and Joni shook her head.

"I'm coming with you!" she whispered.

Slake grunted and both continued down the stairs. The sounds of things moving ceased and heavy footsteps stomped away to another room. Slake grabbed Joni by the hand and both raced down the corridor to the next flight of steps.

Hurrying down them, a shotgun suddenly blasted through the house and Joni screamed in terror when another explosion sounded, blowing away part of the wall above them.

As the intruder reloaded, Slake pulled Joni ahead, racing for the house's front and opened the door. Pushing her outside, Joni stumbled down the porch steps and turned around, only to get the door slammed in her face. She ran away once another gunshot thundered from inside.

Joni shivered in the cold walking down the darkened streets while searching for a safe hiding place. The gunshots continued firing every several moments, sending shivers up her spine.

"*Who did Slake piss off?*" she wondered. "*If he doesn't get killed, he's got some serious explaining to do!*" Joni gasped and came to a dead stop when the bloody vision flashed in her mind. "*What if this is what I saw? I can't live with myself if he gets killed right now!*" She turned back for the abandoned house and ran up the street. "*Maybe I can change the course of the future... There's no reason he has to die if I can't stop it!*" A single headlight came on in the distance, forcing her pause. Cold sweat beaded down her forehead and neck and she took in a shallow breath, backing away when an engine turned and started. "*I hope whoever is there isn't the lookout for the one with the gun!*" Joni prayed.

The vehicle slowly crept up the street and Joni clenched her teeth as she looked around, seeking an escape. She stood her ground when the engine revved and the unknown vehicle came closer. Joni shielded her face once the light became too bright to face.

"Hey," said a familiar voice, "need a ride home?"

Joni put down her arms after the beaming light switched off. "Signe?" she questioned cautiously.

"The one and only," Signe answered and chuckled. "Your Mister Harmless!"

Joni approached the motorcycle. "Do you know what's going on? Slake invited me to his house to show me around and someone broke in..."

Another gunshot resonated faintly in the distance. Signe stiffened, slightly disturbed. "Yeah, Martel called me," he said nervously, "and he told me that he saw someone bust the window and go in."

"Are you going to check it out?" Joni worriedly wondered. "What if Slake gets hurt?"

"Will you be all right?"

"Yes, now go!" Joni grabbed at Signe's arm. "Please, make sure Slake doesn't get killed."

Signe pulled out of his cycling jacket and handed it over to Joni. "I will, I promise... and that's a nice dress." He grinned. "Will you do a striptease for me later?"

"Not now!" Joni took the jacket from his hands, blushing. "But thanks, though..."

"Hm, that one's a winner."

Joni waved him away. "Stop drooling."

"Can't help it."

Another gunshot resonated through the air, cutting the nighttime silence. Signe suddenly clutched his side, hissing in pain.

"Are you alright?" Joni cried, touching his arm.

Signe nodded, grimacing. "You're right... I have to go check on him. I'll see you tomorrow, okay?"

Joni stepped back as Signe started the motorcycle and watched him speed off.

"*What kind of response is that?*" she mused, pulling into the jacket and hurried for home.

CHAPTER ELEVEN

Reaching the cottage, Joni found the inside lights were out, except for the warmly beaming porch light as she ascended the steps. She instinctively went for her pockets and cursed under her breath realizing she left her coat.

"Damn, no keys to get in," Joni grumbled. "I did all this walking for nothing!" She paced, formulating a plan to enter her house. "*Signe must've stopped by and found I left everything unlocked,*" Joni considered. "*I'm so glad I've got him as a friend, creepy as he can get sometimes!*"

Noticing a fist-sized stone on the porch's edge, Joni picked it up, only to turn when she heard harried footsteps down the path. Relieved when she spotted Slake running toward the house, Joni hurried down the stairs.

"I was about to bust a window to get in there," she said, meeting him. "Maybe you can help?"

Slake nodded and bent over, hands on his knees, panting hard for breath. Joni returned toward the steps and dropped the rock back into the garden.

Slake stood upright and motioned Joni to follow. She came after him, walking around the cottage's side and approached a tree offside nearest to it. He grabbed the lower branch and lifted himself then walked across to the roof. After several paces, he turned to Joni, beckoning her to climb.

"You're nuts," Joni snapped. "I haven't climbed a tree in years!" Slake held out a gloved hand again. She sighed, jumped and gripped the branch, hoisting herself into the tree. Standing perched on the branch, Slake lent a hand and Joni grabbed it, getting pulled toward him. "Either you're very strong or I'm really light!" she quipped once she hurried onto the roof.

Slake snorted and took her hand, guiding Joni carefully around the frost-covered roof toward her bedroom window. Letting go, he knelt down, tapping lightly at the glass.

Joni gasped when shadows moved about and she grabbed Slake's arm when a ghostly hand reached forward, unlocking the bolts. She felt cold steel at her fingertips and looked down, finding metal at the edge of Slake's sleeve. Joni pulled it back, revealing a metal bracer with a glowing dark red orb in the wrist.

"What is that?" she murmured as Slake gently pushed her away and pulled up the windowpane. He leaned over as Joni silently hung from the roof's edge, swinging her feet into the pane and climbed in. Once stepping into her room and brushing off her dress, Joni quickly surveyed her darkened room for signs of the mysterious shadow. "Where did it go?" Hearing a small jingle, Joni turned and found her ring of keys on the window's ledge.

"Take care," a low voice said softly.

Joni gasped and looked out her window, finding Slake gone.

Joni sat on her bed's edge and picked up her beside phone's receiver. Dialing Greta's number, she twisted the cord around her fingers while waiting for Greta's answer.

"What is it?" Greta moaned after several rings. "It's after midnight!"

"I need Randy's number," Joni said breathlessly. "All I've got is Ryan's and Signe's busy tonight!"

"What the hell, Joni?" Greta complained. "What makes you think I've got his number?"

"You're friends, right?" Joni pleaded. "Come on, give me Randy's number! I swear; I'll never call unless it's a real emergency!"

"What is it?"

"Please, Greta!"

"I hope somebody's bleeding to death the next time you call me this late!" Greta groused.

"Please don't say that." Greta told her the number and the line cut off with a slam. Joni then dialed Randy's number and it picked up after the first ring.

"Joni?" he said sleepily.

Joni swallowed hard, feeling as if her blood froze in her veins. "H-how," she sputtered, "how did you know it was me calling?"

Randy snorted. "I've got a caller ID service," he drawled. "Come on, now! You thought I was psychic or something?"

"Well, come to the house," Joni said, ignoring his comment. "I need your help!"

"Now?"

"Yes, now! The door will be open, okay? Just come over!"

Randy grumbled under his breath and the line disconnected. Joni hung up the receiver and hurried to the kitchen, pacing frantically.

Moments later, she heard the back door handle turn and rushed over, switching on the overhead lights. Unlocking the bolts, she opened the door, revealing Randy disheveled in his varsity athlete jacket and flannel pants on the other side. On his feet he wore unlaced sneakers and on his face, he wore dark glasses.

"How did you get down here this fast?" Joni asked, peering outside. "You don't drive and I live three miles away from Pleasant Valley!"

"Make this quick," Randy complained, avoiding Joni's question. "My uncle threw a major fit and promised to bury me in the morning."

"I just need help getting out of this dress," Joni said as Randy entered and she shut the door behind him. "It's got, like, a thousand buttons in the back." Coming out of Signe's cycling jacket, Randy blew a suggestive whistle.

"Wow, where'd you get this?"

"Stop drooling!" Joni punched his shoulder and Randy laughed, rubbing at his arm.

"Hey, with a punch like that, you can be sexy *and* scary!"

"*Anyway*," Joni continued, rolling her eyes, "Slake invited me over to his house and I tried it on for him."

Randy cleared his throat loudly and motioned for Joni to turn around. She turned her back toward him and he started taking the buttons out of the eyelets.

"So Mister Stoneface actually *talked* to you?" Randy questioned, incredulous. "Should I look for pigs flying and checking if Hell froze over yet?"

"Not really... anyway, Slake's got a brother you know. I don't know if he's any older or younger though."

"Why didn't you ask him?"

"I didn't feel like it at the time!"

Randy snorted. "What did you two do after you posed for him?"

"We danced."

Randy scoffed and knelt down, finishing the last of the buttons. "No way," he exclaimed. "Now you're shitting me for real."

"Yes, we danced around to elegant music and then he had to send me home because his rowdy neighbors showed up."

"Really, huh?" Randy stood upright. "Stoneface must throw some awesome parties from the sounds of it!"

"I'll invite you next time."

"Alright, I'm done. So what happened after he dropped you off?"

"He told me good night," Joni admitted, facing him.

Randy howled in laughter. "I don't believe you," he ridiculed. "That guy's chances of talking are like finding a needle in haystack: almost nil!"

"Well, laugh all you want; Mister Stoneface likes me!"

"Why bother with that freak show?"

"I'm interested in why he's always asking about me."

"If you end up on the news being hacked to pieces in his deep freezer, I'll be the first to tell them, 'she's the only gal that's ever shown any *real* interest in him and see where it got her!'"

"Randy, go home!"

Randy continued giggling and opened the door. "Wait until he asks to marry you; that'll be hilarious!"

"Get out of here before your uncle kills you!"

Randy gasped for breath, laughing even harder as he headed outside. Joni rolled her eyes, shutting the door behind him. Switching off the light, she slipped off the dress and headed to her bedroom, leaving it on the couch along the way.

Waking up to a buzzing alarm, Joni reached over, slamming a fist over it. After another bang, she shut it off and sat up groggily, yawning. Joni stretched, then stepped out of bed, shuffling to her closets. Hearing a tinny harsh voice yell expletives from her father's room, Joni let out a scream.

"*See, you've scared her again,*" complained the other.

Joni stomped into the room and yanked open the drawer. The red vial pulsed brightly.

"*When are you going to let us out of this desk?*" the rough voice demanded.

"Am I crazy?" Joni asked.

"*I wouldn't know the answer for that,*" answered the cool voice hesitantly.

"Argh! Shut up!" Joni kicked the drawer shut. "I've got school to deal with too, you see!"

"*And we're not important enough for you?*" came the muffled answer.

"I will break you, I swear!"

Joni stormed out the room, irritated.

Later at school, after Joni left her homeroom, she waited outside Slake's locker and spotted Randy and Greta walking down the hall toward their base class. Joni clenched her teeth as Bobby approached and said several words to them, making the two laugh in response. Randy looked up and waved at Joni for her to come over. She blew a disgruntled sigh and stomped toward them.

"Hey, Joni," Randy greeted. "I forgot how freakin' hilarious Bobby was!"

"Ha, ha, ha, whatever," Joni grumbled. "So the fuzz actually let his paperwork through, huh?"

"Like my coat?" Bobby interjected, ignoring her snide comment. He pulled out of his heavy embroidered denim jacket with mohair lining and handed it to Joni. She put up her hands.

"I'm allergic to mohair," Joni spat.

"Hey, don't hate," said Bobby, slipping it back on. "I did the work myself."

"So, I see," said Joni dryly. "You had plenty of free time while in the big house to learn some soft skills." Bobby glared at her over his dark glasses and pushed them up to his face. Joni smirked. "Don't hate," she retorted.

"What really happened to you?" Randy asked. "Was it true you did time in the clink for a while

"No, I didn't unfortunately, though it wouldn't have been much difference," Bobby explained, shrugging his shoulders. "I got sent to some psych ward where they doped me up and did all sorts of terrible experimental tests on me."

"Hey, it must've forced you to improve," Joni cracked. "You're not fat anymore!"

Bobby bared his teeth at her. "Of course," he hissed. Suddenly, Bobby grinned widely. "Let's see what you got."

"What?" Joni jumped back when Bobby suddenly advanced.

"You heard me; let's see what you got!"

"Um, no. You're taller and a lot stronger than me!" Joni backed away into Randy when Bobby lurched forward.

"They say the smaller ones are fast."

"That's true, Joni," Randy agreed as Joni hid behind him while Bobby stood before them, grinning devilishly.

"I can beat up Joni," Greta said, giggling. "She's a crappy fighter!"

"Shut up, Cadell!" Joni snapped.

"Oh, so it's family name only now?" Greta gave a facetious grin. "Just show him your smooth moves for old time's sake."

"Don't start with me!" Joni growled and picked up Randy's backpack. She swung at Greta and she squealed, jumping out the way.

"She'll mess you up like she did that sun porch," Randy warned, stepping away. "She's got dynamite short-range aim!"

Bobby's face etched in anger. "So you're the one who busted my window, huh?" he snarled. Joni let out a yelp when he grabbed her wrist, applying pressure and forced her dropping the backpack. "Let's see what else you can throw!"

"Let me go!" Joni screeched and struggled against Bobby's tight grasp.

Randy scampered out the way. "You can take him!" he cheered offside. "It should be easy!"

"Use all that awesome chop-socky stuff that your sister taught you!" Greta called.

Joni tried pulling back, only to get thrown forward. She stumbled and turned, jumping out the way when Bobby made a grab for her.

"Leave me alone, Bobby!" Joni yelled, slapping away his hand.

"You thought you were so tough back then, huh?" Bobby shouted. "You aren't so tough now, you dumb pixie!"

"I'm not a dummy!" Joni screeched.

"Then try to stop me!"

Bobby charged, throwing Joni against the nearby locker. Joni pound into his back with her fists, only to cough and stagger to her knees when Bobby delivered a powerful punch into her solar plexus. He lifted her up and threw another blow, then let her go when Joni weakly shoved him away. She turned to her side, vomiting painfully on the floor.

"Whoa," Greta said in awe, "he wasn't kidding!"

Randy hurried to Joni's side, taking her by the arm when she faltered. "You didn't have to do that!" he snapped, glaring at Bobby.

"I'm fine," Joni mewed and weakly pushed Randy away. She leaned against the locker, holding her side. "Don't worry about me."

Bobby gave a smug smile as he put his hands to his hips in triumph. "If she knew how to fight," he said plainly, "she would've countered."

"You--!"

Randy stepped forward, throwing a punch and Bobby leaned out the way, capturing Randy's fist then twisted his arm behind his back. Randy yanked out of his grip and Bobby stomped him to the floor.

"Stupid wannabe!" Bobby growled, kicking Randy in the side.

"Hey, look who's coming down the hall!" Greta exclaimed when Bobby geared for another kick. "It's Mister Stoneface, and he looks really pissed!"

"Who's that?" Bobby asked, looking around.

"That's Joni's new silent boyfriend that I was telling you about," Greta explained. "Oh, he's crazy about her, you see."

Slake ran toward them, elbowing Bobby and Greta out the way and grabbed Randy by the arm, hauling him to his feet.

"I'm okay," Randy muttered when Slake appeared concerned and clasped his shoulder. "It's Joni you should worry about."

Joni waved Slake away when he approached, taking her arm in a gentle hold. "I'll survive," she said and gave a weak smile when Slake ran a hand through her hair. "I might not be able to eat anything for a week, though."

"That's the new boyfriend, huh?" Bobby said haughtily. "Doesn't look like much to me." Slake turned to Bobby, giving him a once over. He snorted at him and waved him off. "The hell was that for?" Bobby snapped, offended. "You're just a skinny little bird! You can't touch me!"

Slake's blue eyes suddenly brightened and he grinned brightly, approaching Bobby then gave a firm push against his chest.

"Hey, I think that's a challenge," Greta said. "He touched you."

"So, you fighting me?" Bobby pushed up his sleeves. "Alright wimp, I'm kicking your ass!"

Throwing a punch, Slake ducked and swept his legs beneath Bobby, faltering him. Slake grabbed Bobby's collar as he quickly put out a hand to balance himself and threw him down, also turning away. Slake stood over him with arms folded across his chest as Bobby crashed into the solid tile and his glasses flew from his face.

"Mister Stoneface got a few good moves," Greta said as Bobby turned onto his back, glaring at Slake with cold black eyes. The bell rang and students crowding around watching the fight hurried for their classes. "Too bad we can't finish it now!"

"Yes," Bobby sneered, "too bad."

Randy stepped over Bobby, grabbing for his backpack on the floor. "Come on, Greta," he complained. "We got Class."

Greta held out a hand toward Bobby and he let her help him to his feet. Slake left his side and took Joni by the arm, leading her into their assigned classroom.

CHAPTER TWELVE

Joni found Signe sitting in a seat near the door with Martel sitting behind him, braiding his sandy hair. "Signe," she called, "what's Martel doing in here?"

"Oh, hey!" Signe said brightly as Martel tied the ribbon in his hair. "You've met my brother Martel, haven't you?" Martel waved at Joni and she gave a halfhearted wave back.

"I've seen him before," Joni answered, "but we haven't really met." Slake sat in the seat before Signe and Joni sat across from him. "Why is he in this class?"

"He got transferred out from TriCity," Signe explained. "The divorce is finalized and Martel's staying with us now."

"That's good, I suppose."

"So you're hanging out after school?"

Joni shrugged. "There's nothing else to do."

"That's great! Now I can get my brother in on the fun!"

Joni's face immediately flushed red and her mouth gaped in shock. Stomping on his shin, Signe yowled and crumpled over.

"You'd better not be saying what I think you're saying!" Joni snapped, narrowing her eyes at him in return.

"What is he talking about?" Martel innocently asked. Signe gingerly waved him over and Martel leaned forward, listening with interest as Signe whispered in his ear. Martel's eyes widened and his tanned face flushed red then he punched Signe's shoulder in response. "You asshole!" he harped.

Joni smiled in response. "Thank goodness you're not a sleaze like your brother," she said gratefully.

"Don't let my gentle nature fool you," Martel replied seriously. "I'm as freaky as they get."

Joni blanched and Signe broke out laughing.

Moments later, Bobby stormed into the classroom and stomped up to Signe, snapping his fingers at him. "Give me the seat," he ordered.

"Is your name on it?" Signe shot back, glaring up at him. "Take any one that's free!"

"What happened to your face?" Martel asked, surprised.

"The same that'll happen to yours if you don't move your scrawny ass!" Bobby carped.

"Hey, stop it!" Joni complained.

"Look," Martel said nervously, "let's be civil here and just take any seat that's free, okay?"

"Shut up!" Bobby barked as he yanked Signe's shirtfront and pulled him out of his chair. "You're next!" He grabbed for Martel and Martel quickly got on his haunches.

"Don't touch me!" he yelped.

"What's wrong with you?" Bobby snapped.

"He doesn't like being touched," Signe replied coolly. "Go on somewhere, why don't you?"

"You're coming out of that seat!" Bobby growled and reached for Martel again, only to have his hands slapped away. Grabbing his collar, Bobby pulled Martel forward.

Martel let out a yowl and kicked Bobby in the groin. Bobby grunted, stumbling rearwards. He shook off his stun and made another grab as Martel pulled back, ripping his collar and revealing a gold chain attached to a silver pendant of a winged sword-wielding Aerian. Martel's hazel eyes glazed over as he sank into his seat, gasping for breath. Bobby grimaced and clenched his hands.

"Look, leave him alone!" Signe snapped and stood between Martel and Bobby. Martel shuddered and pulled up his knees,

wrapping his arms around them. "Because you lost a fight doesn't mean you have to pick on my brother to get your balls back!"

"You got a lucky shot in, you asshole," Bobby growled. "Next time, when I'm not feeling like shit, I'm slugging you!"

Bobby stormed away and found another student, pulling them from their seat then plopped into it, forcing the student finding another free chair.

Signe turned to Martel and touched him gently on the knee. "Come on, Martel," he said softly. "You're okay. He wasn't going to do anything."

"But," Martel sputtered. "He almost... and he..." Signe sighed as Martel abruptly fell flaccid, slumping forward.

"Oh boy," Signe murmured and pet Martel gently on the head.

"Will Martel be okay?" Joni asked worriedly. "What happened to him?"

"Nothing," Signe replied flatly.

Joni turned around in her seat, looking at Slake. He stared ahead, silent. "I hope he'll be okay," she murmured.

"They all say that."

Unable to say anything else, Joni crossed her arms, listening to the student's idle chatter as they waited for the teacher's arrival. The teacher soon entered the classroom and Signe gently shook Martel by the shoulder.

"Come on, Bro," he said softly. "The teacher's in and he'll get pissed if you're dozing!"

Martel slowly roused and opened his eyes. Joni gasped, grabbing Slake by the arm.

"*His eyes are red!*" she realized. "*They're not hazel anymore!*"

"Where's Master Covey?" Martel grumbled as Signe stood and pulled him upright.

"Master...?" Joni parroted. Slake suddenly stiffened once she tightened her grip around his arm. "Hey, Slake, what are they talking about?"

"Remember, he's not around anymore," Signe said sternly in a low voice. "We're with Adiaen and Master Corbitt now."

"That's right," Martel mumbled.

"Please turn in last night's assignments," the teacher called.

Slake sprang to his feet in response and pulled Joni to her feet. He hurried out into the hall, dragging her along.

"Wait a minute!" Joni cried as Slake ushered her to his locker. "Who is this Covey guy and why are those clowns calling you 'Master'?"

Slake let her go, saying nothing as he unlocked his combination lock. He pulled out her backpack and his notebooks, handing them to Joni, then came out of his dark overcoat and gloves, revealing a dark brown sports jacket and tan slacks with his usual white shirt. Stuffing the gloves into the sleeves and placing the coat into the locker, Slake slammed the metal door shut and hurried for the men's restroom.

Joni took the notebooks and slung her backpack over her shoulder then headed back to class. Coming into the room, she set the notebooks on her desk and let the backpack slip off her back, banging onto the floor.

Taking one book at random, Joni opened it, finding writing in coded language. She flipped through page after page full of the different text.

"This is just like the writing in that 'Book of Legions'!" Joni determined, astonished.

A flawless pale hand slammed down atop the book and Joni looked up at Slake standing before her, his face drawn in irritation. He snatched up the notebooks and stormed for the classroom's rear, taking an unused seat.

"What's your problem?" Joni grumbled and blew a disconcerted sigh. She then searched her backpack for her needed books.

"Now I've got to find out if he's connected to this Legions thing," she considered, "and why Martel and Signe would call Slake 'Master'!"

Going through her usual routine of core classes, Joni finally received a break when her lunch hour approached and she entered the school corridors, searching for Signe.

"I hope his brother Martel will be okay," Joni mused. "It looked like something major happened to him that he's stuck dealing with... He could use a friend and I'm generally nice."

Approaching Slake at his locker, Joni waved tentatively. "Want to lunch with me?" she asked. "I bet you hate eating by yourself!" Slake said nothing as he opened his locker and stuffed his notebooks inside. "Well, I'm off for a place in line before I get stuck starving near the salad bar!" Slake put a hand on her shoulder before she could turn and walk away. "What is it?"

Slake smiled faintly and let her go, waving her away. Joni slipped off her backpack and handed it over. Slake took it, placing the bag inside then shut the locker close. Taking Joni by the hand, he led her down the corridor toward the cafeteria.

Along the way, an unexpected crash sounded by a classroom door opening and Kipper tumbled out, striking the floor in the hallway.

"What's going on?" Joni cried, startled as Slake tensed.

"Don't touch me, you beast!" Martel's voice screeched from inside.

"It's Master Sable to you!" Kipper growled as he sat up, wiping his bloodied nose across his sleeve.

"Forget it!"

Kipper jumped to his feet and rushed back into the classroom.

"We need to help Martel!" Joni protested when Slake pulled her away for another route. "We can't leave him against that greasy blond!" She bat off his grip and hurried into the classroom, finding

Martel standing on the teacher's desk, holding a solid oak staff defensively. His ripped-open shirt revealed his gold chain with the dimly glimmering silver pendant hanging down his tanned chest that had bloody clawed scratches.

"We all left for a reason!" Martel cried. "We *don't* like you!"

"You are still under *my* control!" Kipper roared and formed the black steel saber in his left hand. "Technically, I still own you and whoever you're with has to duel me to get true ownership!"

"Leave Martel alone!" Joni yelled.

Kipper turned, glaring at Joni. "Why are you here?" he snarled. "Get out of here!" He waved her away with his other hand armed with a bladed knuckle and Joni let out a yelp as invisible forces threw her back against the wall.

"You leave her alone!" Martel shouted and jumped down from the desk.

Vaulting forward with his staff, Martel kicked Kipper in his chest, sending him crashing into the floor. Kipper scrambled to his feet as Martel brought down the staff and slashed back, cutting into the wood. The staff glowed briefly when his sword made no dent and Martel swung around, hurling Kipper over into empty desks.

"The hell!" Kipper yowled.

"This one can't break easily," Martel teased and tapped his staff in his hand.

"You bastard!" Kipper kicked a chair aside and staggered to his feet. "There's no way you should be able to use Shenja; I'll break you both, I swear!" He charged with a horizontal strike and Martel leaned back, forcing Kipper stumbling forward.

Martel slammed the staff across Kipper's face and Kipper spiraled onto the floor, dazed. Martel stood over Kipper's downed form triumphantly and the staff he held in his hands pulsated dimly.

"*I'll do more than strike you down!*" a voice shouted faintly.

Joni gasped, alarmed. "*That stick he's holding's like those bottles in Dad's drawer!*" she realized. "*How many more of those things exist?*"

"She says she'll do more than that if you cross her again!" Martel snapped.

The classroom door abruptly opened, revealing Slake and Signe.

"Come on, Bro," Signe called, "let's get out of here!" Martel nodded and followed Signe out.

Slake held out a hand to Joni and she took it, getting led out the room. The four of them then raced down the hall to the cafeteria.

"Oy," Martel groaned, clutching his chest.

"What happened?" Signe asked when they approached the serving line filled with other waiting students. He took off his short jacket, handing it to Martel.

"You know..." Martel said nervously as he set the oak staff against the wall then pulled into the coat. "It's the same problem we've been dealing with." Signe nodded, understanding.

"Why'd Kipper want you calling him 'Master' Sable?" Joni demanded. "You called Slake that too!"

Martel stiffened and grabbed the staff, clutching tightly. "Well..." he stared.

"We, um, used to work for his father," Signe explained before Martel could answer.

"Yeah, right!" Joni spat incredulously.

"That's right," Martel insisted, smiling faintly. "We cleaned house and stuff for extra income."

Joni shook her head. "That doesn't sound right," she protested. "That greasy blond mentioned something about dueling him for true ownership, but why would someone do *that* for if all you two did was clean house?"

"Right, cleaned house," Signe countered. "Really good pay and all!"

"Okay, whatever," Joni grumbled. "Look, I'm finding us a place to sit, okay?"

"I'll grab you something!" Signe promised.

Joni nodded and left Slake's side, searching the cafeteria for a place to eat. She spotted Randy and Greta and walked toward them, only to pause in step when Bobby came to their table and Greta scooted over, making a place for him.

"Hey, sorry about that," Bobby said to Randy. "I wasn't myself this morning."

"It's okay," Randy answered and pushed up his dark mirrored glasses to his face.

Joni left, searching for another free table and came across one near the very back close to the canisters. She sat in the available chair, waiting and Signe approached moments later with a tray holding several burgers and pints of milk.

"I can't miss that curly red head anywhere!" Signe quipped and sat next to her. Joni giggled as Signe wrapped an arm around her waist. "Hey, are you hungry at all?"

"Not really," Joni murmured.

"Oh, boy, that food looks really good!" Martel complained once he approached moments later.

"Then eat something!" Joni said and Martel set the staff against the table.

"Sorry, I can't." Martel put up his hands. "I really wish I could though..."

"Why not?"

"It'll run right through him," Signe explained and Martel momentarily appeared confused. He then burst into laughter as Signe nodded and Joni giggled.

"That's right; we don't want things to get messy!" Martel chirped, sitting across from Signe. "I get really bad gas mileage, you know!"

Slake approached the tables, taking a seat next to Martel and grabbed three burgers and a milk from the tray. He placed the milk aside and started eating.

"Wow," Joni said as Slake devoured his lunch, "he's got an appetite like a horse."

"More like a bear or something," Signe replied and laughed harder.

"Breathe sometime, okay?" Martel chided, laughing more. Slake ignored them, focusing on his meal instead.

"How did you all meet?" Joni asked. "It looks like you three are good friends, well, you and Martel notwithstanding."

"We're brothers," Signe clarified. "I was born albino." He shrugged. "Because I look so different than Martel, people assume he's not related to me by blood."

"Yeah," Martel chimed in. "They think we're best friends or were adopted."

"Well, that explains why you wear dark clothes and sleeves all the time." Joni poked Signe's chest. "But what about your eyesight? Wouldn't it be sensitive to light?"

"I can see okay." Signe waved Joni away. "It's not that bad."

"What an understatement!" Martel protested. "After he signed us away, it only got worse for us."

Joni raised an eyebrow at Martel. "What do you mean?" she pressed. "Was the divorce that messy? Is that why you lived away from Signe?"

Signe shook his head. "After the divorce, you know..." He blew a short sigh. "It wasn't too happy, but we were treated well."

"Yeah, in exchange we had to kick major butt in all his battles," Martel interjected. Signe kicked him underneath the table. "Owch!" Martel rubbed at his shin.

"Battles?" Joni asked, raising both eyebrows. "What do you mean?"

"Oops, never mind." Martel waved his hands wildly, his face flushing scarlet. "Look, we really need to get to class. Later!" Martel jumped to his feet and scurried away.

"Don't forget your stick!" Joni called after him.

Signe laughed nervously as he let Joni go and rose to his feet. "We'll talk later," he said gently and grabbed the staff leaning against the table's edge.

"Sure," Joni murmured and Signe hoisted the staff over his shoulder.

"I promise we'll talk more, just not right now."

Joni nodded and Signe left the table. She turned to Slake who sat across from her, hands in his lap. The burgers were gone and the empty milk carton crushed before him.

"What was that about?" Joni demanded. He shook his head in response. "You had to know them for some time, right?" Slake shrugged his shoulders. "Argh, why am I even bothering asking you?" She rose to her feet. "Look, we've got Gym next. Are you playing hockey with us this time?" Slake blew a heavy sigh, also standing ill at ease.

Joni stomped ahead and Slake quickly followed her for the gymnasium.

CHAPTER THIRTEEN

A charged sensation coursed through Joni once she entered the gymnasium. *"There's a lot of magical energy in here,"* she realized, growing uneasy as she grabbed a taped wooden hockey stick from the box resting against the wall. *"I never felt this much power in one place before!"* Approaching where the other students huddled conversing amongst themselves, Joni shuddered. *"I wish I knew where it was coming from... I hope they're not looking for me!"*

"Hey, it's that Warren girl," someone called, "and her new boyfriend, Mister Stoneface!"

"His name is Slake," Joni yelled, "so get it right!"

"Going to sit another game out, Mister Stoneface?"

"No, he's showing up all you turkeys!" Joni turned, spotting Slake standing at the wall. He pinched his nose and shook his head, then sighed and stomped back for the box containing the hockey sticks. "He's the best player around and he'll crush you all easily!"

"Tch, right," Bobby snapped upon entry into the gym. "I am and still the best floor hockey player since fifth grade. Also, I won all the interschool championships to prove it!" He withdrew a pair of dark green fingerless gloves from his jeans pocket and pulled into them. They glimmered softly before dimming as he flexed his hands. "I helped the Nortiniry Valley School District win four straight before I left!"

"Yeah, Milian kicked everyone's butt while you were benched half the time!" said the loud student.

"That's right," crowed Bobby. "Warren was benched *all* the time because *she sucked!*"

Joni gripped her stick tightly in her hand. "Watch it, Bobby," she barked and waved the hockey stick in his direction, "or I'll make you eat those words!"

"Did you enjoy lunch today," Bobby retorted, "or were you still hurting after I twisted your insides?"

Joni took a step forward and a firm hand grabbed her arm. Turning, she spotted Slake next to her, shaking his head. "You're right, he's not worth spending time in Detention." Joni shook loose his grip. "We'll just show him up in a game of hockey!"

"Fall in, you buzzards," called the instructor, "let's get divided here and we'll start."

Everyone split into smaller groups and Randy left the central group, approaching Joni. "Hey," he said, "I'm joining your team. We need five more people though."

"Did we miss the fun yet?" Signe called as he hurried into the gym with Martel running after him.

"Missus Delaney," Joni called, "I have my team right here."

"Warren," responded Delaney, "you'll need at least three more players to do this game."

"Hey, I'll join," called a voice and Joni noticed the slender olive-skinned young woman with long chocolate brown hair and navy horn-rimmed glasses approaching the group. She wore a yellow vest over a black shirt, a matching plaid skirt and low-top sneakers. The agate-leafed bracelet on her right wrist glowed softly as she neared.

"You were on the bus yesterday," Joni remarked.

"I'm in your class too," the young woman said, grinning and held out her hand. "I'm Varuna."

"Hey, where'd you get that cool bracelet?" Joni asked, shaking Varuna's hand. "We'll need another player, of course."

"I found it in one of my walkabouts in the woods," Varuna answered. "I'm surprised it wasn't broken." She turned around and waved at a group of students chatting offside. "Hey, Nadi, let's play!"

A tall athletic young woman with mocha skin and shaggy black hair wearing a rugby shirt, jeans and basketball sneakers looked up from the group. "My friend Nadia loves sports," Varuna said as she waved back then jogged over.

"Varuna, stop it," Nadia complained upon approach.

"You met Joni, haven't you?" Varuna asked.

Joni shook Nadia's hand when offered. "What class are you in?" she asked.

"I'm in your class too," Nadia explained, grinning. "You really keep your head in books, eh?"

"You still need one more player," Delaney said. "We play with eight people on the team for a quick game you see... and you're one player short."

"Hey," Kipper said sourly as he entered, holding his buckled and zippered leather jacket over his shoulder. "You punks forgot about me."

"Mister Sable," Delaney stated, "welcome back from Detention. Join Warren's team and we can get started."

"Forget it," Kipper snapped.

"Then join Milian's team; your choice."

"I'll stick with the losers," Kipper grumbled. "I don't feel like dealing with him."

"You play Goalie and we'll handle Bobby," Nadia declared.

"Whatever." Kipper chucked his leather jacket aside then picked up a stick and headed for the goalie's box.

Nadia and Varuna joined Joni with Signe and Martel following. Randy huddled with them as Joni glanced back at Bobby and his teammates.

"How are we going to do this?" Randy asked and pulled at Joni's hand to have her join.

"What position are we playing?" Joni asked. "We have to figure out what to play so we can effectively kick Bobby's butt!"

Slake approached the group with an open notebook showing a diagram of a playing field and marked positions on the page.

"What's that?" Randy asked.

"Positions," Slake said simply. Everyone in the group grew silent as he tapped at the sheet of paper. "This is our formation."

"That looks like Soccer or Lacrosse or something," Joni murmured.

"But what he's got isn't a traditional formation regarding any of that, even Hockey," Randy protested. "You should know better than that!"

Slake put up a hand to silence him. "Varuna, you play Rear Chaser," he said, pointing to the position listed on the page. "Martel, Signe, you two are Safeties. Choose a Wing."

"I'll be Left and Signe can be Right," Martel replied confidently.

Joni grew uncomfortable when Signe nodded in agreement. "What is Slake even talking about?" she pressed. Signe ignored her as Slake continued assigning positions.

"Randy, Nadia and I are the Drivers when we play defensively and the Backers when we play offensively," said Slake. "The only difference is that two of us will have to switch from which sides we play on when we change our strategy. Someone tell Kipper he's Guard."

"Nadia already told him that he's the Goalie," Varuna murmured and Nadia nodded.

"So, Randy," Slake said, "do you want to be Left Wing or Right for the Driver position?"

"Um, Left, I guess." Randy stammered, slightly startled.

"Then when we switch to Backer, you'll have to play Right." He turned to Nadia. "You're Right Wing Driver and remember, switch to Left when we become Backers. I'm Central."

"Sure..." Nadia murmured. "I'll try my best."

Slake shut the notebook and folded it, returning it back in his rear slacks pocket. "Let's have a good game, then."

"Hey, what position do I have?" Joni asked.

"You're Front Chaser," Slake answered.

"I think that's like a Forward or something," Randy muttered.

Joni nodded, not completely understanding. "If you say so..."

"Class, let's start!" Delaney called and blew her whistle.

Joni left her group, getting into her position on the gym floor and Slake retrieved his stick he left behind. She faced Bobby who towered over her, grinning bitterly. Joni raised an eyebrow, noticing his hockey stick had orange tape on the handle and on the wide edge of the wing.

"All the others have black tape or white," Joni noted. "Why is yours different?"

"What difference does it make?" Bobby snarled. "Prepare to lose!"

Joni narrowed her eyes at him. "Hey, cry to your mother once we kick your butt!"

Joni cringed when Bobby growled and his black eyes glowed dimly in orange. "You're eating dirt!" he sneered.

The instructor Delaney dropped the black plastic puck and Bobby slammed it away before Joni could set her stick at ready. She turned, spotting the puck whiz past Kipper.

"Damn it!" Kipper screeched as it ricocheted off the wall and slammed into his ankle, forcing him down.

"One point," Bobby said, smirking. "Did you forget that I was the most skilled player in junior high? I made at least three points at the start of the game alone."

"I don't care," Joni snapped, facing him.

"Watch yourself. They didn't call me *Miliaria Milian* for nothing!" When Delaney returned with the puck and set it, Bobby flicked his wrist and sent the plastic shooting past Joni once again. "I set the heat 'cause I'm always on fire!"

"I'll kill you!" Kipper howled when the dark plastic struck him.

"I believe that's two points," Bobby said smugly.

"You're cheating somehow," Joni grumbled. "Nobody's that fast!"

"Then try beating me."

Joni set her stick at ready, waiting for the puck to drop. Once Delaney let it go, Joni struggled against Bobby when he tried striking the plastic once again. The hockey stick glowed brightly against her.

Joni sucked in a shallow breath, stunned. "*There's Magic on it!*" she realized. "*What is he?*"

"Forget it, Warren," Bobby growled, breaking her thoughts. "You're not that strong!"

"I'll kick your butt just like back then!" Joni spat.

"Want to know a secret to my success?" Bobby sneered. "I always imagined that your head was the puck and I carved a hole into your skull each and every time I hit it!" He slammed his shoulder into Joni's chest, knocking her back and forced the puck free. Joni fell on her rear and Slake ran up to them, striking the plastic back.

"Hey, you got a point, Joni!" Greta called after it sailed across the room and landed in the marked area on the floor.

"You're straight crazy!" Joni snapped, glaring at Bobby.

"No checking, Milian!" Delaney shouted.

Bobby raised his stick, pointing it at Joni's throat. "If only this were razor sharp," he hissed, "then I could use your head for real!"

Joni gasped when the end of his hockey stick changed into a sharpened blade. Slake pointed his hockey stick at Bobby's chest and it glowed dimly in gold light.

"Not this time," Slake snarled.

"You want a real game, Stoneface?" Bobby crowed. "You got it!"

Slake pulled up Joni and waved her back. She took his former position in the rear as Slake stood before Bobby, waiting for the puck's return. Joni rubbed at her eyes and looked again, noting the hockey sticks changed to normal.

"I'm seeing things," she muttered. "I'm not even sure if I saw that crazy vision right!" Joni shook her head. "It was so disjointed in the first place..." She sucked in a shallow breath and blew an uneasy sigh.

"You okay?" Randy asked from offside. Joni glanced over to him. "You look ready to hurl or something."

"I'm fine," Joni replied. "I'm not in pain still, thanks."

Randy gave a nervous smile and looked ahead, standing at ready. Joni also returned her attention to the game, clenching her teeth when she watched Slake grip his stick tightly in his hands. Delaney dropped the puck and Slake shouldered past his opponent, guiding the plastic along the floor. Bobby turned, growling.

"Let's go, Joni!" Randy called and ran after Slake.

Joni nodded, following him with Nadia coming up on her side. Slake maneuvered freely through the other students who failed blocking against him. Approaching the goal several feet away, he arched back and slammed the hockey stick down with force, driving the puck past Greta. She shrieked when it whizzed past her, ricocheting off the wall.

"Hey, isn't that what you call a slap shot?" asked Randy, grinning.

"You're even, Joni," Greta called and retrieved the puck, returning it to the teacher.

"Let's take it to eleven," Martel said brightly upon passing.

"What?" Joni asked and hurried to her position, racing after the plastic passing by her.

Signe caught the puck with his stick and passed it to Martel who stood open on the other side of the playing area. Martel ran down the side and flicked his wrist, passing it to Randy.

"Send it home, Joni!" Randy called and immediately passed it to her.

Bobby hastily shouldered into Joni and slapped the plastic away. "You're not showing me up!" he snarled and stormed past her.

Joni raced after Bobby. "You creep!" she yelled and Bobby rammed his elbow into her face, knocking her down. Joni cried out when she struck the floor and sudden pain shot through her nose. She cupped her hand to it, feeling warmth drip down and looked at her palm, spotting blood. "You busted my nose!" she shrilled.

"It was an accident," Bobby said curtly.

"Incoming!" Martel called. Joni shrieked and ducked as the puck returned, sailing past her. Martel stood between them, panting for breath. "You're losing, aren't you?" he quipped and held out a hand to Joni. She took it and he easily pulled her to her feet, then pushed her behind him.

"Why you...!" Bobby's dark eyes flared orange and he grabbed for Martel's throat, only to pause once the gloves brightened. Martel stood ready on the defensive, breaking into a cold sweat.

"*I know you!*" abruptly cried a voice Joni didn't recognize.

Bobby stepped rearward, flashing a devious grin. "I see..." he muttered and turned away, then unexpectedly whirled around, whacking the hockey stick into Martel's chest with lightning speed. Martel crumpled to the floor without a sound.

"Martel!" Joni wailed, kneeling for him.

"Milian!" Delaney barked. "Outside! Two minutes!"

Bobby laughed. "Loser," he spat and stomped away, heading for the penalty box.

"Martel!" Joni cried. "What did he do to you?" She pulled him up as he wheezed for breath.

"Hey!" Signe cried and ran up to them both. "Is he okay?"

"My ribs..." Martel moaned.

"I'll take him to the nurse's office, okay?" Joni nodded as Signe looped an arm around Martel's shoulders. "Hey, your nose..."

Joni gasped when Signe touched her nose lightly and she felt cool energy from his fingertips. She pulled away, stunned.

"Get going," Joni scolded. "Don't worry about me; worry about Martel, okay?" Signe nodded and helped his brother out the room. Joni touched her nose, surprised.

"It's *not broken anymore*," she thought. "*Did he actually* heal *it?*" Joni shuddered as dread coursed through her.

"Hey, Warren," a fellow student called, you okay?"

"Not really," she replied, tossing her stick to them. "I'm out this game. Take my place, okay?"

"Sweet!"

Three others ran onto the floor, immediately taking Joni and her friend's respective places, then resumed game play.

CHAPTER FOURTEEN

Joni made her way for the wall and folded her arms across her chest, leaning against the bricks. Surrounded by other students clustered offside, her apprehension deepened, also mixed with overall worry while watching the match continue underway.

"*What did Bobby do to Martel?*" she wondered. "*What kind of power does Bobby have? I can't even begin to believe that crackpot crank is anything like me!*"

Joni cheered for her friends as they scored more points than Bobby's team.

"Man, they're scoring like no tomorrow!" a nearby student whooped. "I mean, they've already got five points to Bobby's three!"

"I know," Joni replied. "That's one fast hockey game!"

Delaney blew her whistle and Bobby went back in, heading straight for Slake. Signe ran back in from his momentary absence and the student who replaced him tossed him a stick.

"You're screwing up our strategy," Signe called as he raced for a place between Randy and Nadia.

"Y'all playing too fast for me," the student wheezed and he returned for the wall, slumping on the floor with his head between his knees.

Slake's back tensed as he stood across from Bobby, panting hard for breath. Bobby readied his stance and his eyes glowed dimly in orange behind his glasses, glaring back at Slake.

"You son of a bitch," Bobby growled. "You're not even playing the game right!"

Slake shrugged his shoulders in return and Delaney tossed the puck. Slake quickly slapped it away, sending it sailing across the room.

"Go! Go!" Joni called as Randy raced ahead, catching up with Signe after their heels. She cheered when Randy gained control of the puck and passed the plastic to Nadia who passed it to Signe.

"I'm open!" Varuna called. Signe struck the puck to Varuna and she maneuvered around other players.

"Watch out, Varuna!" Joni called when Bobby charged at her.

Varuna faked a left as he tried to block in return and she turned away, picking up the puck with the edge of her hockey stick and passed it behind her. Signe picked up the puck on the edge of his stick, flipping it up and slammed it hard, sending the puck to Slake. Slake caught it on the rear edge, flicking his wrist and arced it into the goal. Greta ducked when the black plastic ricocheted against the wall.

"Better be glad that's not my face!" Greta yelled and Joni laughed, clapping her hands.

"Six points!" Signe whooped. "This is too easy!"

The players reassembled as Bobby took center and growled at Slake. Slake wiped the sweat from his forehead and held his stick firmly with both hands.

"Whatever game you're playing," Bobby snarled, "you're going to regret it!" Slake stepped back after Bobby slapped at the puck once it dropped.

"Turn it around guys," Signe called, hurrying after Bobby.

"Play defense!" Joni yelled as the player who filled in for Martel slammed into Signe. She ran out to the field, taking the stick from the downed player once Signe turned out unhurt.

Joni ducked, twisting out the way, passing others attempts at blocking her while she searched for the puck's controller. Bobby ran past Joni and Signe advanced, taking the puck away from him.

"Joni, get open!" Signe called. Joni jumped over Bobby's stick aimed to trip her and she received the puck. She let out a yelp as Bobby charged for her. "Slake's open!" Signe yelled.

Joni surveyed her surroundings, catching sight of Slake who stood ready for the shot. She passed it to him and a forceful shove knocked her down. Looking up, Joni faced Bobby standing over her, baring his teeth.

"I'll do more than break your nose once I'm done!" Bobby sneered and stormed away.

"Player down!" Signe called and hustled up to Joni, grabbing her by the wrist. "Not fragged this time, are you?" he asked, pulling her up.

"Huh?" Joni shook her head. "You're not making any sense!"

"Signe, get clear!" Slake yelled.

Signe quickly stood at ready, passing the hurling puck back once it came his way. "Nadia, get open!" he called as the plastic went to Nadia. She passed it to Varuna who ran up to the sidelines.

"Slake, watch out!" Joni howled when Varuna passed it to Slake.

Bobby slammed his stick in the back of Slake's knees as he prepared to send the black plastic into the goal. Slake faltered and Signe left Joni's side, darting over near them. He pointed his hockey stick at Bobby's throat before Bobby advanced.

"Back off," Bobby growled.

"You first!" Signe spat. Slake staggered rearward and shook his stick at Bobby.

"I'm warning you, don't mess with me!"

Delaney's blew her whistle and the other students cleared the play area. Slake ran off in the opposite direction and Signe backed away, glaring at Bobby.

"This isn't over," Signe threatened.

"I'll mess you up next time!" Bobby vowed. "Just you wait!" He raised his gloved hand and Signe grabbed his fist coming for his face.

"So, try," declared Signe.

Joni ran over to Signe and grabbed is sleeve. "Stop it," she protested. "Let's get out of here." Signe let go and Bobby swiftly backhanded him across the face. Signe grunted as gold light sparked between them, forcing him staggering back, stunned. He whipped around to throw a punch and Joni pulled him away. "Let it go, Signe!"

Bobby laughed darkly and hoist the hockey stick over his shoulder as he walked away.

"He busted Martel's ribs!" Signe screeched. "My brother could've punctured a lung from the likes of that bastard!"

"But he's okay, right?" Joni pulled Signe closer and took in a shallow breath when she noticed that he had no scar on his face, not even an imprint or bruise from Bobby's strike.

"Damn," Signe moaned, touching his nose. His eyes rolled around in his head and he staggered rearwards. "The piece of shit...!"

"That was one crazy game!" Randy said upon approach. "Can you believe it?" Joni walked Signe toward the sidelines with Randy following. "I never played floor hockey that fast or that intense before!"

"Jeez!" Signe moaned, slumping against the wall.

"Hey," Randy said in concern, "is he alright?"

"What do you mean?" Joni asked.

"Look at him. He looks paler than he usually is!"

Joni touched Signe's shoulder and he winced. "Are you going to be okay, Signe?" she asked gently.

"I'm alright," Signe murmured, "really!"

"Yeah, tell me a new one!" Randy snorted, raising an eyebrow. "You look ready for death!"

"Get out of here," Signe griped.

Joni took Signe's hand. "Are you sure you're alright?" she implored and Signe nodded. Joni clenched her teeth, noticing the color faded from his skin and a pale blue hue began to form.

"Shit man," Randy cried, "are you sure you can breathe?"

"Joni, come on!" Signe begged. "Get me out of here, *now!*"

Joni pulled Signe's hand and both ran out the gymnasium. Following close behind, formless shades rushed after them.

"Where do you think you're going?" Kipper sneered as he broke the swirl of shadows and appeared at the hall's end, blocking their path. His leather jacket glowed dimly in silver light.

"We don't have time for this!" Joni yelled. "Get out of our way, you greasy blond! Signe needs to get to the nurse's office."

"No nurse can cure him and you know that, right Signe?" Kipper teased and laughed darkly. "Or should I call you Naezalesi?" Reaching inside his pocket, he withdrew a small black rod. "Moon Staff, reveal to me!" It transformed into a glistening short-handled ebony sickle gleaming in navy light.

Joni stood in front of Signe who wavered. "You're not hurting him with that – whatever that thing is!" she said evenly. "Let us pass!"

"Fight me first!" Kipper twirled the sickle in his hand as it flashed in dark light, the handle growing longer and turned into a scythe. He pointed it ahead in their direction, grinning. "He's too weak to be of any help! One strike and he's mine!"

"Holy crapola!" Martel's voice cried. Kipper turned as Martel ran toward them.

"Martel, stay back!" Joni called. "Kipper's armed and really dangerous!" Martel skidded to a stop once he saw the scythe.

"Heh, you're weakened too!" Kipper snapped. "Your eyes prove it!"

"*That's right,*" Joni determined as Martel backed away, frightened. "*His eyes aren't hazel anymore... they're* completely red!"

"Take this!" Martel pulled a silver vial from his jeans pocket and tossed it to Signe. He caught it and thumbed the cork, flipping it open. The powder it contained poured out as a pile at his feet on the floor.

"Oh no, you don't!" Kipper thundered and struck the scythe to the floor, releasing a blast of force throwing all three against the wall.

The silver powder scattered into the air and Joni fell back as Signe struck the wall and spiraled to the floor, unconscious. Martel also struck his head and staggered forward before collapsing to his knees, moaning.

"*That's like the two in Dad's drawer!*" Joni realized as the silver powder settled down as dust, glowing brightly on the floor.

"Joni," Martel called, "pick it up!"

"No!" Kipper shouted and rushed toward Joni as she reached out, touching the powder.

The sand glimmered in saffron light and the powder shifted, its scattered grains reforming as a pile. Floating upwards, the granules swirled around Joni's hand before transforming into a large flat ring with a molded handle and a sharpened outer edge.

"Beat it!" Joni snapped and thrust the weapon ahead as Kipper slashed down, forcing dark light sparking when their weapons made contact.

Kipper struggled bringing down his scythe and his eyes widened in disbelief as the scythe glowed brightly before powering down into the sickle again after slicing. "No way!" he screeched.

"*That's the same one that cut Kipper before!*" Joni recognized as the sharpened ring pulsed in faint silver light.

"*Aye,*" a familiar voice grumbled in return, "*I suggest you leave us be!*"

"Get out of here, you greasy nut job!" Joni shouted as she pushed against Kipper, forcing him stumbling rearwards. "I'll slice you to ribbons with this, I shit you not!"

"Joni," Randy's voice called, "are you alright?"

"I'm out of here, suckers!" Kipper growled and withdrew a yellow pouch. He threw it down to the floor, exploding white smoke that quickly fogged the corridor.

Joni clamored to her feet and ran after him, instead finding nothing there. She looked around, stunned at Kipper's disappearance.

"Joni," Randy called again. "What happened?"

Joni turned, hiding the ring behind her back as the fog dispersed. "Kipper fought Signe and Martel and I tried breaking it up," she called back, sensing the weapon grow warm then instantly become cold.

Randy came down the corridor and came to a pause, his expression neutral. "Where are they?" he demanded.

"They..." Joni searched around, finding Signe and Martel had vanished. "Oh no," she thought in horror, "did he take them with him?"

Hearing a faint clink of glass, Joni looked down at her feet, finding a dark blue vial and a black vial with silver specks near her shoe. She noted she held the silver vial once again and reached for the small containers, picking them up. All three disappeared in pale violet light once Randy approached as she rose upright.

"Well?" he pressed.

"They chased after him once I came onto the scene," Joni lied.

"I hope they'll be all right," Randy replied and ran a hand through his shaggy mullet. "They both looked really wiped out!"

Joni nodded. "I wonder where Slake disappeared off to," she said instead.

"Probably went to the nurse's office to check on them." Randy shrugged his shoulders. "You know Kipper fights dirty."

"Yeah, I'll go check on them. Thanks!"

Randy scratched his head as Joni took off down the hall. "Okay," he called after her, puzzled.

Leaving the main corridor, Joni hurried into a side hall and headed for the men's restrooms. Glancing to her left and right, when she saw nobody else watching nearby, she slipped into the room. Once the door clicked shut, Joni heard a sneeze and jumped, turning around.

"Goodness," a voice moaned.

Joni crept into the main area near the sinks and saw several canary yellow feathers on the floor. Another sneeze resonated loudly in the room, followed by a bang against the stall door.

"Are you alright?" she called and heard a yelp then the stall door locks suddenly clicked. "Slake, are you in here?"

"He's in Study Hall," Slake answered.

"Liar!"

"Please," Slake mewed, "go away!"

Joni picked up the fallen feathers and approached the locked stall, knocking lightly. Another sneeze followed and several yellow feathers floated out from underneath the door. She picked them up, surprised when she saw that they matched the ones in her hand.

"Are you working on an art project or something?" Joni asked and entered the next stall. Standing on the seat, she looked over, spotting Slake sitting on the commode with a wad of toilet tissue paper in his hand. His dark brown suit coat lay draped across his lap and his white dress shirt unbuttoned, revealing his broad pale chest.

"What are you talking about?" Slake murmured.

"Are you okay?" Slake nodded and he blew his nose, then folded the used tissue, setting it aside. He looked up, his cheeks flushed slightly at the sight of her. "You're sure?"

"I'm alright," Slake answered.

"Are you allergic to feathers or something?"

"What now?"

Joni dropped a feather and it floated down to him, landing in his hair. Slake grabbed for it, looking down at it in slight revulsion. "Hey, it matches your hair," she remarked. Slake grunted. "So, are you feeling any better?"

"Thanks for checking up on me," he replied softly.

"Any time!" Joni said brightly.

"You're being a bit weird, however..."

Joni snorted. "Blame Signe," she said then jumped down from the toilet and exited the stall. The toilet flushed next to her and Slake unlocked the door. He stepped out, pulling into his blazer and Joni handed him the feathers. Slake immediately recoiled in disgust. "Do you want these?"

"Goodness, no!" he yelped. "Get that away from me!"

"Argh, you act like these are radioactive or something!" she complained and walked over to the nearby trash can, throwing them away.

"They're just..." Slake shook his head. "No, just no." He buttoned up his shirt as he made his way toward the door then immediately backed away when the panel slammed open and Bobby stomped in, growling under his breath.

"You son of a bitch!" Bobby screeched, throwing a punch with his glowing gloved hand. Slake leaned out the way and Bobby struck the wall instead.

Joni cringed near the sinks when she heard the bones in his hand break from impact. "What, are you a little ticked off because Slake showed you up at some weak hockey game?" she snapped. "I thought you were better than that!"

"Shut up!" Bobby yelled. "This is between me and the idiot, stone-faced bastard!"

"He's not an idiot!" Joni snapped.

"You thought you had me at the lockers, huh?" Bobby sneered as he advanced and Slake backed away, bumping into the sinks. Joni grabbed his sleeve and Slake pushed her aside. "You're going down!"

Slake stared down Bobby in defiance once the young man stood close to him, glaring hatefully back. Joni swallowed hard, noting the difference in height between them as Bobby towered slightly over

Slake. Fearing a vicious fight, she stepped away near the urinals, steering clear of them.

Bobby snapped his fingers, forcing a slender silver rod with a golden key on its head appearing in his left hand. Slake elbowed Bobby and made a mad dash for the door. Bobby threw the staff at Slake's back, releasing bronze sparks.

Slake cried out once shocked and fell, seizing on the floor. Bobby stormed over to Slake and kicked his side. "Good luck showing me up tomorrow!" Bobby spat, kicking Slake again. He picked up the staff and slammed it down into Slake, forcing him wailing in agony when shocked once more.

"Stop it!" Joni screeched and ran up to Bobby, shoving him aside.

Bobby grinned devilishly as he pointed the silver scepter in her direction. "Don't touch this," he warned, "unless you like getting stung." Joni stepped away, hesitant. "That's right, Baby, back away." Bobby turned toward Slake and picked him up by his shirt collar then jammed the golden key into Slake's chest. Slake screamed as the bronze light charged through him.

"Don't kill him!" Joni cried.

"Shut up!" Bobby roared, dropping Slake. The door opened moments later and Randy entered. He immediately put up his hands as Bobby pointed the silver scepter in his direction.

"Hey, now," Randy said nervously, "I'm not into that game."

"Get this bitch out of here!" Bobby bellowed.

Randy grabbed for Joni's arm, pulling her out with him.

Joni cringed, hearing Slake's anguished howls when led away from the restrooms. "What is he doing to him?" she demanded as the door swung shut behind them. "Bobby's clearly hurting him with that *thing*..."

"There's nothing I can do about it," Randy grumbled, leading her down the hall.

"It's like a stun gun, right?"

"I don't know, but getting zapped by that thing is the last you need!"

"Then what am I doing standing out here while Slake gets slaughtered?" Joni yanked out of Randy's grip and threw a punch, whipping back his head. The force threw his dark mirrored sunglasses, sending them flying from his face and he held his stinging cheek. Randy glared back at Joni and she gasped, realizing his eyes were blind white.

"Have you lost it today?" Randy snapped.

"No," Joni retorted, "I might lose a good friend instead!"

"I wouldn't even come close to touching Bobby as long as he's got that!" Randy charged. "You're the senseless one if you're even *thinking* of touching him!"

"Slake's getting hurt by that crackpot crank and we're just standing by and doing nothing!" Joni stomped back for the restroom. "I don't want my friends getting hurt!"

"You don't understand what you're getting into!"

"I don't care!"

"Look!" Randy ran up to Joni, grabbing her firmly by the arm. "Listen to me; not everyone can *see* what you see!"

"What do you mean?" Joni shook loose his grip. "That thing Bobby has, only *we* can see it?"

"Not just *us*," Randy said in a low voice. "Listen; just don't go near him as long as he has it. It can hurt *you* a lot more than it's hurting Slake and I don't know what it can do if you get zapped by it!"

"Is it different from person to person?"

"Possibly!" Joni pushed Randy away and hurried to the restrooms. "Wait, Joni; you can't fight him as long as he has that thing!"

"I'm trying anyway!"

Joni kicked in the door, finding Slake on his hands and knees, panting weakly for breath while Bobby stood over him, grinning haughtily.

"How many days will that be, huh?" Bobby jeered and kicked his side, sending Slake crashing to the floor. "You can't do shit to me as long as you're weakened!"

Slake staggered to his feet and clenched his hands. "Lysisner," he hissed, "take power and come in hand."

"You can forget calling on your weak power," Bobby spat. A golden vial slowly appeared before Joni, floating unsteadily and she gasped, stepping away in mute terror. "See! Your stupid pocket nightlight didn't even form!"

Joni swallowed hard and found her courage. "Leave him alone!" she hollered, grabbing the vial. It glowed brightly and a golden broadsword quickly formed in her hand, shining brilliantly in white light. Bobby let out a vicious yell and charged after her.

"*Ay, you heathen you,*" a voice with a thick brogue accent snapped as Joni shielded herself when Bobby brought down the silver scepter. Golden light released on contact when he struggled against the sword. "*What're you doin' fighting alongside that bastard, eh?*"

"*I had no choice!*" a high voice cried back in response. "*He destroyed my former Master!*"

"*No kidding!*"

The light shone brighter and Bobby cried out, going blind. Joni kicked him away with a forward stomp, sending him spiraling onto the floor and the silver scepter clattered away from his reach.

"Come on!" Joni yelled, grabbing for Slake. He took her by the arm and she pulled him up. "Let's get out of here before he regains his sight!"

Slake nodded and they both ran into the corridor, bumping into Randy who had his mirrored sunglasses on.

"Hey!" Randy yelped, jumping back. "Put that away before you put an eye out, okay?" Joni dropped the sword and it clattered onto the tiled floor, flickering dimly.

"*Owch!*" it yelped. "*Watch it, missy!*"

"Sorry!" Joni cried.

"Lysisner, go," Slake muttered. The golden broadsword vanished into particles of golden light.

Joni pulled out of Slake's grasp. "I want an explanation!" she demanded. "What's going on here?"

"We'll explain it after school," Slake grumbled, then suddenly moaned and slipped to his knees. The door burst open and Bobby staggered out.

"You're finished!" Bobby roared.

Randy grabbed Slake's arm, draping it over his shoulders. "Go!" he yelled and Joni took off in the opposite direction.

CHAPTER FIFTEEN

Joni skipped her remaining classes, unable to concentrate on anything else but Bobby. She hid in Study Hall, mindlessly flipping through books while Randy's haunting words disturbed her.

"No one else can see what we see," Joni mused. "How is that possible? Why hadn't I sensed his Magic before then?"

When class let out for the day, Joni took an alternate bus home and breathed a sigh of relief when the route was similar to her usual bus, though on the opposite side of town.

After getting off on a familiar street corner, she spotted Bobby ahead on the path, standing across from Randy who tapped a golden staff against his palm. The scepter glimmered in the afternoon sun's light, its glare reflecting back from Randy's mirrored sunglasses.

"I saw what you did to Slake," Randy snapped. "You're paying for that!"

"Back off," Bobby growled, shoving Randy aside. "I've got stuff to do."

"You leave her alone!"

Randy swung the staff at Bobby and he swiftly turned away. The rod struck pavement, breaking free bits of cement.

"What the hell?" Bobby screeched.

"You beat him up 'til he could barely stand!" The staff cracked across Bobby's jaw and he stumbled over his steps, stunned. "How's 'bout I beat on you 'til *you* can't even take another step?"

Bobby growled, cupping his mouth then ran a hand across his busted lip, glaring at Randy. "Do it," he sneered and spat blood on the ground, "then I'll break your damn legs for even trying!"

Randy charged and faked a right, then whacked Bobby across the face with the staff on his left, causing him falling back onto the ground before he had a chance to react. Bobby rose to his feet unsteadily, rubbing at his jaw as Randy pointed the head of the golden scepter at his throat.

"You'd better watch your step," Randy snarled, "or next time, I'll break your legs!" He stormed away down the street.

"Randy, wait up!" Joni called.

"You want a piece of me too?" Bobby yelled as Joni caught up to Randy, taking his arm. "Yeah, walk away," he called after them. "You know you can't handle this!"

"Are you okay?" Joni asked. Randy shook his head. "What's that you have there?"

"Remember when I told you that not everyone can see what we see?" Joni nodded. "This weapon is one of them."

"Where are we going?"

"I'm going out to Lakeview."

Joni frowned. "I thought you lived in Pleasant Valley!"

"My uncle has a two-storey cabin across the lake out that way," Randy explained. "He likes going there to relax and draw, away from the hustle and bustle of Downtown."

"That explains why I see you out there sometimes."

Randy broke into a wide grin. "You seriously thought I was spying on you?" He tousled her hair. "Someone's got a huge ego!"

"Stop it!" Joni exclaimed and pushed off his hands. Randy chuckled. "I just didn't know, okay? For a while there, you were totally freaking me out."

"You do have a wild imagination, like Greta said."

Joni grunted and looked away. "Will you take me there?" she said instead.

"Sure!" Randy took Joni's hand and they headed for the woods beyond the dead end markers.

Randy and Joni approached a large cabin created of treated pines and maples off a dirt road. Joni waited on the steps as Randy opened the door for her.

"You can come in," Randy said, stepping inside. "I think he's out today."

Joni poked her head in the doorway, astonished at the myriad of art supplies jammed in the corridor. "I thought your uncle ran a comic shop for a living, not draw!" Joni said in awe. "There's a lot of art stuff here!" She entered the hall and found more papers and paints scattered across the parlor.

"Well, that's mine," Randy replied. Joni turned to him and noticed his slightly flushed cheeks. "Uncle just draws posters for the shop, while I paint for extra income."

"How can you paint...?"

"I'm not physically blind, if that's what you're wondering," Randy said softly and leaned against the doorframe. "But people mistake me to be because of... well, my condition."

"I noticed you saw Martel across the way when Kipper tripped the alarm," Joni noted, "but I didn't know what to say..."

Randy chortled. "I suck passing for a blind guy, huh?"

"Still, that's a nice hustle, getting folks to buy paintings from some blind kid."

Randy snorted. "Mahoney's got that covered in spades," he drawled. "I do it for kicks, that's all."

"What's wrong with you anyway then?"

Randy's face flushed darker scarlet. "I never told anybody about it because I didn't think other people with Magic existed around here," he answered. "I mean, I used to go on message boards with like-minded others, but they didn't believe me either thinking I was some role-playing yahoo."

"You mean to tell me that's why your eyes are like that?"

Randy shrugged his shoulders. "Your guess is as good as mine," he replied. "I think the more I use my Magic, the more I'm changing." He grinned and tapped at his head. "I mean, look at me, I'm starting to look like Signe these days."

"Yeah, he *is* on the pale side," Joni agreed, "but he told me it was because he was born that way."

Randy scoffed. "I call bullshit on that one, but whatever." He grinned. "That's why I wear the sunglasses. I can fake being blind..." Randy snorted. "I mean, that's what people presume when your eyes are like this..."

"But doesn't it freak them out?"

Randy sighed, shaking his head. "You have to learn to live with it. Hell, I even have a laptop with a text-to-speech program to make it more plausible." He waved Joni away. "But what's the point of adapting to the mundane world when the mundane refuses to adapt to you?"

"How do you deal with school then, especially for exams?"

"I got a pen that tells me what I'm writing."

"How is it you can play football, then?"

"Super tactile fingers and superior hearing supposedly, remember?"

"I... I guess you're right." There was a sudden crash in the house's rear and Joni turned around, frightened. "What was that?" she cried.

Turning for Randy, Joni sucked in a shallow breath, finding him gone. Noticing shadows swirling near the stoop, she raced for the front door once the shadows parted, revealing Kipper.

The black crescent-shaped blade lodged in the way of the door and frame once Joni slammed into it with all her weight, resisting against him from the other side.

"Let me in!" Kipper snarled.

"What are you doing here?" Joni demanded. "How'd you get over here?"

"What does it matter?" Kipper spat. "You have something that belongs to me!" A strong push tossed Joni to the floor in the hall as the door slammed open. "I just felt them activate... Hedos and Cian are hiding out somewhere near here!"

"You can't have them!" Joni yelled. "They're with me and they're not going with you!"

"I beg to differ!" Kipper stormed inside, holding the black scythe at ready. "You're not strong enough to defeat me!"

"If I have to, I'll try!"

Kipper chuckled and pointed the enchanted tool at Joni. "Then try!"

Joni let out a cry as invisible forces lifted her in the air and Kipper jerked his scythe forward, throwing her into the parlor. Joni slammed into the couch and hurtled over onto the floor. She scrambled to her feet, spotting Randy running downstairs.

"*When did he go upstairs?*" Joni wondered as Randy came to a pause once Kipper pointed his weapon at him.

"Moon Staff," Kipper called, "cause distortion!" A low drone resonated in the room and Randy let out a pained cry, cringing as he gripped his head.

"Leave him alone!" Joni screamed, rushing toward Kipper.

"Moon Staff, gravity bind!" Kipper slammed his enchanted threshing tool onto the floor, releasing black threads of dark light.

Joni let out a shriek and stepped up to the wall, jumping the banister. Grabbing the ledge, she climbed it and darted upstairs. Kipper growled and kicked Randy aside, sending him tumbling down the steps then raced up the stairs after Joni.

Entering a room with its door already open, Joni grabbed a golden long sword lying across the bed and held it at ready as Kipper stood in the middle of the doorway, sneering.

"Get out of here, you grease ball!" she hollered.

"Give up, lame-ass," Kipper spat. "Cian and Hedos are mine!"

"You lost!"

"Really?"

Joni jumped on the bed as Kipper advanced, slicing at her with the scythe. She leaped out the way, avoiding the blade and slashed down, cutting open Kipper's jacket sleeve when he turned and pierced the mattress.

"You suck!" Joni yelled and kicked Kipper's head, throwing him back against the wall. He loosened his grip as he stumbled, leaving the crescent blade lodged in the mattress.

"You wish!" Kipper roared. "Kuroiken, reveal to me!" A black saber formed in his left hand, cackling in indigo energy. "You want a sword fight, you've got one!" Kipper charged and Joni jumped off the bed as he struck the black steel into the scythe, vanishing the weapon. "The darkness overpowers the light, stupid girl!"

"Light makes the darkness disappear, you dummy!" Joni jammed the long sword into Kipper and he staggered rearward after she let go in a stupefied daze. The golden sword glowed dimly in yellow light as it protruded from his body.

"You stuck me, you bitch!" Kipper howled. "That's it! You're through!"

"Anlace, Combine Chaos!" Randy's voice called.

Kipper let out a pained scream as fire flared beneath his feet and white-hot electricity charged through him. He collapsed to his knees and the golden long sword disappeared.

"Is that all you've got?" Kipper wheezed. "It felt real good!"

Randy came up the stairs and stood outside the door, gripping the golden long sword in his hand. "Joni, get out of here!" he commanded. "He's too strong to fight at your level!"

"Chaotic Seal!" Kipper called and thrust forward his hand, generating a glowing dark navy-violet pentagram underneath Joni. She stepped away as black threads appeared from the light and cried out when the strands latched onto her limbs, tying down her arms and legs. "I'll drain you myself until you die!"

"Randy, do something!" Joni wailed when the mystic yarn glowed brightly and she felt herself weakening. "He's killing me!"

Kipper thrust his dark saber into the floor and rose unsteadily to his feet. "Give me the Legions you own and I'll let you go," he demanded, "otherwise, you're good as dead!"

"Don't give them to him!" Randy protested. "He'll kill you anyway!"

"Shut up!" Kipper yanked up the sword threw it at Randy who instantly turned immaterial. "She doesn't need your help!" The blade struck the wall where Randy once stood.

"I'm getting some help!" Randy's voice called into the room.

"You don't deserve them!" Joni screeched, struggling against the glowing binds. "Once I get out of here, I'm kicking your greasy butt into next week!"

"Good luck!" Kipper crowed. The threads flashed in bright blue light, transforming into heavy chains. "You can't control them!" Kipper raised his hand. "Hedos, Cian, return to me!" The blue steel short sword and the cherry scepter appeared in front of Joni. "Damn it, I command you: return to me!"

"They refuse, you greasy blond!" Joni snapped. "They're not going with the likes of you!"

"You don't know how to use them!"

"Well, the last I've checked," Slake's voice said into the room, "she's a quick learner." A flash of golden light flared and he appeared beside her. "Lysisner, grant me your power!" The golden broadsword formed in his right hand, cackling in bright energy.

"What the hell?" Kipper squawked as Slake struck at the chains, breaking them.

Joni jumped on the bed, immediately getting out of Kipper's path as he formed the black long sword in his left hand and charged Slake.

"Joni, take them!" Slake called, quickly defending against Kipper's frontal strike.

Joni picked up both weapons and gasped, noting how the blue short sword felt frigid, while the cherry scepter felt scalding, yet she had no adverse physical reaction on her hands.

"*One's hot and the other's cold!*" Joni realized. "*Like fire and ice...*" She cringed when Slake became unbalanced from Kipper's continued furious blows. Kipper sliced into Slake, shredding his shirt and blazer with unchecked fury.

"What do I do?" Joni called.

"Tell them what to do!" Slake commanded and kicked Kipper's side, sending him tumbling across the floor.

Joni thrust forward the short sword. "Let's cool him off some!" A blast of icy water slammed into Kipper, knocking him down.

"You bitch!" Kipper shrieked and spat water. "I swear!"

"Fry him!" Joni thrust the staff ahead, expelling a fireball. Kipper screamed when the flame struck him and he collapsed to the floor.

"I'll throw you in a world of pain soon!" Kipper roared once the fires dissipated on contact. "Those weak attacks can't do shit to stop me!"

Slake dropped the golden broadsword and leaned against it, panting hard for breath. "Combine them to make them stronger!" he called. "Hurry before he gathers his senses!"

"Get out!" Kipper held out his hand. "Kuroitougane, combine and transform!" The black steel saber and the black long sword vanished from their respective places and reappeared before Kipper, glittering in soft navy light. Suddenly glowing brighter, they merged, changing into a heavy dark blue steel broadsword flaring in violet energy. He grasped the blade and struggled upright. "Now know the fury of the Kurokonoha!"

Slake took up his blade in guard. "Order them to evolve!" he yelled.

The golden broadsword pulsed in response. "*Aye, that's the spirit!*" Lysisner cheered.

"You stay out of this!" Kipper thundered and lashed at Joni.

"Lysisner, shine brightly!" Slake cried, striking the blade into the floor. A blast of white light engulfed the room, charging everything with an intense washed-out color. "Now, Joni, while he's weakening!"

"You're not getting out of this!" Kipper thundered and chucked his broadsword. The blade bulleted ahead, striking Slake in the side and pinned him against the wall. Slake howled in agony and gripped his side as dark red-violet blood soaked his shirt.

"Slake!" Joni cried.

"Star Staff, reveal to me!" Kipper commanded and a silver staff with a golden pentacle appeared in his right hand. "Smoke screen!"

"You're not doing that disappearing act on me!" Joni yelled as the room began filling with dust. "Cian, Hedos, evolve!"

The weapons glowed brightly, turning into orbs of blue and red light. Both merged turning violet and a new weapon emerged. From the light revealed a dark violet staff with a wide flat blade made of dark blue steel on the end and a black orb on the top of the scepter with an indigo handle in the center.

Joni grabbed the newfound weapon and rushed Kipper, slamming the orb into his rapidly fading form. Indigo lightning unleashed, thundering loudly as it covered the floor.

"You missed, stupid bitch!" Kipper's voice faintly cried. "Next time, you're through!" A pile of dull golden ash lay on the floor where Kipper once stood.

Joni fell to her knees, devoid of energy. The bladed scepter glimmered dimly in response in her hand.

"Joni..." Slake moaned.

Joni looked up as Slake fell against the wall, gasping weakly for breath. "Stay up!" she called and rushed over to his side. The golden broadsword he held glimmered dimly before vanishing into a vial of golden powder then fell to the floor with a dull clunk. Joni touched the black broadsword and dark blue light shocked her in response. "I can't touch that thing!" she cried, recoiling in pain.

"Use Hedos and Cian to weaken it!" Slake commanded.

"But it'll zap you too!" Joni protested.

"Do it anyway!"

Joni gripped the bladed scepter in her hands, ill at ease as she stepped away. "Please don't hurt him," she pleaded and tightened her grip, then gingerly touched the orb against the sword's handle. Indigo lightning discharged, surrounding Slake and he screamed.

Joni cringed and shut her eyes, sensing pressure against her weapon. Slake's tortured shriek died and he moaned before falling weakened to the floor, collapsing on his face.

CHAPTER SIXTEEN

Joni opened her eyes and gasped when she spotted the canary yellow wings sheltering Slake's body as he lay unconscious on the floor. She crouched at his side and turned Slake onto his back, finding his dress shirt ripped apart and a gold chain with a silver pendant of a winged Aerian possessing a sword around his neck.

"*That's the same necklace Martel has,*" Joni considered. "*Why would Slake have one like that too?*"

"Is the coast clear?" Randy's voice called into the room and he reappeared near the door. "Whoa!" he yelped, kneeling beside Slake. Touching the side of Slake's neck, he sighed in relief. "Good, he's still alive." Randy looked up at Joni. "You're not hurt, are you?"

Joni shook her head. "I'm fine, but I'm worried," she answered. "Slake made me use this thing called a Legion against him and he's knocked out cold!"

Randy's face shadowed in worry. "Why would Slake have you use *that* against him? That's dangerous!" Joni explained the events leading up to the conclusion and Randy shook his head in disbelief. "I don't know what to say..."

Joni grabbed his sleeve, clutching tightly. "Why does Slake have wings, Randy?" she cried. "Wings!"

"I..." Randy blew a sigh, gently pushing her away. "You can see them too, huh?"

"Yes!"

"He must be an Aerian..."

"You mean like an Angel or something?"

Randy shook his head. "No, I mean like a winged being who is a protector of Magic..." Joni gave Randy a blank look. "He's like a really, really big elfin fairy with feathers."

Joni scoffed. "Stop kidding!"

Randy winced once hit again. "Look, he looks like this because his power's probably used up."

"What do you mean?"

"What, don't you know?" Joni shot him an annoyed glare. "Aerians have the power to look like Humans," Randy replied flatly, "but it takes so much energy. If they get tapped out, their wings show."

"How did that happen?"

"Probably when he fought Bobby and got cooked by that key weapon," Randy explained. "I mean, he's been through a lot today and most likely used the last of it to protect you."

"He didn't have to!"

"You would've wound up *dead* if he didn't!"

"I did okay!"

"Only with his help!"

Joni blew an angry sigh and rose to her feet. "Look, we need to help him; I can't leave him like that on the floor!" She gestured toward the door. "Is there a room he can stay in?"

"My uncle will kill me if I let him stay here!"

"Didn't you say your uncle didn't come out here often?"

"Don't put words in my mouth!" Randy grumbled.

"Please, Randy!"

"Why can't he stay with you? You stay at your Dad's house... Besides, aren't you supposed to be staying with your aunt anyway?" Joni kicked at Randy and he fell back on his rear. "Hey!"

Joni stood over him, balling her hands into fists. "Shut up!" she snapped. "You don't know anything about me!"

"Sorry I said anything," Randy grumbled, getting to his feet. "Help me, will you?" Joni set the dark violet scepter aside and grabbed Slake's feet while Randy held Slake's arms.

Carrying him across the hall, Joni nudged open the door and pressed her shoulder into the light switch, turning on the lighting. With Randy's help, she set Slake onto the bed then took off Slake's loafers, setting them aside on the floor and Randy pulled out the bedspreads, covering up to Slake's shoulders.

"How long will he be like this?" Joni asked worriedly.

"I'm not sure," Randy responded.

"You're not sure?" Joni cried, punching Randy in his back.

"Hey," he yelled, pushing her away, "my uncle will be coming back later and if he finds that I have anybody not related by blood in this house, be it guy or girl, he will bury my scrawny ass alive!"

"Just keep the door closed and he won't suspect a thing, okay?"

Randy clenched his hands, growing agitated. "If I get into trouble," he snarled, "I'm kicking your ass personally!"

Joni waved him away and stomped back across the hall. "What can I do with all these weapons?" she called, grabbing the scepter.

"You tell them to go away," Randy called back.

"Just like that?" Joni asked in disbelief. "You're yanking my chain."

"Without a doubt!" Randy scoffed. "Why, you thought Magic was supposed to be all complicated and drawn out?" He snorted. "It's not like on television, you see."

Joni picked up the lackluster golden vial on the floor and it glimmered faintly in her hand. "Please get some rest, okay?" she said and the golden vial vanished. Joni faced the dark violet scepter. "Look guys, thanks for helping me out." The black orb glowed dully in violet light. "Without you guys, I would've probably become mincemeat out there!" The black orb darkened, losing its luster. "Look, don't worry, we handled it well! I just hope Slake will wake up soon..." The black orb flickered. "Yeah, I agree. Well, you guys can go too. Try to rest up and don't worry so much." The bladed scepter faded into particles of light.

Hearing a soft clink, Joni turned, finding two vials of blue and red resting near her foot. She sensed someone watching her and looked up, spotting Randy standing at the doorway. He waved a hand and left down the hall.

"Never mind," he called over his shoulder.

"Can't you go home?" Joni asked as she picked up the vials. "I guess you hate that drawer, huh?" The vials pulsed dully and Joni placed them in her pocket. "It's okay; I'll carry you in my pocket, if you don't mind."

Hearing a sudden unexpected bang from below, Joni raced downstairs, entering the parlor. She came to a stop and took in a weak breath, catching sight a short young man with long waist-length wavy blond hair, wearing a multicolored patchwork shirt, white flared jeans and black riding boots. Standing in the middle of the corridor with his arms folded across his chest, he leaned against the nearby couch with his back turned to her.

"Who are you?" Joni demanded and the young man turned, looking down at Joni with light blue eyes. He had a small narrow nose and high cheekbones. "Are you Slake's brother?"

"You got it," the young man answered warmly with a slight clipped accent.

"What's your name?"

"Labraccio Meherin," Labraccio replied. He walked up to Joni and she took a step away, apprehensive. He paused, standing across from her. "I heard what happened and cut my assignment short to hurry down here. I thought he might need some additional help..."

"How did you hear about it?" Joni waved Labraccio away. "It just happened! There's no way, unless you have Randy spying for you or something!"

"Who's Randy?" Labraccio shrugged his shoulders. "He didn't tell me anything. Lysisner did."

Joni scoffed. "Yeah, right!" she spat. "Don't lie to me."

"How long will he be like this?" Labraccio demanded, cutting Joni off.

Joni grew apprehensive. "How do you know about Slake?"

"Can't you hear, girl?" Labraccio narrowed his eyes. "Lysisner told me!"

"Then I don't have to tell you anything!" Joni put her hands to her hips. "Now get out of here before I kick your butt like I did that greasy blond!"

Labraccio growled, forming a pair of silver longswords in his hands. Joni let out terrified cry and took off down the hall. Labraccio charged after her then vanished in a flash of light. Reappearing before Joni, he kicked her rearward against her chest, throwing her against the wall with a hard thud.

Joni screamed, cringing when Labraccio jammed both swords near her head, pinning her between him and the wood. Joni swallowed hard, noting he stood a head taller than she.

"Tell me!" Labraccio growled, "or I won't hesitate in skinning you alive!"

"I don't know!" Joni yelped. "I don't know anything!" She winced once grabbed by the shirtfront. "If you're his brother, don't you have wings too?"

"What?" Labraccio released his grip, stunned.

"Is there any way for him to get rid of the wings?"

"He can always cut them."

"No!" Joni shuddered. "Would that hurt?"

"At first," Labraccio replied. "But if you did it often, you'll get used to it."

"What?"

Labraccio shook his head. "You won't understand."

"You mean Slake cut them before?"

"It's a long, drawn-out nasty little story," Labraccio responded. "I have no business telling." He grabbed the blades embedded in the wall and they vanished into particles of white light.

"How long are you going to be here?" Joni asked cautiously. "Randy doesn't want any trouble!"

"I see..." Labraccio turned away. "I'll be here until I no longer need to be," he answered cryptically.

"Will you be here long?" Joni pressed. "I have to get going and sort out the details..."

"What, you never did this before?"

"Not this heavy into Magic," Joni complained. "I know simple spells and that's it!"

"Well, from what I can tell, you're a lot stronger than you look."

"Well, I'm not, so deal with it!"

Labraccio snorted. "You're honestly serious!" he murmured. "You have so much potential!"

"Tough cookies." Joni pushed Labraccio aside and entered the corridor. Labraccio followed at her heels and grabbed Joni's arm before she reached the front door. "What is it?" she snapped.

"I'm trying to think," Labraccio answered. "Why have this much power and let it go to waste?"

"Maybe Dad didn't want me to be in this deep." Joni pulled out of Labraccio's grip. "Listen, go away or help him."

"I can't help him right now."

"Then go away."

"I can't until he recovers. I'm assigned to you."

"Now you're really lying."

"It's to make sure you don't get your butt into trouble, that's what!"

Joni let out a short laugh. "What kind of trouble can I get into?" she spat incredulously.

"All kinds," Labraccio answered.

"Tell me a new one!"

Joni opened the door, making her way outside into the cold evening air. Moonlight shone between the leaves, giving the woods an unearthly glow. Labraccio stepped out, shutting the door behind him.

"Your life will be constantly threatened as you're contested for your Powers," he continued. "So be grateful you have someone willing to help you."

"You've got to be kidding me!" Joni protested.

CHAPTER SEVENTEEN

Approaching the path in the woods, Joni made her trek home with Labraccio walking in step. The faint moonlight came through the tree's leaves, casting shifting shadows around them. "Why would I be contested constantly?" she inquired.

"How can you ask such silly questions?" Labraccio answered. "You have strong spirit weapons you're not using. Of course nasty mages want to take that away."

"Strong spirit weapons?" Joni huffed. "Dad never told me anything about it!"

"What a stupid thing to do! After that nasty fight, I thought he'd learn his lesson." Joni glared at Labraccio standing nearby and he nodded. "That's right. Your father was a troublesome mage and got his head in things beyond his ability."

"How is that even remotely possible?" Joni threw up her hands. "It doesn't make sense! Why would I have people trying to kill me over stuff I know little about if it's supposedly my dad's fault?"

"The weapons, silly girl," Labraccio said in exasperation, rolling his eyes. "He made some evil stuff folks are killing to get - I would too if I didn't have to abide by rules." The Aerian shrugged his shoulders. "That's why I'm here to deal with you dangerous little powerful monster. Since you're without a clue, put into the wrong hands and we've got major trouble."

"So you're calling me trouble?" Joni retorted.

"Without training, you could be!"

"I'm not liking any of this," Joni griped, "and I really don't get what you're talking about!"

"Ooh, you're a slow one aren't you?" Labraccio blew a hard sigh. "Your father broke some rules and created spirit weapons not sanctioned by the Assembly. Then he had a big battle against jealous mages who wanted to steal it. Now he's dead and gone and you're his only heir, so they're coming after you too. Since you're dumb as a box of rocks, it's up to me to get you up to speed if you still want to breathe and such."

"Stop calling me stupid!" Joni complained. "Not knowing is completely different!"

"Then pay attention, girl."

"But fighting with weapons like that!" Joni shook her head. "It's illegal... and dangerous!"

"These weapons are created with spiritual energy," Labraccio explained, rolling his eyes. "So not everyone can *see* them. To the normal mundane human, you'd be holding *nothing* in your hands. To the trained magician, or anyone dealing with spiritual energy for that matter, they'll see you're holding a kick-ass weapon."

"So, for example, if I took Hedos and Cian in their evolved form to school with me, I wouldn't be thrown out?"

"No, because most of the student body wouldn't be able to see it."

"But you said Dad broke some rules making them," Joni countered. "Wouldn't it still make them *illegal and dangerous*?"

"Well," Labraccio hedged, "yes and no."

Joni groaned and kicked at a nearby tree. "This is too much!" she groused.

"Well, it's not like you have a way of getting out of it."

"There has to be a clause or something!"

"Well, there is..." Labraccio folded his arms across his chest. "You ordain them a new Master and send them on their way."

"But I wouldn't know whom or what to give the Legions to!"

"Then I guess you're stuck with them!"

"Argh, this is too much!" Joni kicked the tree again.

"How much do you know about Battle Magic?" Labraccio suddenly asked.

"What?" Joni glanced at him. "How much do I know?" She shrugged. "Dad told me Battle Magic was dangerous and never taught me anything."

"Do you know at least some self-defense moves?"

"I know some basic protection spells."

"Great, we're back to square one," Labraccio grumbled, throwing his hands into the air.

"Why do you have a problem with that?" Joni demanded.

"Basic protection spells aren't worth the energy against these evil mages coming for your Legionnaire," Labraccio griped. "You need spells of all kinds - negation, absorption, breaking, and that's just basic Battle Magic." Joni clenched her hands, growing incensed as Labraccio went on. "If you get cursed before you even obtain the highest degree with the power..." Labraccio made a slicing sound as he ran a hand across his throat. "You're done, soul and all."

"What are you saying, that even my soul won't exist anymore?" Joni snapped. "Well, sorry to spoil everything for you! I really didn't *want* to get into this mess!"

Labraccio growled and clenched his hands. "This is the first time I personally had to deal with someone with almost zero ability," he said evenly. "Slake always got them up to speed with the basics and I was able to handle the rest."

"So now you're blaming me about Slake's condition, is that it?"

"If he didn't have to *like* his dim-witted charges, he wouldn't be nearly dead each and every time trying to *save* them!"

Joni picked up a nearby rock and threw it at Labraccio, bouncing it off his chest. "Slake doesn't like me!" she argued. "We're just friends and nothing but!"

"Friends, huh?" Labraccio cracked and gave a devious grin. "I heard a different story."

"Shut up!"

"Make me." Joni growled under her breath and Labraccio snorted at her in return. "You're not a threat to me."

"I'll have you know that I used those Legions today and put up a pretty good fight!" Joni said smugly. "My power was so strong, it knocked out Slake! You can see for yourself!"

Labraccio's smile faded and his face darkened in anger. "You sent my brother into that state?" he said in a controlled voice. "Lysisner told me that Slake was in a fierce battle that stripped his ability... but he never told me that *you* did that to him!" Silver light glowed around his hands. "Liang, Contis: release your power and evolve!" A blue steel short sword formed in Labraccio's right hand, cackling in neon blue electricity.

Joni jumped away in fear. "What are you doing?" she cried, backing away as Labraccio advanced.

"Maybe you'll appreciate seeing what it's like to be in a comatose state, stripped of all *your* abilities!"

"It was an accident!" Joni wailed and stumbled over a gnarled root as she tried keeping her distance.

"No accident can strip abilities away for nearly a week and a half!"

"Look, I didn't do it!"

"It had a mark of a Legionnaire all over it!" Labraccio thundered.

"Keep your voice down!" Joni hissed. "You'll wake everybody!"

"I don't care. You're abusing the Legions and their abilities and you're going to turn corrupt eventually! I might as well put a stop to that right now!"

"Don't!" Joni yelped. She tripped on a nearby stone and struck the ground, then crawled back, overwhelmed in terror as Labraccio stepped forward. "I didn't do it; Bobby did! He had some kind of

key-shaped weapon and used it against Slake... She told Lysisner that she had no choice!"

Labraccio sneered and pointed the electric blade at her throat. "Really?" he seethed.

"Ask Lysisner yourself!" Joni wailed.

Labraccio grunted and held out his left hand. "Lysisner, lend me your Magic and bestow me your Power!" he commanded. The golden vial appeared in Labraccio's outstretched hand and his eyes widened, disturbed. "What the hell happened to you?" he marveled. "You're weakened!" It glimmered dimly in response. "Is this girl telling the truth? Did you really battle Aecean?" The vial pulsed dully. "Did Aecean really say she had no choice?" It glowed brightly for a moment in pale red light and disappeared. Labraccio growled under his breath and withdrew the electrical sword.

"I hope I get an apology for this!" Joni grumbled. Her eyes widened and she leaned back when Labraccio pointed the blade swiftly at her nose, grazing the point against her skin.

"Don't push me!" Labraccio snarled. "I *don't* have to keep you alive!"

"Sorry!" Labraccio then turned away, gripping the blade's handle tightly. The sword's energy cackled brightly in response. Joni slowly rose to her feet, noticing Labraccio clenching and re-clenching his left hand. "What's wrong?" she asked carefully.

Labraccio grunted. "Why do you care?" he grumbled.

"Why are you doing that with your left hand?"

"I am a dual-blade fighter!" Labraccio snapped. "I know this particular two-sword technique and because of my superior knowledge of such, it makes me unrivaled in battle!" He sighed and kicked at the ground.

"But you only have one sword!"

"The two Legionnaire creating the counterpart to Contis and Liang were defeated..."

"What is the counterpart to Liang and Contis?" Joni inquired.

"The flaming long sword," Labraccio responded. "Separate, all four Legionnaire are weak on their own, with the exception of Liang for he is the strongest of the group. When teamed together, they are nearly unstoppable!" A copper-plated steel fan slowly appeared in Labraccio's left hand, glowing dimly.

"What's that?"

"This is Voldec," Labraccio explained as he flicked his wrist, opening the fan and revealed steel points from within the folds. "When he touches anything on contact, he ignites immediately."

"He's pretty dangerous," Joni said nervously.

Labraccio nodded. "He worked in tandem with his wife, Flasai... she was a disarming weapon that smoldered when thrown. Together they formed a formidable team."

"What happened to Flasai exactly?"

"She became separated in battle... I had no choice but to leave her behind." Labraccio flicked his wrist, snapping shut the fan. "Afterwards, Voldec refused to fight until she returned... but that doesn't matter anymore - that's in the past."

"Voldec seems to worry about you," Joni said as the copper-plated war fan continued glowing. "Otherwise, he wouldn't have shown up without calling!"

"He misses his wife," Labraccio said flatly. "It's as simple as that." The war fan dimmed and faded away.

"What about Contis and Liang?" Joni asked. She approached offside and the short sword's energy sparked as she neared. Joni clenched her teeth and kept her distance. "Are they also husband and wife?"

"No, they're brother and sister."

Joni nodded as the sword's neon blue energy darkened. "What are they like when they're separated?"

Labraccio tossed the blade into the air. "Liang, Contis, disengage!" he commanded. The sword flashed in bright blue light and evaporated. In Labraccio's right hand formed a silver saber surging in electric blue energy. Strapped to his right arm formed a set of three emerald green darts with golden tips. Joni stepped away when Labraccio pointed the saber in her general direction and the energy surrounding the blade dimmed slightly. "Liang says 'hello'." The green darts glowed softly in response. "Contis also sends her greetings."

Joni waved slightly. "Hi," she said in a weak voice.

A sudden creak resonated from in the woodlands and Labraccio abruptly vanished in silver light, reappearing at the path's end, holding the darts in his left hand.

"Show yourself!" Labraccio roared.

Joni raced the narrow trail, spotting the darts flickering wildly. "Wait!" she called as Labraccio bared his teeth and threw them forward. An alarmed cry followed and branches cracked in response when a body fell against it.

"Contis, zap him!" Labraccio ordered. The darts glowed dimly in pale olive light.

"*She won't do it!*" Joni thought, pushing Labraccio out the way and ran to the track's end. She cried when a hand weakly grabbed her ankle and she tripped forward, striking the ground on all fours. Joni reached out in the darkness, touching sticky warmth and overwhelmed by a strong scent of sandalwood.

"Why are you hurting me?" Slake's voice moaned.

"Brother!" Labraccio yelped. "I didn't recognize you!"

"What did you expect?" Slake grunted as he sat up. "I have no Magic for you to sense me by!"

"Contis, return closely!" The emerald darts appeared in Labraccio's hand, lacking luster. "Forgive me; I am sincerely sorry!"

"I can never forgive you!" Slake snarled. He pushed Joni gently aside once he sat up, struggling for breath.

"I told you, I'm sorry!" Labraccio protested. "Contis, go!" The darts vanished from out of his hand.

"Why did you leave?" Joni asked. "You're supposed to be resting!"

"I thought I sensed something unpleasant," Slake grumbled.

Joni rose upright and held out a hand to Slake. He ignored her as he rose to his feet and stormed toward Labraccio, his wings straining stiffly against his back. Joni followed Slake once he approached Labraccio, towering over him.

"Oh, I'm the unpleasant one, eh?" Labraccio spat. "You're the one to talk, brother!"

"You are never sorry!" Slake hissed, baring his teeth. "Never!"

"I am this time!"

Slake grabbed Labraccio's throat and threw him to the ground.

"Slake, stop it!" Joni yelped and grasped his arm. "Don't kill your brother!"

Labraccio placed the edge of the dimly glowing saber to Slake's neck. "Brother, let me go," Labraccio said sternly. Slake tightened his grip, lifting him up and Labraccio said nothing as the color drained from his face.

"Slake, please!" Joni protested, gripping his free arm tightly. "This isn't worth killing your brother over!"

Slake shook off Joni, growling and turned, throwing Labraccio spiraling onto the ground. Labraccio immediately vanished in a flash of silver light and reappeared behind Slake hovering above him. Joni backed away, frightened.

"You must want to be drained of everything you have," Labraccio declared as he aimed the electric saber at Slake's back. "I did it before and I can do it again!"

"I'm already nearly there!" Slake snarled, clenching his hands. "Try and I make sure you stay in Hell!"

"Yes or no?"

Slake turned and Labraccio slashed down, slicing across his chest. Slake grunted when a sudden jolt jarred him and he stumbled rearwards. He struck the ground, dazed and his eyes rolled to the back of his head as he fainted.

"You didn't have to do all that!" Joni cried.

Labraccio pointed the blade at her as he lowered to the ground and she backed away, hesitant. "This is between me and my brother," he said sternly. "Unfortunately, you haven't mastered invulnerability or immortality, so I suggest you stay out of my way!"

Joni clenched her hands, shaking in fear and anger. "What the hell is wrong with you?" she yelled. "You're really pissing me off!"

"I suggest you bone up on your magical skills if you ever want to defeat me!"

"You're so cold!"

Labraccio twirled his sword, smiling haughtily. "It's a job."

Joni shoved Labraccio away and scurried down the path, hurrying for home. "*Labraccio's lost it!*" she thought, pushing aside branches tearing at her sweater. "*I hope they won't trash Randy's house with this crazy fighting...*" Sudden tears streaked down her face, cooling against the wind cutting around her. "*Please be alright, Slake,*" she prayed, "*Don't die on me!*"

CHAPTER EIGHTEEN

Joni resumed her classes while Slake remained absent, relieved when she heard nothing from Labraccio. She took careful notes in class for Slake and put in her frustrations helping the Nortiniry Knights practice when they needed it.

Joni noticed Bobby and Kipper steered clear of her path as she continued her studies and struggled earning decent grades. Joni also noted Martel and Signe were noticeably absent and it worried her further.

When her favorite day of the week came around, Joni dumped all her work in her locker and went with haste to the stands, picking out a good seat close to the action.

Joni cheered on Randy until she grew hoarse, enjoying the tense match between the Knights and another county school full of large beefy players. After the game, she fought the frenzied crowd, running onto the field and approached Randy who had a cracked helmet.

"That guy ran you down like he was on fire!" Joni remarked. "At least you made the winning goal before he tried breaking you in half!"

"I'll be fine," Randy replied and chortled. "I never thought they'd smash me on the punt return, but at least we made them fumble and ran it in for seventy-two yards!"

"Aren't you going to the afterparty tonight?" Joni asked, walking in step with Randy toward the school. "You know that Coach Oran'll ride you harder to get your head back in after that spectacle!"

"Why bother?" Randy grumbled and pulled out of his helmet. "That first game was just a fluke! All the other games after that were flukes too!"

"But that first game was what they needed to get the Knights out of their slump!" Joni pressed. "Did you look at the stands, Randy? They're jam-packed; everyone's attending these days!"

Randy blew a raspberry. "I'm just a kicker!" he complained. "I don't run; I don't catch... I just warm my spot on the bench watching the Knights get creamed from playing trench warfare, moving barely inches down the line!"

"But you can kick it in on fourth down from midfield, Randy! Mid-friggin'-field!"

Randy shrugged his shoulders. "What's the point when Ryan's not there?" he groused. "He can get those guys playing even when we're losing and they just want to throw in the towel. What if we have a loss? What if we get three in a row? Then four and so on, then what? Without Ryan, that team will fall apart!"

"So go out there and kick ass and then tell Ryan about it! He might want to know how good the Knights are out there for a change and will himself to get better!"

"Fine, whatever."

"Hey, I'm going to visit Ryan later," said Joni once they approached the school's rear. "Want to come with me?"

Randy blew a heavy sigh, rolling his eyes. "Sure, why not?" he muttered.

"He needs our support!" Joni snapped and punched Randy's arm. "Being in a coma must suck major!"

"I know, okay?" Randy winced and rubbed his arm. "I heard people stuck in that state can still see and hear what's going on around them."

"So let's go over there and tell him the awesome details!"

"Fine, I get it!" Randy ran his free hand through his sweat-drenched hair. "You're too damn persistent!"

Joni chuckled. "Can I come over and check on Slake?" she inquired.

"Sure. Wait for me, okay?"

Joni nodded and sat outside on the nearby bench as Randy went inside. Moments later, she sensed a strong presence and immediately stood with her hands clenched at her sides.

Kipper exited the building, twirling a chain in his hand. He came to a pause, noticing Joni. "Waiting around to do the team?" he teased. "I'd doubt they'd screw you – you might break in half with that tiny ass of yours."

"Got rejected so you're picking on me, huh?" Joni retorted. "Never thought you like guys like that."

"Don't you start with me!" Kipper barked.

"Shut up." Joni turned away. "I'm waiting for Randy."

"Oh, dumping your boyfriend for a new model?" Kipper laughed. "You're such a slut!"

"Why are you hassling me?" Joni snapped, narrowing her eyes at Kipper.

"I just came to warn you, don't mess around with stuff you know nothing about!" Kipper approached Joni and snapped the chain at her, wrapping it around her throat. Joni pushed Kipper back as he leaned in. "You'll hurt yourself real bad!"

"I'll kick your greasy face again like last time!" Joni declared. "I'm not scared of you!"

"You better be scared!"

Joni punched Kipper's chest and shoved him away, throwing him to the ground. She yanked off the chain and threw at Kipper who caught it. He snapped the chain again and Joni held up an arm to block, crying out when the steel cut her sleeve.

"Stop messing with me!" Joni spat as Kipper chortled darkly and sprang to his feet, wrapping the chain around his hand.

"There's more to me than you think!" Kipper crowed and Joni backed away as he advanced.

Randy returned dressed in jeans, sneakers and his hooded sweatshirt as Kipper made a swing at Joni. She leaned out the attack, stumbling rearwards.

"Beat it," Randy shouted. He ran up to Kipper, grabbing him by the collar. Kipper swung at Randy, releasing his grip and Randy grunted as he let go when the chain slammed against his chest.

"I'm kicking both y'all's asses," Kipper vowed and backed away, pointing at them both. "Watch your backs! You can't hide from the shadows!"

"Get lost, scum!" Joni shouted.

"You can't fight in your sleep, remember that!"

Kipper whipped the chain at Randy and Randy leaned back as the metal struck his glasses, snapping them off his face. Kipper cracked the whip again and Randy easily sidestepped the attack, turning away.

Randy whirled around, unleashing a golden dagger in his hand. He hurled the glowing blades before Kipper could retaliate and the knife struck the ground, releasing a flash of light.

Kipper let out a stunned cry. "You son of a bitch!" he roared.

Randy ran over to Joni and took her hand, pulling her away from the scene. They left school grounds at a fast clip, gaining considerable distance. Randy glanced over his shoulder, finding Kipper wasn't behind them then slowed to a stop and Joni let go.

Joni doubled over with her hands on her knees, panting hard for breath. "I wish you'd stop saving me," she moaned between gasps of breath. "I'm sorry for being totally lame!"

"Be careful dealing with him," Randy warned. "He looks weak, but that nutcase is too strong to fight at your current level!"

"You told me that before." Joni rose upright. "How can you tell?"

Randy shrugged his shoulders. "It's hard to explain."

"I can't keep running from the likes of him all my life." Joni continued down the walk with Randy following. "I don't know why Dad didn't warn me about all this…"

"So you *do* know about Battle Magic?" Randy asked, surprised.

Joni shook her head. "I really don't. Dad only taught me basic protection spells and healing techniques… and even that's not so great!" She blew a hard sigh. "When I needed to use those healing Powers the most, I couldn't!"

Randy took Joni's arm and turned her toward him. "Why would he fail to mention Battle Magic to you?" he demanded. "Wasn't he a Mage Knight?"

Joni shook out of his grip. "I don't know what that is."

Randy grew silent and they continued their walk for Lakeview.

Approaching the cabin in the woods, Randy opened the door and let Joni entry.

"Go check on your boyfriend while I get some stuff," Randy said and entered the parlor.

Joni grunted and stomped upstairs, heading for the guest room. Finding the door open, she stepped inside and gasped once she found Slake standing at the window, wearing only his slacks. A deep raised red scar appeared across his shoulder blades and down his back.

"Are you okay?" Joni asked nervously.

"No," Slake answered in a dead tone, "I'm not."

"Did you--?"

"I had to…" Slake blew a hard sigh. "I lost…"

"What kind of punishment is that?" Joni yelled. "That nut job's got a serious superiority complex; because he's your brother doesn't mean he can trash you like that!"

"Forget it, Joni," Slake grumbled. "We've been doing this for years and nothing's going to change. One fight lasted one hundred and thirty-eight days!"

"Both of you are insane!"

"Thank you for checking on me... I appreciate it."

Joni shook her head and stormed downstairs.

"Heading out?" Randy called after her.

"Yeah," Joni called back.

"I'll be there in a second!"

Joni opened the front door and let out an alarmed cry at Labraccio standing on the porch with light gray wings twitching lazily across his back.

"Labraccio!" she yelped and frowned when she noticed his deep red scars covering his bare chest and arms.

"What?" he replied, glancing at Joni. Labraccio stepped aside as Joni exited onto the porch with Randy following. "You act like you've never seen an Aerian before!"

"Well--!" Joni ran a hand through her hair. "You can't be walking around like *that*!" she complained.

"I'm trying to relax here," Labraccio grumbled and blew a heavy sigh. Joni timidly reached forward to touch a feather and he stepped away, growing tense. "Pull one out and I'm *seriously* hurting you!"

"Can anyone see you when you're like this?" Joni asked, placing her hands into her coat pockets.

"Unfortunately, yes. We're not completely spiritual energy like the Legions."

"Aren't you cold?"

"Not really."

"Well, put them away if you're going to the hospital with us."

"Why? Who's sick?"

"I'm visiting a friend. I thought you might want to tag along or something."

Labraccio snorted. "You're a strange little girl," he murmured. "Give me a few minutes."

Joni left the porch with Randy walking along her side and they headed for the trail. "Those wings are really large," she admitted.

"They are," Randy agreed. "Did you know that an Aerian's wingspan is double their height?"

"Really?"

"So, if an Aerian is six feet tall, his wingspan would be twelve feet!"

"I thought it would be just the length of their arms."

"That would be hard to fly with all that weight!"

"I guess you're right." Joni glanced to Randy. "Have you ever met Labraccio before?" she questioned.

Randy shook his head. "First time I ever saw him," he answered.

"He's Slake's brother, apparently."

"Hm, I figured there was some semblance."

CHAPTER NINETEEN

Continuing walking in silence, Joni and Randy reached the woodlands edge and emerged, happening upon the dead end markers. Joni clenched her teeth as they approached Greta and Bobby coming their way.

Greta wore her familiar pink parka over jean leggings, purple leg warmers scrunched at her ankles and dark brown short boots. Bobby wore a black short coat with a fur collar and large brass buttons, tight stonewashed jeans and red high-top sneakers. Randy quickly reached into his pocket and slipped on a pair of dark glasses, hiding his eyes.

"So, Bobby's your new boyfriend, huh?" Joni cracked.

"You're asking the wrong person," Greta answered, rolling her eyes. "I'm not telling you anything so you can steal him too!"

"What the hell?" Joni squawked, clenching her hands. "I didn't *steal* any of your boyfriends and if you got your ideas right, I didn't *ask* them to bug me and pester me for my number! Besides, I *always* turned them down!"

"Yeah, tell me a new one!"

"Even your last one, Slake, never spoke to me and he just liked hanging around... I mean, what do you want me to do? Shoo him away?"

"Yes, Joni; shoo him away!" Greta glared at Randy. "So now you're with Randy too these days? Damn, girl, keep this up and the whole school will think you're whoring around!"

"Whoring around?" Joni screeched. "How can I be when I haven't even kissed a guy yet?"

"Oh my gawd, you're still a virgin?" Greta laughed. "Then stop using guys to build up a nonexistent rep! Those horn dogs will get the wrong idea and rape your skinny ass!"

"For your big fat information, we were going to catch the bus to visit Ryan." Joni stepped forward, shaking her fist at Greta. "What's with you these days? You act like I'm not allowed to have more than one friend!"

"You keep turning them into something else other than that!"

"Maybe it's all in that empty head of yours!" Joni leaned away out a backhanded slap. "Hey, what's with you, Cadell?" she shrieked.

"Why are you letting her trash Joni?" Randy demanded as Bobby smirked and withdrew his dark green gloves from his rear pocket.

"Why should I intervene?" Bobby replied smugly. "Watching two girls fight is such a turn-on." He sniggered, pulling into his dimly glowing handwear. "Alright, girls, get out of my way. You know what I'm about to do to you, Alister."

Randy charged Bobby and plowed into him, throwing the young man onto the ground. Bobby struck the pavement hard, forcing his horn-rimmed glasses falling from his face.

"I'm breaking your legs!" Randy snarled, kicking Bobby's chest.

"Randy, stop it!" Joni cried when Bobby grabbed Randy's foot and flicked him back. Randy stumbled backwards and quickly gained his footing, standing at ready with his fists up, ready to fight. "You know Bobby's been in the Detention Center for three years! He can really mess you up!"

"That's right," Bobby snapped, rising to his feet. "I can really hurt you... and you really don't want to see the extent of my ability!"

"Randy, let's get out of here!"

"They were heading for your house," Randy snapped. "He's got something planned!"

"Is that true?" Joni demanded.

"No," Greta retorted. "We were just walking around!"

"I live on the other side of Pleasant Valley, three miles away!" Joni yelled as Greta picked up Bobby's fallen glasses. "Why come out to Lakeview if you're just 'walking around'?"

"Maybe we wanted to check out the lake," Bobby retorted. "It's not on private property."

"You know what," Greta spat as she approached Bobby's side, "Bobby said Slake attacked him and he was hiding at your house!" She handed him his glasses and Bobby nodded, taking them from her. "So I went with him to watch him kick his ass!"

Joni's mouth fell open in disbelief. "What the hell?" she squawked. "Get it right - Bobby attacked Slake! He's trying to recover from what Bobby did to him!"

Greta glared at Joni. "Oh, so he is at your house, you skank!"

Randy put out an arm before Joni as she lurched forward, making a swipe at Greta. "Cool it, girl," he said, then sneered at Greta and Bobby. "You get out of here," Randy growled, "or I'll make you."

"Try it," Bobby snarled, his black eyes glowing dimly in orange as he set the glasses atop his head. "You're worthless without that stick of yours!"

"Suck it, Milian!" Randy yelled and rushed Bobby again. Bobby crouched down, scooping Randy as he geared for a kick and turned, throwing him down into the pavement. Randy tumbled overhead, landing awkwardly on his back.

"You could've broken his neck!" Joni cried, running up to Randy. "Are you okay?" She pulled him up and gasped when she noticed Randy holding a glowing golden dagger in his clenched hands. "Randy, don't do it!" He nudged Joni aside, standing more steadily on his feet.

"We can go like this all night, ladies," Bobby said curtly, beckoning to Randy. "Like I said, without that stick, you're nothing!"

Charging again, Randy threw a reverse roundhouse kick. Bobby immediately grabbed his foot and slammed him down on the ground, twisting his ankle. Randy howled in agony.

"Don't break him!" Joni screamed.

"He said he was going to break my legs!" Bobby shouted as Randy struggled beneath him and slashed at his arm with the dagger, slicing his sleeve. "I might as well beat him to it!" Bobby adjusted his grip as the gloves glowed brightly in response and gave a swift turn, followed by a sickening pop. Randy screamed and the dagger burst into particles of light.

"You bastard!" Joni screeched, running up to Bobby. She kicked at his back and Bobby stumbled forward.

Turning out on his feet, Bobby stood at ready in his fighting stance. "You want a piece of me too?" he bellowed. "I'll give you plenty to work with!"

"*I can take you,*" a hollow voice hissed.

Joni clenched her teeth as she advanced. "I don't care if you beat me into a bloody pulp!" she yowled and dropped low for a shoulder tackle. "You don't do this to my friends!"

Randy hunched forward, gripping his leg. "My knee!" he cried.

"Come on!" Bobby roared. "I'm only giving you one shot - then it's over!"

"Joni, forget it!" Randy called after her. "He'll destroy you!"

"Screw this!" Joni shook her fists at Bobby. "You crackpot crank!" She hastily approached Randy's side, holding out a hand. He grabbed for her, getting pulled unsteadily to his feet. "You just leave us alone!"

"I don't have enough power to use the Anlace!" Randy said weakly and grimaced. "He's got something that stripped my Power somehow..."

Joni helped him stand and slipped his arm over her shoulders. "Why didn't you stop him, Greta?" she yelled, glaring at her former friend.

"Hey, I had nothing to do with it!" Greta protested, putting up her hands. "It was between you and him!"

"Better have more control of your man, Greta," Randy snapped. "I'll forgive you just this once!"

"Come on, Randy," Joni said, "We'll just have to miss seeing Ryan tonight." She helped him down the street as he hopped on his good leg.

"Hey," a familiar voice called, "I was going to ask if you kids wanted coffee."

Joni glanced up, spotting a slender young man with frizzy blond hair approach the sidewalk, wearing yellow boots, a floor length white denim coat with silver buttons, tan driving gloves and a yellow and navy plaid driving cap perched on the side of his head.

"Labraccio," Joni called, "don't worry about us, okay? We're fine!"

"Fine, my ass!" Labraccio snapped upon approach. "What happened to him?" The coat and gloves he wore glimmered softly.

"*That's really got to hurt!*" a rough low voice said faintly.

"*Don't worry,*" a voice with a clipped accent responded. "*We've got this covered!*"

"Bobby dislocated Randy's knee or something," Joni answered. "I'm too upset to even look, let alone trying to heal him from it!"

"But he shouldn't be able to do that," Labraccio said, giving Randy a critical look. He perched at Randy's side and gently touched his knee. Randy tensed, shying away.

"What are you trying to do?" Randy mewed. "Don't touch me!"

Labraccio narrowed his eyes after he let go and rose to his feet. "I see," he said simply. "Pardon me."

Joni stepped aside as Labraccio walked past them and turned, watching him come within reach of where Greta and Bobby stood.

"Labraccio, what are you doing?" Joni called after him. "Don't think about revenge; we can handle this!"

"Hey short-stack," Bobby jeered, grinning as he placed his glasses over his face. "Are you another one of that dumb pixie's groupies?"

Labraccio's face became unreadable as he clenched his hands and his gloves glimmered brighter.

"*Get ready!*" the voice with the clipped accent cried.

"Labraccio, don't!" Joni wailed.

Labraccio ignored her, swiftly delivering a jumping palm slap into Bobby's face. He then turned away, wrapping his other arm around Bobby's chest before he could stumble back and pulled him down, placing his hand to Bobby's chin while turning it at a painful angle.

"Damn, he's fast!" Greta yelped as Bobby struggled against Labraccio.

"Do you want me to break your neck?" Labraccio growled in his ear. "I have no problem giving you the same punishment you delivered to my unfortunate comrade."

"Holy shit!" Bobby screamed when Labraccio pulled back.

"Yes or no?"

Bobby flailed his arms wildly. "No!" he screeched.

Labraccio snapped his arms back, flipping Bobby's body down on the ground. Bobby groaned and rubbed at his neck as Labraccio stepped over him, returning to Joni and Randy.

"You go on home," Labraccio said gently, "and I'll make sure your friend gets treated."

Joni let Randy go as Labraccio took hold of him and both returned to the woods. Blowing a sigh in relief, Joni approached where Greta stood and poked her chest with a firm finger. "What the hell is your problem?" she snapped.

"My problem?" Greta retorted, appalled. Bobby rose to his feet and elbowed past them, storming away. "What are you doing with that nutcase?"

"That nutcase is Slake's older brother," Joni replied. "So if Bobby was going to fight Slake again, he's got *him* to contend with!"

Greta grunted. "That guy's pretty strong for someone your height!"

"Probably so."

"Look, I'm..."

"Don't apologize to me," Joni grumbled. "Either you make up your mind about who your friends are or don't bother hanging around."

"You know what; I don't have to stand for this." Greta stormed away, leaving her side.

"Who do you think you are?" Joni yelled after her. Greta flipped an obscene gesture over her head. "Back at you!" Joni snapped angrily.

Suddenly an engine roared and Joni whirled around, spotting the dark cycle speeding around the corner. She folded her arms across her chest when Signe pulled up and idled near her.

"Hey," Signe said brightly and flipped up the helmet's visor.

"What are you doing here?" Joni asked, flabbergasted. "I thought Kipper laid you out!"

Signe shrugged. "I looked for you at the party and couldn't find you," he said instead. "So I thought maybe you was hiding out here."

"Thanks for thinking about me," Joni murmured.

"I think I spooked Greta when I barreled 'round the bend back there," Signe teased. "She totally ducked behind that car up the street." He chortled and Joni shook her head, rolling her eyes. "What's the matter? You usually laugh at my lame jokes."

"It's nothing important." Joni muttered.

"Where are you going?"

"I was thinking about visiting Ryan at the hospital." Joni blew a heavy sigh. "But I'm just not in the mood right now..."

"Come on, I'll take you there." Signe held out a hand. "He probably misses you!"

"Argh, fine..." Joni took his hand, getting pulled alongside him.

"Then maybe afterwards we can do something fun," Signe murmured as Joni held on around his waist. "You can play sexy nurse and I'll play horny patient."

"You try that," Joni warned, "and you'll be playing one *dead* patient!"

Signe chuckled and flipped down his visor. "Hey," he quipped, "I keep trying."

CHAPTER TWENTY

Arriving at the hospital with Signe, Joni grew uneasy as she entered through the double doors. After getting clearance from the nurse's station, Signe waved her off and took a seat in the waiting room while she headed for the room Ryan resided in.

Joni entered the antiseptic-scented colorless-tiled space and cringed at the sight of Ryan lying in the hospital bed, surrounded by machines that beeped, buzzed and whooshed.

"*He looks like a corpse,*" she thought nervously, noting his pallid appearance. "*I shouldn't think thoughts like this. But it reminds me too much of Dad before he passed on...*"

Joni shuddered, grasping her necklace then carefully approached the bed and picked up Ryan's cold hand. "Ryan," she said softly, "I hope you're doing okay in there..." She felt slight warmth from his hand and patted it gently. "Hey, the Knights are winning these days. We haven't lost these last several games. Hell, we even beat down East Nortiniry tonight and you know they always had better players. After tonight, Randy, now our only infamous kicker, is starting to get nervous."

Joni sighed and shut her eyes. "*I hope you pull out of this soon and get back to us,*" she prayed. "*I miss you... we all miss you!*"

"I miss you too," a faint voice said from behind.

Joni gasped and opened her eyes, turning around. Her mouth dropped in shock, astonished to see Ryan in his hospital gown faintly standing near the bed. "What are you doing over there?" she yelped. "Why aren't you in your body?"

"You can see *and* hear me too?" Ryan cried. "I've been trying to get those nurses and the doctor's attention for days!" He touched his chest, his eyes growing wide. "I'm not dead, am I? I can't be..."

"You're not dead," Joni said calmly. "See, there's that silver rope sticking out of you." Ryan looked down and gasped when he noticed a shiny silver cord extending from around his waist. Giving it a gentle tug, the nearby machine monitoring his pulse abruptly beeped erratically in response. "Hey! Don't yank it out or you *will* end up dead!"

"Ah, what's going on; why am I like this?" Ryan wailed. "I want back in my body!" He gestured wildly at the bed. "Look at it, it's a mess; I look like a damn statistic!"

"I don't know how to get you back in, but you've got to calm down. Freaking out won't help!"

Ryan let out a cry and grasped his wrist. "Hey, what's wrong with my hand?"

Joni looked down at Ryan's hand and realized she gripped tightly. "Sorry," she muttered, slackening her hold. "I was squeezing it."

"Joni, I don't know what's going on," Ryan protested.

"Tell me about it," Joni mewed.

"Get me back in my body, soon! Please, Joni!" Ryan approached and grabbed at her arm, only to pass through it. Joni clenched her teeth, watching Ryan's arms twitch slightly in response. "There are these weird shadows that keep following me..."

"What weird shadows?" Joni demanded. "*I hope they're not Agents of Death or something!*" she thought as Ryan shrugged.

"I don't know what they want and I couldn't get the nurse's attentions, but since you're here..."

"I, well..." Joni shook her head. "I don't know what you're talking about!"

"Are they dangerous?"

"Let's hope they're not." Joni stood. "Ryan, stay in this room and don't leave near your body! If you go too far away and that cord gets cut..." Ryan nodded ruefully. "Listen, if someone tells you to go into the light, *don't do it!*"

"Got it!"

Joni let go of Ryan's hand and his apparition faded. Leaving the room, a strange chill suddenly coursed through her and she turned around. She spotted Ryan's varsity athlete jacket hanging from the small bin tagged with a sticker bearing his name on the side. Joni picked it up and a gold chain with a silver pendant fell out from the pocket.

Picking up the chain, Joni studied the silver pendant: a silver-toned skeleton key with a small iridescent gem embedded into the head. The key rapidly heated and her vision became cloudy as darkness enveloped the room. Joni let out a cry when grabbed firmly by the arm.

"He's mine!" Kipper's voice snarled behind her.

Joni turned and pushed him away. "What are you doing here?" she demanded. "Why are you hurting Ryan?"

"Who said I was?" Kipper replied, smirking.

"What are you doing to him?"

"Something you shouldn't concern yourself with!" Kipper shoved Joni away, the force sending her flying across the room. She struck the wall, stunned when she watched her own body slump forward on the floor as a heap. Kipper approached, grinning sneeringly and his gray eyes dimly glowed in ruby light. "What's wrong, eh?" he heckled. "Don't like playing in my world, huh?"

"Why are you attacking Ryan?" Joni spat. "You tell me right now or I'm kicking your greasy butt again like last time!"

The darkness swirled around Kipper and he held out his hands. "Yeah? Give it a shot. I'm all yours!" Joni growled and rushed over, dropping down for a tackle. Her body passed through him and Kipper laughed. "You forget that I control the shadows, stupid girl! This is *my* domain!"

Joni faced Kipper, clenching her hands. "What do you want with Ryan?"

"He's got something that belongs to me."

"What, that key thing? Take it and leave him alone!"

"Not without punishment... You'll see why you should've returned Cian and Hedos!" Kipper's hands glowed in red light and he snapped his fingers, forcing the room around them instantly darkening and turn into empty space.

"You leave Ryan out of this!" Joni rushed Kipper again and he turned away with ease.

"Ha," Kipper crowed. "Give me one good reason why I shouldn't seal your ass away right now!" Joni stepped rearwards, shaking slightly as fear and panic rose through her. "I can feel they're in the room somewhere so you can forget calling on them to help you; they're too weak to fight for you now!"

"*He can sense they're weak from fighting him earlier!*" Joni thought in horror. "*He can't find out I've got them in my pocket!*"

"Look, girl, you should stay out the way – this is too heavy for you to deal with; I can tell you don't know anything about the Legions!"

Joni backed away, overwhelmed. "*He's right!*" she considered. "*The only reason that greasy blond keeps attacking me is so they'd get worn down and have no choice!*"

"Too scared to talk, eh?" Kipper teased and pushed his bleached hair out of his gray eyes. "I'll tell you what, if you just hand them over, I won't send the shadows after your soul!"

"No way," Joni spat. "You'll just go back on it!" She shook her fists at him. "Look, you move your greasy self somewhere else and leave my friends and these Legions out of it!"

"Forget it!" Kipper's thrust forward his glowing hands, releasing a dark sphere of black light tangled with dark violet and navy lighting.

Joni screamed and ducked down, cringing as the light flung toward her. Suddenly the light hurtled back, blasting out of the shadowy world. It ripped a hole in the side of the dark wall, revealing the hospital corridor. The light arched upwards, slamming into the fluorescent lights and the energy crackled as the cover burst, raining down glass and sparks.

"What the hell?" Kipper screeched.

Joni looked up from her crouched position, spotting Ryan's faint form standing over her, baseball bat in hand. "Ryan!" she cried.

"Looks like a home run to me," Ryan quipped and ran a hand through his messy hair, tucking a flyaway lock behind his ear. "See that, next time that'll be you!"

"I'll kill you!" Kipper roared and dashed forward.

Joni sprang to her feet and grabbed Kipper's arm, reversing him using his momentum. He grasped Joni's wrist and pulled her forward, then threw her overhead, sending her back against the wall. Joni fell head over heels and struck the floor, surrounded by shards.

"Joni!" Ryan cried.

Kipper turned for Ryan and let out a stunned cry when the bat smashed across his face, knocking him down. "You son of a bitch!" he howled, jumping to his feet. Throwing a charged swing with his glowing hand, Ryan sidestepped the swipe and delivered another swift strike against Kipper's legs, downing him.

"You sicko creep!" Ryan yelled, bashing the bat over Kipper's head. "Leave her alone!"

"You should worry more about yourself, weakling!" Kipper snarled. Ryan raised the bat again as the shadows darkening the room departed, forming into a humanoid shape. "Aratas, destroy him!"

Ryan backed away from a large shadow looming over him. The phantom transformed into a large cape, stretching wide and Ryan swung his bat as it hovered over him. He found to his horror it had no effect once his clubbing weapon disintegrated in white light. The cape captured Ryan, winding tighter around him.

"Ryan!" Joni screamed, watching helplessly as her friend struggled underneath the sheet of darkness.

Kipper got up on his knees, laughing at Ryan fighting in vain against the darkness tightening harder around him.

"Look closely, girl," Kipper crowed. "The more he fights, the weaker he gets!"

The machines attached to Ryan's unconscious form emitted high rapid chirps in response. Joni scrambled to her feet and pushed away the swirling darkness, clearing her view. She watched his body twitching involuntarily.

"Ryan!" Joni wailed and raced to his bedside. "Don't struggle; he's killing you!"

"Hear that?" Kipper sauntered. "See how erratic it'll get?"

Joni grabbed Ryan's involuntarily twitching hand. "Ryan," she pleaded, "please don't die!"

"Hedos and Cian are still under my command," Kipper growled from behind. Joni turned and threw a punch at Kipper and he leaned back, grabbing her fist. "They may be fighting for you now, but the power belongs to *me*!" Kipper pushed Joni to the floor.

Joni kicked Kipper's shin as he towered over her. "I'm not giving them up," she snapped, "no matter what you do!"

"Facing my true power's a side of me you *don't* want to see!" Joni grunted when kicked in the side. "Look closely and see what I'll do to him."

"No!" Joni screeched as Kipper formed the black saber in his glowing hands. She sprang to her feet and Kipper thrust the blade at her as she tackled him, releasing a spark of indigo light. Both fell against the wall and Kipper kicked Joni off. She slipped to her knees, clutching her side as red stained the floor around her.

"You're lucky I wasn't aiming to kill you this time," Kipper snarled, sheathing the saber into an invisible scabbard, making it fade in dark light. "But next time, you won't be lucky." He stalked off, laughing manically and faded into the darkness.

Joni looked down at her hand, surprised when she found no blood staining her fingers. "*It hurts, but I'm not bleeding*," she thought and struggled upright. "*I don't understand it!*"

The red and blue vials appeared faintly in front of Joni, floating unsteadily. Joni grabbed for them and they pulsed in dim light. "You guys saved me again!" she cried. "Please, don't do that again; you might die!"

"*You can't do this alone*," the cool voice whispered.

"*We made a promise*," the harsh voice croaked.

"Who did you promise?" Joni heard no response when the vials faded in faint purple light. Turning to Ryan, she watched terrified as the shadow's struggles grew weaker, then began crumpling, crushing her friend. "Ryan, wake up!" Joni wailed and ran to the shadow as it became more compact.

The shadow faded in a puff of smoke and Joni cried out when a low tone resonated in the darkened world. The swirling darkness began dissipating and Joni returned to Ryan's bed, finding a heavy dark aura surrounding his body.

"Please, don't die," she begged. "I promise to get stronger and beat down that greasy blond!"

Joni ran away, returning to her slumped body in the hospital room corner. Touching the top of her body's head, Joni's red-stained world faded away into whiteout.

Sitting bolt upright, sounds of sirens and buzzing of the various machines attached to Ryan assaulted Joni's ears. Several nurses and a doctor flocked in, surrounding Ryan's comatose body going through a seizure. An orderly approached Joni, appearing concerned.

"Are you alright?" the orderly asked.

Joni nodded and the orderly grabbed her arm, pulling her to her feet. She pushed him away and escaped the frantic scene, rushing for the cafeteria.

Collapsing at a nearby table, Joni put her head into her arms and broke down in tears, sobbing into her sleeve.

"*I don't know why Dad left me those awful things!*" she thought. "*Those things kill! They probably killed him and it's going to kill my friend too!*"

"What are you crying about?" a familiar voice called.

Joni sniffled and sat up, yelping in surprise when she faced Labraccio standing over her. He wore his coat unbuttoned, revealing an open oversized red blazer revealing his pale narrow chest, with blue suspenders underneath holding up his black slacks. His yellow and navy cap hung from his coat pocket and around his neck he wore a silver necklace with a golden pendant of a winged sword-wielding Aerian.

"You've got to stop scaring me like that!" Joni yelped and kicked the nearby chair. Labraccio caught it and turned it around, plopping into it. "You're aiming to kill me too!"

"Who said I was trying to kill you?" Labraccio chortled. "There's plenty of other people out there who can do that for me."

"Sicko creep," Joni grumbled.

"Well, hey, at least you stopped crying!"

"Shut up!" Joni turned away, crossing her arms. "What do you want?"

"Well, I decided to come over since you were so kind to invite me. At least there's only one hospital in town."

"So you're here."

"Anyway, my job is to keep tabs on you. I don't necessarily have to keep you alive."

Joni glared at Labraccio. "I've got enough crazy people keeping tabs on me!" she spat. "They're trying to kill me and my friends and I don't have time for your stupid antics!"

"Are you saying you need my help?" Labraccio grinned. "Just say it and I'll be willing, for a fee."

"Really?" Joni snarled. Labraccio grunted when she poked his bare chest with her fingers. "Does your fee have something to do with you not having a shirt on?"

Labraccio rolled his eyes. "My shirt is my business," he retorted.

"Yeah, right."

"Really!" Labraccio protested and put up his hands. "If you decline, that's fine. It's not like you can pay me with money or anything."

Joni's face turned red and she stood indignantly to her feet. "Are you serious?" she thundered. "The only way you'll help me fighting Kipper and Bobby is if I sleep with you?" Joni kicked his chair. "You're completely sick!"

Labraccio snorted and folded his arms along the chair's top edge, leaning forward against it. "How else are you going to pay me?" he complained. "You got any better ideas?"

Joni clenched her hands, growling, unable to say anything in return.

"Hey, Joni," Signe called upon entering the cafeteria, helmet tucked under his arm. "I can hear you screaming all the way out in the waiting room!"

"Sorry," Joni spat, jutting a thumb at Labraccio. "But I'm this close to kicking that nasty bastard's ass over here!"

"Is he a friend of your dad or something?" Signe asked. "He looks too old to go to Nortiniry."

"He's Slake's brother."

Signe nodded. "So, what did I miss?" he said instead.

"That!" Joni gestured down the hall. "Ryan's in serious condition; I can't handle it."

"I understand," Signe murmured. "I'll peek in there and give you an update, okay?"

"Thanks."

Signe left her side, walking the corridor's end.

"While he's out," Labraccio said, "let's find a nice place to get more intimate."

"What?" Joni squawked. Labraccio stood and grabbed Joni by the wrist. She struggled against him and suddenly their world warped around them. "What's going on?"

"Hang on," Labraccio commanded.

Joni let out a cry when bright light abruptly blinded her and she felt a moment's weightlessness. Suddenly her vision cleared and she stood in cramped darkness.

"W-Where are we?" Joni sputtered.

CHAPTER TWENTY-ONE

"Damn," muttered Labraccio, "I miscalculated."

A door opened and bright light filtered through. Stepping out, Labraccio waved at Joni to follow and she cautiously exited into the open. Turning around, Joni found she formerly stood within a closet.

Once her eyes adjusted to the light, she looked about her surroundings. Across from the closet rest a single desk with a desktop computer, stacks of papers and small stuffed animals of various types cluttered on the other side. Pale rays of the afternoon autumn sun streamed through the frosted windows.

"Why are we in this office?" Joni asked. "You're not trying to fulfill some sick teacher-student fantasy, are you?"

Labraccio snorted. "Thanks for the idea," he replied, "but this office belongs to a friend of mine, Greg Shorthand." Labraccio sat in a chair against the wall and crossed his legs at the knee. "Before you ask, yes, that's his real name, and no, he's not the guy who invented that atrocious stenographer's writing style." He motioned at Joni and several chairs in the room. "Take a seat. He's probably on break."

"I'm not doing him too!" Joni snapped. "Get that sick thought out of your head!"

Labraccio shrugged. "Hey, the option's still open if you want to."

"Ugh," Joni spat and shuddered in disgust. Approaching the desk, she picked up a stuffed golden gryphon with white wings and beady black eyes. Giving it a gentle squeeze, a small squeak emitted from the toy. "Is something wrong with Greg?"

"Why do you ask?"

"Why does he collect these toys?"

"They're not toys," Labraccio said in annoyance. "They're pocket monsters!"

Joni scoffed. "I can see that they're mini beasts," she retorted. "He likes mythical monsters or something?"

"Oh, so you notice that some of his collection consists of animals from legend," Labraccio answered. "That's because he was able to capture them and control them."

"Stop kidding around." Joni placed the gryphon back and picked up a black hound with short pointy ears and beady red eyes. She squeezed it and it also squeaked.

"I wouldn't do that if I were you, manhandling them all like that," Labraccio warned. "They don't like that!"

"How would you know?" Joni set aside the hound and picked up a silver tiger with beady orange eyes.

Labraccio gave a shrewd grin. "You'll see."

The office door opened and a tall middle-aged man with short dark blond hair entered, holding a tray of food in his hands and a fork between his teeth. He wore a dark gray suit with a chain hanging from his rear pocket and a gold pendant of a winged Aerian pinned to his blazer's lapel. His dark brown eyes narrowed as he set the tray in the chair next to the door and pulled out the fork from between his teeth, pointing it at Joni.

"Put that down!" he barked.

"I didn't ruin it!" Joni yelped, dropping the silver tiger. It struck the floor with a squeak, rolling towards Labraccio.

"Afternoon, Greg," Labraccio greeted as he picked up the small silver tiger.

Greg kicked the door shut and snatched up his tray. "Get out!" he snapped, storming toward his desk. Joni backed away when he towered over her, glaring down with blazing amber eyes.

"Why are you in such a bad mood today?" Labraccio asked innocently. He stroked the head of the small stuffed tiger. "How can you deal with that meanie weenie, Tigris?"

"You know why!" Greg said through gritted teeth. He pierced the fork into the desktop near Joni's hand and she recoiled, noting the metal stood upright in the wood. Joni took a nervous step away.

"I know you can't stand me." Labraccio pet the tiger on the head. "Is that right, Tigris?" he cooed to the toy.

Joni shot a nasty look at Labraccio. "Is that monster your friend?" she spat, incredulous. "You're a sick man, Labraccio!"

"If you won't leave," Greg thundered, "I'll force you out of here!" He thrust forward a hand at Labraccio. "Tigris, transform!"

Labraccio tossed the silver tiger in the air as it flashed in bright white light. A large dark gray tiger with silver stripes appeared in the office's central area, growling softly as it faced Labraccio. Joni let out terrified shriek and ran to the office's rear. The tiger's ears flicked and it turned around, sniffing the air.

"Don't let it bite me!" Joni cried and shuddered in fear when the beast padded past Greg's desk, coming closer. The tiger approached and looked up at her with bright orange eyes. The beast purred softly, gently nudging at her hand with its head.

"Hey, Joni," Labraccio said brightly, "Tigris likes you!"

"Why did you come here?" Greg demanded and set his tray aside on his desk. "You're lucky she's a part of the Arcana Assembly, otherwise, you know he would've shred her on sight!"

"Well," Labraccio said wryly, "glad to know Tigris can tell!"

"W-What?" Joni stammered. "What's this Arcana Assembly? Why would Tigris hurt me?"

"The Arcana Assembly is a council of Magicians and Mage Knights," Labraccio replied. "You're a part of that, did you know?"

Joni slipped to her knees, suddenly lightheaded. The tiger licked at Joni's face. "I never heard about any of this," she said weakly. "Dad never told me..."

"I'm surprised he'd keep you in the dark like that. He was a high-ranking Mage Knight."

"Really...?"

"Be glad that Tigris didn't eat you, because he'd totally destroy you by now if you weren't a part of that." Labraccio grinned brightly. "Cool beans, eh?"

Joni raised a wary eyebrow at Labraccio. "Are you telling me these pocket monsters can destroy on command?"

Labraccio nodded. "Pretty much."

Joni held her sides. "I think I'm going to be sick!" Tigris left Joni's side and pushed a small metal trash canister toward her with its nose. "Um... thanks."

"Well, these little guys only attack mundane people and enemies of the Assembly," Labraccio went on. "We can't have people talking about how stuffed animals are real, now do we?" He chortled.

"What about people with Magic?" Joni asked. "Don't they still count?"

"They're not allowed to destroy people with Magic, unfortunately," Greg grumbled. "They can fight until the opponent is drained, but not to the point of death."

"Unless they're that weak to begin with," Labraccio piped. "But hey, that's not our problem at that point."

Joni shook her head. "The insanity!" Tigris knelt down on the floor, placing its head in her lap. She pet it gently. "Um, nice kitty?"

"Now if I can only get Tigris to destroy *you*!" Greg spat and pulled out his seat, sinking into it. "Then you can finally leave me alone!"

"I can't help it if all your pocket monsters like me," Labraccio said, smiling brightly. "I'm just that charismatic!"

Greg waved Labraccio away. "Don't you have some other place to be or someone else to pester?"

"Not yet." Labraccio leaned back in his chair. "I came to report that Sable and Milian are on the prowl, kicking up trouble." He blew a sigh. "Sable's the one I'm more concerned about at the moment. He's a total loose screw, giving this redhead some problems."

"So what of it," Greg spat. "I have him on record as having gone through the toughest reform school the Assembly had to offer! He can't do anything while on probation!"

"What?" Labraccio squawked and gripped his seat, leaning forward. "You mean that's not an Animer?"

"In the flesh," Greg affirmed.

"What's an Animer?" Joni asked.

"A spiritual projection," Greg answered. "Like so." He withdrew a small blue orb from his pocket and threw it at Labraccio. The orb crashed against the wall and Labraccio leaned out of a swipe when a pale copy of Greg appeared in a flash of cyan light, swinging at him.

"How the hell he's on probation?" Labraccio snapped and punched the copy in the groin, forcing it bursting into particles of light. "Demons like him aren't supposed to leave Starsky's Reformatory!"

"Now hold on!" Greg shouted. "I didn't release him – someone *else* on the Assembly did!"

Labraccio narrowed his eyes and abruptly rose to his feet, his body tense. Tigris stiffened and let out a deep throaty growl. "There were strict rules that Sable was to *never* get off that island after *that* incident!" Labraccio turned and kicked the chair, overturning it to the floor with a clatter. "Check your damn papers once in a while, Greg!"

"Tigris, revert!" Greg commanded. The tiger growled softly and it flashed in white light, vanishing back into a small stuffed tiger with tiny orange eyes in Joni's hand. "I'll look into it... it's probably a minor filing error."

"You'd better!" Labraccio fumed. "Joni, let's go." She squeezed the stuffed tiger, making it squeak. "Tigris will get you later," Labraccio reprimanded as Joni got up and set the stuffed animal on the edge of Greg's desk. "I told you not to squeeze them!"

"I can't help it," Joni said sheepishly. "They're cute!"

"Sometimes the cute ones have a nasty bite!" Labraccio stalked to the office door, throwing it open. "They're not so adorable when they're chomping on your neck!"

Joni stepped out and followed Labraccio through the maze of various gray cubicles, finally reaching the main door. Labraccio turned the handle and it snapped off. Growling under his breath, he gave the door a hard stomp, slamming it open. Storming ahead, he entered a white-walled corridor.

"What was all that back there?" Joni asked, walking in step with him. "From what I understand, I know these Aerians are like some kind of mystic protectors..."

"We work for the Assembly and keep files on people who use Magic," Labraccio explained. "We know about you and your father Terrell."

"This is some pretty heavy stuff!" Joni exclaimed. "I don't know why he didn't tell me about all this, especially if he worked with you!"

"I'm not quite sure either... Maybe it has something to do with the last war over the Conjunction Arts."

"Conjunction Arts? War?" Joni came to a stop and grabbed Labraccio's sleeve. He grunted and pulled out of her grip. "What are you talking about?"

"Nothing that concerns you right now." Labraccio smirked. "It's a nasty little story."

"You and these damn stories!" Joni punched Labraccio's arm. "One of these days, I'll get you to tell me!"

"If you can defeat me in combat, I'll tell you whatever you want." Labraccio gave a mischievous smile. "But at your rate and your nonexistent knowledge, that won't be happening any time soon."

"Argh!" Joni punched him again.

Labraccio chuckled and brushed off his sleeve. "Now then," he continued and made his way down the long hallway while Joni reluctantly kept pace behind him. "Would you like to know more about how Aerians work?"

"I guess," Joni muttered.

"Ever since the public's awareness of the paranormal, they've opened their eyes to the arcane world. Most magicians worry about themselves and use self-serving spells, while others use Magic to help people, but you always have some kind of wingnut lusting for power and fighting other magicians or harming innocents, summoning demons, causing all sorts of nasty things – disease, war, plagues, whatever..."

"Are you saying this Arcana Assembly was put together to keep the world in balance?" Joni blew a raspberry. "Tell me a new one!"

"Fine, don't believe me."

Approaching a single door in the corridor, Labraccio opened it, revealing pale blue-violet energy filling the doorway.

"What's that?" Joni inquired.

"A portal back into the Material World."

"You mean--? We were--!"

"Yes, and don't tell anybody," Labraccio said sternly. "I'll lose my job if word got out!"

Labraccio took her hand and they stepped through the pulsing light. Joni's world washed out in white then descended into darkness.

A flash of light blinded Joni and she cried out, shielding her eyes. Once her vision returned, Joni found herself in the hall outside the hospital cafeteria and Labraccio gone from her side. She spotted

Signe coming down the corridor with his helmet tucked under his arm and ran up to him. Signe held her gently with his free hand when she fell against him.

"Hey, I wondered where you ran off to," Signe said, concerned. "I know it's scary when your friends are in a situation that's out of control."

"It's been so hard," Joni moaned and hugged Signe tighter as tears streamed down her face.

"I understand, but Ryan will be okay. I asked around and they said that seizure he had, it wasn't life-threatening. The doctors think he had a weird reaction or something to some sort of painkillers or antibiotics they switched him to."

"Of course..."

Signe ran his hand through Joni's hair. "It'll be okay," he murmured.

"It won't!" Joni wailed and broke away from Signe's hold. "Don't get close to me, Signe. You'll only get hurt!"

Signe raised an eyebrow. "What are you talking about?"

"Anyone who gets close to me always get hurt," Joni bitterly spat. "I don't want you to get hurt too!"

Signe gave her a blank look and ran his hand through his hair. "What brought this on?" Joni explained the fight near her home and he frowned. "The Knights still have a chance and they'll play again," Signe said cheerfully. "I'm sure Randy's knee isn't seriously messed up."

"This is serious!" Joni squawked and slapped a hand against Signe's chest. "That crackpot crank Bobby really put the hurt on him! He's dangerous."

Signe pet her head, smiling. "Hey, we'll get Bobby for messing up our team's secret weapon. It's not right for him to waltz in and start hurting others like that..."

Joni shook her head vehemently. "No, Signe, it's not that easy. Normal fighting methods aren't going to work on him..."

"Oh?"

Joni hesitated and her heart fluttered in her chest. "What about Ryan?" she said instead. "He was fine before that guy started sacking him in the last quarter!"

"I don't know too much about that guy or familiar with TriCity's players, but that's not what we're concerned about."

Joni frowned, though the constricting tightness refused to dissipate. "What about you?" she said weakly. "Bobby busted your brother's ribs and you got seriously hurt!"

"Just a little concussion, is all," Signe remarked and shrugged his shoulders. "At least it wasn't majorly severe or anything. I'm just worried about Martel... He's the one that got badly hurt."

Joni nodded numbly. "You're always so cheerful..."

"I have to be." Joni fidgeted and Signe blew a short sigh. "Do you want me to take you home?" he asked, breaking the tension. "You're always welcome to crash on my couch if you like." Signe gave a playful grin. "I can play doctor with you instead of Martel."

"What?" Joni yelped and her face turned bright red. "Damn it, Signe!" She punched his arm and he giggled.

"There's my favorite redhead," Signe teased.

"Please drop me off at home," Joni pleaded.

"Sure, I'll take you there." Signe took Joni by the hand and escorted her to the hospital exit. He frowned when he noticed her deep in thought. "What's bothering you?" Signe asked softly.

"I need to go back and check on Randy," she answered. "See if he needs anything or whatever."

"Why not let me drop you off at Randy's place?"

"He's at one of those vacation cabins in Lakeview. I'll tell you how to get there."

"Good to know."

Reaching the outdoors, Signe let go of her hand and put his helmet on then they approached his motorcycle parked in the lot. Joni got on behind him once he readied the motorcycle and he took off through the darkened streets.

CHAPTER TWENTY-TWO

Joni jumped off before Signe had a chance to shut down the engine and left him behind in the driveway, running up the cabin's steps. She knocked on the door then leaned against the wall, waiting for an answer.

The door opened moments later, revealing Labraccio with his torso and chest in bandages, in bare feet and loose-fitting jeans.

"What?" he grumbled.

"What happened to you?" Joni cried. "Did you and Slake fight again?"

"Doesn't matter."

"Is Randy okay?"

"He's fine."

"How's Slake?"

"Fine."

Joni put a foot in the door as Labraccio tried to shut it close. "Wait," she snapped. "I came here to talk to you."

Labraccio blew an annoyed sigh and held open the door. "About what?"

Joni fished through her pockets, revealing the two dark vials. "This, Labraccio!" she snapped. "I need to know what's going on, why I'm stuck dealing with them, and why Bobby and Kipper keep coming after me!"

"It's a long story that you don't want to get involved in!"

Joni stomped her foot and chucked the vials at Labraccio, pelting them at his chest. They clattered to the floor behind him and vanished. "I'm involved in it *now*," she shouted, "so why can't you help me?"

"It's not my problem and I can't help you."

"Well, *make* it your problem!" Joni placed her hands on her hips. "This is getting dangerous for me and my friends! Don't you *understand* how serious this is?"

"Of course it's serious," Labraccio spat. "Magicians killing each over powerful elemental spirit weapons that don't require training; I'd kill for it too."

"Ryan's barely hanging on, Randy's knee is almost destroyed and the Legions are stripped so they can't do anything right now to help me if those two lunatics come back again." Joni blew a hard sigh. "I don't know when they will ever get their power back..."

Labraccio rolled his eyes. "What do you want me to do?"

"I thought you were supposed to help me!" Joni yelled. "You're a Protector, right? Then do your job!" She kicked Labraccio's shin and he grunted in response. "Don't give me any more shit about having to sleep with you or combat you to get any help, you sleaze!" Labraccio clenched his hands and turned away, grumbling under his breath. "What's with you?" Joni continued. "If you helped my dad, then why not help me?"

"I'm not assigned to your case!" Labraccio growled.

"What are you talking about? You said you were when we first met!"

"So, I lied." Labraccio turned, glaring at Joni. "Aerians are assigned to people they must watch over," he said evenly. "If they screw up, then it's their problem. I'm not allowed to get involved!"

"Then break some rules and help me since you're apparently good at it!"

Labraccio bared his teeth. "You snippy little girl," he snarled. "You have Slake assigned to you, so you don't need me!"

"Why?"

"Slake is supposed to be enough!" Labraccio slammed the door in her face.

"You've got to drop this long-running feud you have!" Joni called and banged on the worn wood. "I know Slake's stripped right now so he can't help me. Please, work together to protect me."

"I'm not getting demoted for his failures!" Labraccio's voice snapped from the other side.

"What do you mean, 'demoted'? Are you trying to cover for him in some demented way?"

The door opened, revealing Labraccio who appeared annoyed. "What are you, clueless?" he thundered. "You know what 'demoted' means!"

"You guys have ranks or something?"

"Yes, we have ranks," Labraccio said irritably and snorted. "When you do what you're told, you advance. If you can't handle the pressure, you are given something you can deal with! Apparently, the both of us can't even manage your case and that idiot brother of mine is in the highest rank there is in relation to the Legions!"

"What happens if you both get demoted?" Joni asked softly.

"You're a smart girl," Labraccio sneered. "What do you think?"

"Will you two get reassigned to somebody else?"

Labraccio huffed and stormed indoors. Joni walked in after him, following him into the parlor. "Why are you bothering me?" he muttered and looked out the window, facing the darkness of the night.

"Please help me!"

"How many times do I have to keep telling you that it's none of my business?"

"Please, Labraccio! It's obvious that you've got greater skill than Slake out here dealing with these nut jobs, even if he is higher ranking than you!" Joni pleaded. "You must care a little to go through all that trouble to attend to Slake when he got hurt and to pester Greg when you needed information."

"I owed Greg a favor," Labraccio grumbled. "Besides... I'm done with this."

"Please, Labraccio," Joni appealed and grabbed his arm as he began glowing in silver light. "Just this once, I'm begging you. I won't bother you ever again!"

"You owe me," Labraccio snapped and brushed Joni's hand aside. She blew a distressed sigh, watching him disappear in a flash of silver light.

"What's wrong with him?" Signe's voice called into the room.

Joni turned about face as he entered the parlor. "I don't know what's going on," she said dejectedly.

"How's Randy?"

"I haven't checked yet; Labraccio claims he's okay."

"Come on, he needs our support."

Joni nodded and followed Signe upstairs. She paused in step once Slake exited a room wearing a dark navy suit with white dress shirt.

"He's stable if you're wondering," Slake replied as he passed by Joni and Signe in the corridor.

"Are you okay?" Joni inquired, touching Slake's arm. He looked down at her, his expression neutral.

"I'm fine," he answered.

"How is he?" Signe asked.

"Better."

Slake pulled away and headed downstairs. Joni hurried after Slake and grabbed for him as he vanished in golden light. Her vision temporarily washed out and the feeling of weightlessness took over.

Suddenly Joni's sight cleared and Slake pushed her away, placing a hand to the hilt of his sword harness that materialized around his waist. Before Joni could open her mouth, he withdrew the glowing silver long sword and pointed it in her direction.

"What are you doing here?" Slake shouted.

"I--!" Joni put up her hands and took a step away. "Slake, I just needed to talk to you!"

"You're not supposed to be here!"

"I can't leave because I don't know how!" Joni put down her hands. "What are you going to do, kill me?"

Slake clenched his teeth and lowered his weapon, growling under his breath. Joni looked about her surroundings, noting that she was back in the space of white walls and gray cubicles and they stood before an office door with the nameplate 'G. Shorthand' on the front.

"You're going to cost me my job!" Slake snapped as he sheathed his blade.

Joni rolled her eyes in response and snorted. "Well, tell that to Labraccio," she said dryly. "But don't worry. You won't get demoted if nobody finds out!"

"What?" Slake hissed. Joni nodded and he turned away, shuddering in silent fury as he clenched his hands tightly at his sides. "He thinks he can be lax and do whatever he wants. I'm scrambling to keep by the book while he's always breaking the rules around me!" Faint light charged through his hands, coursing around his arms. "I swear; he's driving me crazy!"

"Slake, please calm down," Joni said softly, placing a hand at his back. "If you stick too hard to the rules, you'll only drive your own self insane because everyone else around you keeps breaking them."

Slake pushed Joni away and knocked on the door. The door opened slightly and Slake entered with Joni following behind. She spotted Greg staring into a mirror showing distant images across its glass surface.

"Mister Shorthand," Slake called, shutting the door behind him. "I really need to talk to you!"

"What is it?" Greg demanded and turned away from the mirror, dissipating the images inside the silver-painted glass.

"*Does he have the same talent I have?*" Joni wondered. "*Greg must be powerful if he can see things in a mirror instead of water like I do...*"

Slake stood on the desk's other side and gripped the edge. "Have you been made aware of what's going on?" he inquired.

"You must be in some kind of trouble if you're asking," Greg replied.

Slake grunted and narrowed his eyes. "What do you think?" he snarled.

Greg approached his desk, gripping the edge firmly. "What do you want me to do?" he demanded in an even tone. "You got yourself into this mess, so you get yourself out of it. I'm in charge of Records, remember?"

Slake lowered his head, blowing a hard sigh. "I need you to get involved," he muttered.

"Ha!" Greg pushed against Slake's chest, shoving him away. "Why should I bother?"

"I seek out your advice on this matter."

"Admit it, you've screwed up majorly!" Slake bared his teeth and pushed Greg with a charged hand, forcing him slamming against the far wall. "Oh, with that kind of attitude, I'm not helping you!"

"Sometimes I wonder why I even bothered," Slake grumbled.

Greg shook off his initial stun and stepped forward, picking up a small stuffed gray and white husky with beady light-blue eyes. He squeezed tightly, forcing it squeaking in response.

"Then why did you come here?" Greg demanded.

"You should make it your care to lend a hand, Greg!"

"It's Mister Shorthand to you," Greg retorted. "Anyway, I don't care what you do or what happens to you." He grinned darkly as his eyes gleamed. "I'll actually appreciate watching the glorious Mister Rulebook fall apart and get demoted to the rest of us desk jockeys!"

Slake's eyes narrowed and he clenched his hands that flared in gold light. "You wouldn't dare!" he spat.

"You're making all of us look bad, Corbitt!"

Joni ran toward the desk, snatching up the silver tiger. "Then how would you like it if I destroyed something you cared about, Mister Shorthand?" she threatened. "They would really hurt if they were damaged in this form, right?" Greg bared his teeth at her. "Even if you were able to fix them somehow, they wouldn't be at their strongest because they'd be forever hurt, never to heal up right!"

"You don't know which ones I control," Greg sneered through gritted teeth, "and which ones are merely toys!"

"I know because Labraccio told me." Greg growled under his breath as Joni pointed to the small husky he held in his hand. "Labraccio told me that the legendary animals are the ones you own. Also, they don't like to be squeezed."

Greg set down the husky with trembling hands. "The bastard!" he hissed and punched his desk in frustration.

Noticing the tiger's orange eyes glittering faintly in her hand, Joni continued. "Tigris wouldn't want Labraccio or Slake to be in trouble," she said gently. "Please, just this once! We won't bother you ever again!"

"You owe me," Greg snapped.

"*Great, two favors!*" Joni thought as Greg gripped the desk's edge.

"As long as that girl goes without training," Greg said in a low tone, "she'll constantly be contested for the Legions."

"What is it with these Legions that make them so great?" Joni complained. "Did they have anything to do about some war Labraccio mentioned?"

Greg's face suddenly blanched and he glared at Joni. Joni stepped away, hiding behind Slake who stood there with a blank expression. "Now what do you know about that?" he snarled.

"Nothing, obviously!" Joni cried.

Greg left his desk and opened the door. "Tigris, to me!" he ordered. The stuffed tiger vanished from Joni's hand, reappearing in Greg's. Greg pocketed the animal then stepped outside.

"What's with that response?" Joni asked. Slake shrugged his shoulders and left the office with Joni at his heels. They hurried after Greg, following him through the maze of cubicles. Exiting onto the long corridor, the three approached the portal at the end glowing in dark green energy. "Why are the colors different on this one?"

Greg glared at Slake and he immediately put up his hands.

"This is Labraccio's fault," Slake said quickly. "I know nothing about it."

Greg shook his head and stepped through. Slake took Joni by the hand and bright light washed over them as they stepped forward into the pulsating field.

CHAPTER TWENTY-THREE

Emerging into a large library, Greg turned, facing both Joni and Slake.

"Now you two don't wander off," Greg said sternly, "especially *you*." He firmly poked Joni's chest with his finger. "If you snoop and get any classified information, it will cost us our jobs and we *will* be on your head!" Joni nodded, opting to stay silent. "You stay put until I get back. I'll give you any information you want to know about the war." Greg stalked off and Slake directed Joni to a set of tables and chairs.

"Sit here," Slake commanded and hurried away. After several moments, he returned carrying a single large hardbound with a black wooden cover and metal hinges, setting it on the table with a bang.

"My dad has a book just like this!" Joni exclaimed. "The inside cover read '*Book of Legions*' but I couldn't read the rest of the writing."

"Well, here is the original copy," Slake grumbled, gesturing toward the book. "Depending on your power level, you should be able to read it."

"Why can't I read Dad's version?"

"Perhaps he encoded it with a spell so that you can't decipher it until you're strong enough, or wrote it with a cipher in general. It all depends..."

"That's smart, either way."

"Just read." Slake left her side, pacing as Joni opened the book and turned several pages, skimming its contents.

"*There's detailed information about the Legions in here,*" Joni thought. "*There's fifty total; with half offensive and the other half defensive.*"

"Learn anything?" Slake asked moments later, sounding bored.

"It seems that it doesn't matter which set of Legions I have; since they're as only as powerful as I am," Joni said as she scanned the material. "I can choose which ones of the fifty I want. That seems flexible enough." She looked up from reading at Slake. "With that in mind, why is there so much fuss over Cian and Hedos?"

Slake shrugged his shoulders. "Your guess is as good as mine," he replied.

Joni returned to the book, turning pages. She paused on a watercolor drawing of an armored knight in blue steel plate armor with a closed-face helmet only revealing his intensely staring aquamarine eyes. In his right hand, the knight held a blue steel short sword.

"*The Legionnaire Cian,*" Joni read on the following page. "*This warrior controls the Water Element.*"

She turned the page onto another watercolor drawing of a fighter with light brown hair and hazel eyes wearing a black face mask depicting a demon, red outer jacket, black wide-legged horse-riding trousers and black sandals with white socks. In his hands, he held a cherry staff affixed with a large ruby orb on its end.

"*The Legionnaire Hedos,*" read the entry. "*This warrior controls the Fire Element.*" Turning to the next page, Joni found a single passage. "*When the combined forces of Water and Fire become Rain and Thunder, the magus can control any Legionnaire under his command.*"

"Hey, Slake," Joni called, "what does this mean?"

Slake approached from offside and read the text. "That means Hedos and Cian can work together to become stronger," he answered. "You already know that they have the ability to conjoin."

"What does it mean that the magician can control any Legion under their command with Cian and Hedos?"

"When fighting for control over different Legionnaire, you have to weaken the Legionnaire's bond with its former master and break its confining spell."

"How would that work?"

"The Lightning element seems to be the easiest to do so, since it shocks, stuns, blinds, burns, drains, and weakens all at once." Slake folded his arms across his chest. "After that, you can control the newly weakened Legionnaire by giving it a new ability. As long as you have the knowledge and the use of the new power, the Legionnaire can't go to anyone else."

"Why did Bobby say they were overrated?"

"Hedos and Cian were the strongest because the original magician using them favored them."

"But what about the ones Bobby owns?"

The pages began glowing in response and turned on their own, stopping on a painting of a pale-skinned young woman with long white hair and gray eyes wearing a black kimono. Around her neck she wore a thin gold chain with a green skeleton key and in her hands, she held a thick weighted silver chain. Joni scanned the passage, taking in the information.

"*The Legionnaire Aecean*," the entry read. "*This warrior has the ability to take away Energy and use it for other means.*" The pages turned again, revealing a young man with short lime-treated hair and green eyes. He wore a black and yellow plaid kilt with deerskin leggings and leather short boots. Tattooed on his upper body were blue swirls extending from his chest, down his shoulders and arms. "*The Legionnaire Oisine*," read the title. "*This warrior has the ability to take away Power and use it for other means.*" Joni grew uneasy once she noted the lone paragraph at the end of the following page: "*With the combined forces of Spirit and Chaos, the magus can control any physical familiar under his command.*"

"What does this mean?" Joni asked, tapping at the book. "So far Bobby was able to strip both you and Labraccio as well knock out Contis, Liang, Hedos and Cian!"

"It means that he can take away our Powers for a short amount of time, as well as take the essence of anyone he touches," Slake explained. "If they are Magical, then their mystic abilities are gone for any unspecified time." Joni grew increasingly worried and grasped her necklace as his expression changed from neutral to terse. "If they are just normal regular people without Powers..."

Joni shuddered in horror. "So, Cian and Hedos aren't the only ones that can evolve like that?" she asked faintly.

"There are twenty to date altogether of known conjunctions, but it's up to the user what they want to put together and keep separate," Slake clarified. "Any new ones are recorded in the magician's spellbook. Then after they die, the Aerians will take their copy and scribe it in the master, the one you're holding."

"I see..." Joni studied the watercolors of the warriors inside the book. "Were these Legions once real people?"

Slake let out a short laugh. "You can't be serious!" he crowed.

"Slake, please!"

"No," he answered. "They are merely manifestations of past magicians who created the Legionnaire. Those voices you hear and forms you see if they choose to take a human appearance is just the essence of its creator."

"So Hedos and Cian were brothers in real life?"

Slake nodded. "They worked well together and fought constantly."

"Just like you and Labraccio."

Slake turned away, growing tense. "Just so you know, only high ranking magicians are capable of crafting Legions," he grumbled. "These fifty that we have are the results of study and hard work."

"How can someone create a weapon that's made entirely of spirit energy?" Joni inquired.

"If you become a dedicated magician, you have to cover all aspects: spiritual warfare, magical creation, magical negation, and curse breaking," Slake responded. "There are tests that the magician can go through to advance in power, if the Aerian assigned to them feels they are ready to take."

"So are there ranks with magicians too?"

Slake nodded. "Only when you master the highest degree of Magic, then you are allowed to create two weapons of your choice: one offensive and one defensive. If it can pass the ultimate test, then they are recorded into the master and are part of the Order of the Mage Knights." Slake shrugged. "However, in my time, only eight magicians have been successful creating new Legionnaire and there hasn't been any new creations in the past three years."

Joni stiffened, as if the blood in her veins froze. "Wait, did I hear you right?" she asked, wincing when her stomach churned. "Did you say the past three years?"

Slake turned to Joni, concerned. "Why, what's wrong?" he gently asked and Joni shook her head.

"*Bobby was put away for three years for making threats to the school,*" she thought, grasping her pendant. "*That's also around the time Dad got sick...*"

"Are you alright?" Slake called to Joni, taking her out of her thoughts.

"What exactly happened three years ago?" Joni murmured.

"A battle between the best Magicians, Mage Knights, and other Magic Users took place over the forbidden information about the Legions and their conjunction abilities," Slake explained. "This battle caused a lot of disturbance on the Material Plane that almost broke the rules of existence."

"The rules of existence...?"

"Out of that battle," Slake continued, ignoring her comment, "a highly skilled Mage Knight took the flak from the Arcana Assembly in order to destroy the exposed evidence..."

"What are you saying?" Joni demanded, grabbing his sleeve. "You mean Kipper and Bobby were involved in that fight and my dad died because of some lame Magic School wanted to keep the peace?" The color drained from Slake's face, though he gave no response. "But why did he give *me* the Legions and this book without any warning? What am I supposed to do with it?"

"He left nothing else?"

"Nothing else."

Slake shook his head. "I don't know how to help you. Terrell Warren clearly stated that he wanted to retire as Mage Knight and didn't want you to take his duties of such... But if others find that you may have the forbidden information somewhere, you *will* be constantly threatened."

"I don't even know if I have that, let alone be able to read it if I did!"

"The best I can do is try my hardest to help," Slake said, smiling faintly. "We'll find out together!"

"You're just as clueless as I am!" Joni spat and released her hold, then rose to her feet. "First of all, you're going to teach me how this Legion thing works. Second, you're going to tell me what this forbidden information everyone's killing to get is about!"

"I can tell you a bit about the forbidden information that I know of, but I can't teach you." Slake put up his hands. "I'm not a trainer. Labraccio however is, and I really don't advise you train under him."

"Why not? He's clearly better than you!"

Slake's face shadowed in irritation. "He is *not* better than *me*," he snarled through gritted teeth. "His cockiness is his downfall!"

"Alright, whatever!" Joni huffed. "I believe you." She waved him away. "Now, what is this about the forbidden information?"

"You want to know *now*?" Slake spat irritably.

"Might as well!"

Slake blew an annoyed sigh. "Certain Legionnaire can conjoin under certain circumstances," he described, "whereas some merely increase their Power while others enhance their Elements; for example, take Voldec and Flasai. Labraccio put them together to improve their flaming sword technique."

"What about Hedos? Isn't he Fire?"

"Yes, but he will most likely take a different form when paired with Voldec or Flasai. How that is, I have no idea. Out of the fifty original Legionnaire, the possibilities are endless!"

Joni nodded. "I think I get it, so what is it that makes these different magicians want to kill each other?"

"Since you have to put so much power into a Legionnaire, it grows stronger as you grow stronger, therefore you may have a certain set of two you enjoy fighting with that may also evolve, if able. However, if you put together two separate Legionnaire of different elements and abilities, *and* if you have enough Power and experience, you can *create* a new talent for that Legionnaire. Even rarer, you can even create a new element!"

"That's interesting..."

"Well, the book itself lists only six elements that the Legionnaire have: Earth, Wind, Fire, Water, Light, and Dark. That doesn't mean there aren't any *more*; it's just that some people fail to write things down."

"Why does element matter?" Slake pinched his nose, shaking his head. "Hey, I'm not stupid!" Joni complained. "Nobody taught me this stuff!"

"So a crash course…"

"Right!"

Slake let out a frustrated sigh. "Everything has a strength and weakness," he muttered. "Water puts out Fire, Wind blows away Earth, Earth slows down Water, and Fire eats away at Wind. You see, these things matter if you want to live."

"This is too much to handle at once," Joni grumbled and turned to the dimly glowing book. "I need to go home and think about this some more…"

"That's fine."

Joni pushed the book away and tensed when Slake approached her from behind. "So you're not pissed at me for not knowing this stuff?" she wondered aloud.

"I find it a bit jarring that Terrell didn't teach you this." Slake grabbed Joni gently by the arm and turned her around. "There has to be a reason."

"Can't we do it later?" Joni protested, prying off his hand. "My skull might break if I learn too much of this stuff all at once."

Slake rolled his eyes in response. "Fine, I'll wait," he said. Taking her hand, he escorted Joni toward a portal at the end of the room. Suddenly pausing in step, Slake hurried to a nearby bookcase, dragging Joni along and stood rigidly at it, putting a finger to his lips. Joni nodded and squat beside him as he listened.

"… You'll have to make sure she gets killed," Greg's voice said in a low tone behind the bookcase. Slake crouched down and pulled out two books at waist level, peering through the slat. Joni craned her neck to get a better view, seeing Greg standing across from a man wearing a black overcoat, dark navy jeans and dark brown leather boots.

"Why you want me to get bothered with some punk girl?" snapped Greg's indescribable visitor. "It's obvious she doesn't know what she's doing or what she's fooling with. Let her have an accident, okay?"

"Listen to me, she's that Spellforce Legionnaire's daughter," Greg hissed. "She's asking too many questions and she's probably got those Force Remnants with her somewhere!"

"Force Remnants don't exist; they're just legends!"

"They do and I should know; I worked in the Arcana Assembly's archives and records center for years," Greg snapped. "We covered that up so nobody without the right credentials can obtain that kind of Ascended Mastery!"

"Hold on, hold on, how can that girl be *related* to *that* Mage Knight?" the mysterious visitor exclaimed. "If she really had those Force Remnants, then there's no way she'd be constantly getting her ass kicked by weaklings like Sable!"

"Obviously she doesn't know how to use them - that's why I need you to get her out the way and take those things before someone else finds them!"

"What's so great about these Force Remnants anyway?"

"If I told you that, then I'll have to get rid of you too."

"Damn, so that means I've got to get on the ball."

"Remember, everyone out there is in danger because of this witch. You make sure she doesn't get any powerful *now*!"

"Right, right, I'll go in for the kill." Greg's acquaintance chortled. "It won't even be messy! Like you said, 'Magic accident'."

"Remember; make sure she can't reincarnate! Destroy everything – including her soul!"

"What about her sister?"

"Her too."

"I'll torch everything into nonexistence, heh..."

Joni felt her breath escape her and Slake placed the books back on the shelf. He grabbed her hand then hurriedly pulled her for the nearby portal. They stepped through and everything washed out in white.

CHAPTER TWENTY-FOUR

Emerging through the other side, Joni and Slake returned inside Joni's parlor and she collapsed on the couch, stunned.

"Why is Greg trying to kill me over these Legions?" Joni moaned, holding her head in her hands. "What about these Force Remnants he's talking about? I know nothing about any of it!"

"Nothing at all?" Slake pressed.

"Obviously!"

"What about your sister?"

"Kacey was a natural fighter and Dad sent her away to train," Joni explained. "At first he supported her then suddenly turned a complete one-eighty, saying how Battle Magic was dangerous and how I shouldn't get myself involved in it. Dad said Healers shouldn't get involved in fighting."

"Did she write you at all while she was away?"

Joni nodded. "She used to write us a lot, then the letters became less frequent and after Dad got sick, I didn't hear anything else from her." Joni blew a heavy sigh, leaning forward. "After her last exam, I got this weird-sounding letter from her. It didn't sound like her at all."

"May I see it?"

Joni nodded and left the couch, heading for her bedroom. Slake followed and stood at the doorway, watching her rummage through the desk. Joni came across a shoe box containing dozens of worn papers and handed them over to Slake. He picked one to scan, then read the next one underneath.

"Kacey and Dad were always close, but after that, she didn't even bother to address letters to him anymore," Joni went on. "I don't know what caused them to get so icy like that; Dad didn't tell me and I hadn't heard from Kacey in almost four years." Joni folded her arms across her chest. "The last one I got from her spooked me to no end. All she wrote was: '*When the shadows speak to you, don't answer.*'"

"When was the last letter dated?"

"Well..." Joni clenched her teeth and put the heel of her hand to her forehead, trying to recall. "It came a few days before that weird phone call..."

Slake raised an eyebrow. "What phone call?"

"It seemed to come from myself, but in the future, trying to alert me about a death of someone close to me." Joni sighed and looked at Slake, putting her hands to her hips. "Three months later to the day, Dad died and school ended for the summer."

"Do you have the ability to see the future?" Slake suddenly asked as he took one letter and slipped it into his jacket pocket.

"Only the future," Joni admitted, taking the box he handed back to her and tossed it aside on the desk. "I can't see the past."

"How many variables have you always seen of the future?"

Joni shrugged her shoulders. "I don't know," she said. "I look once and don't look again. Dad always told me the future isn't set because of the many choices one can make to change the outcome."

"He's right," Slake said firmly. "I'm possibly over-thinking these things, so I won't worry about it too much."

"What are you worrying about?" Slake shook his head in response and Joni took a seat on the edge of her bed, slightly depressed. "It's beyond a scary thought, though. I just don't see why he'd do this..."

"We'll find out eventually..."

"Whenever we do, will it be terrible?"

"Let's not think that way."

Joni clasped her hands on her knees, growing apprehensive. "Will you tell me why these Legions are so important?" she asked timidly.

"I will," Slake said in assurance. "I'll tell you whatever you want to know."

"This is getting so crazy - it's bad enough dealing with Bobby and Kipper and their strange weapons..."

"It'll be okay," Slake said gently, entering the room.

Joni looked up as he ran a hand through her hair. *"Why are they so intent on killing you too?"* she thought as her face grew warm when he ran a hand down her cheek and cupped her chin. *"You're not supposed to be bothered with me! You'll die if you stick around..."*

Joni pulled away from Slake when she heard an engine turning loudly outside. She pushed past him, running for the front door. Opening it wide, she spotted Signe getting off his motorcycle.

"There you are!" Signe said brightly as he made his way up the walkway. He lifted his visor. "Did I miss the fun?"

"What are you talking about?" Joni asked guardedly once Signe approached.

"You ran out of here so fast with Slake, I thought you were--!" He burst out laughing when Joni punched his arm.

"Shut up!" she wailed, punching him again. "It's not like that!"

"Of course I was worried and everything, but you seem to be fine now." Signe tousled Joni's hair. "You had something important to talk about and didn't want me to overhear, right?"

Joni blew a sigh and nodded. "I got it straightened out for right now," she replied.

"I'll see you tomorrow then." Signe grinned and Joni gave a modest smile. When he didn't leave, Joni blew a hard sigh and embraced him. Signe chortled and gave her a firm squeeze. "Next time," he murmured in her ear, "I'll bring my brother along and it'll be a great party!"

"Ugh!" Joni cried, pushing away. "Stop it, you tease!"

Signe pulled away with a wolfish grin. "So you're seriously thinking about it?" he wheedled.

"You total sleaze!" Joni harped and Signe laughed when she bat him against his chest.

"I can't help it!" he yelped.

"Go home!"

"Whenever you need my service, you know my number!" Signe returned to his motorcycle, giving it a start.

"Tell Martel I wish him well!" Joni called after him.

"Sure thing!" Signe called back. After flipping down his visor, he waved at Joni then took off into the night.

"It's getting late," Slake said from behind. Joni turned and gave him a tense smile as he touched her gently on the arm. "I should get going. Will you be all right tonight?"

Joni nodded. "I will," she answered.

Slake walked past her, heading down the path. Joni returned indoors, overwhelmed by feelings of dread.

Plagued by nightmares of shadowy creatures chasing her, Joni awakened with a start and kicked off the sheets tangled around her legs then sat up, drawing her knees to her chest. She broke out in cold sweat as she looked around her darkened bedroom, worried about returning to the realm of dreaming.

Her heart nearly jumped in her throat when she noticed swirling shades in her room, and tensed, fearful Kipper may be on the attack. She immediately stepped out of bed and crept toward the door.

"I don't have anything to fight with," Joni considered. "Without Cian and Hedos, I'm dead!"

Peering down the darkened corridor, she blew a sigh when she saw nothing out of the ordinary. Joni shuddered when a sudden chill passed over her and hurried down the corridor, entering the parlor. She noticed a small red light emanating from the end table behind the couch.

Wondering how she could have missed a call as she approached the sleek slate-gray touchtone model with built-in answering machine and speaker phone function, Joni pressed the button and a series of digital pips filled the air, followed by a smooth, soft silky voice she didn't recognize.

"I know you're all by your lonesome," said the voice. "I've been watching you carefully..." Joni gasped and backed away from the telephone. "There's no where for you to run, no where to hide... I'm everywhere and nowhere at all."

Joni drew in a shallow breath as her heart thudded in her chest. She ran to the parlor window and pushed aside the heavy curtain, looking out into the pitch darkness of the night. The cold autumnal winds were high, blowing limbs of pines in the surrounding woodland. Joni stiffened, hearing a rustle and turned back, facing the couch.

"I know when you're awake, when you're asleep," continued the soft voice on the machine. "I know all your family, your friends, your enemies even... They can't stop me, no one can."

Hearing a shuffling sound, Joni bit her hand, keeping in her scream. The wind was still blowing outside and she heard skittering across the roof. Joni strained to hear, trying to make out the noise and hoped it wasn't just someone out there on the other side prowling around in the middle of the night. She hoped it was just some *thing*, maybe errant branches or the squirrels she hated.

Joni moved soundlessly from the door with her clammy hands clenched at her sides. She broke out in cold sweat, quickly going through a mental check if all the doors and windows in her house was locked.

"There's nothing you can do to me, Joni," said the cold, soft voice. "I can get close to you and you'd never know it. I know everything about you: your wishes, your dreams, your hopes, your desires, your fears..." Joni sank to her knees and clutched her sides as her stomach churned in severe dread when she heard the sinister chortle on the other end. "You'd better be careful in the next few days, Joni... Accidents can happen, especially at home."

Accidents can happen...

Joni doubled over, moaning in distress. "*There's no one I can call this late,*" she realized. "*Who would believe me?*" Joni sucked in a shallow breath, trying to check her tears. "*My friends are already hurt and I can't put them in anymore danger!*" Overwhelmed by fear, the tears ran down Joni's face full force.

CHAPTER TWENTY-FIVE

After spending the weekend avoiding going out and having her phone unplugged, also spending two fitful uncomfortable nights sleeping in her closet, Joni felt uneasy once she resumed her classes. Slake appeared tense and kept close by, along with her friend Signe and his brother Martel.

Joni loathed Bobby's presence and felt generally creeped out when he stared at her, grinning knowingly in her direction. She hardly hid her disgust at the sight of Greta always hanging around Bobby, running her hands through his hair or touching his arm or leg.

"You're so not making me jealous," Joni spat at Greta as she pushed past them in the hall. "Just sick!"

"Whatever," Greta retorted and stuck her tongue out at Joni.

Entering her next class with Slake and Signe at her side, Slake stiffened and grasped Joni's arm.

"Wait," Signe murmured and Joni glanced around, finding the classroom as it usually was.

Joni's sights fell on the teacher running a hand through her nape-length feathered dark red hair as she stomped about the classroom. She wore a black dress shirt with gray buttons, black slacks with white pinstripes and black leather boots that had a narrow cut with buckles on the sides. On her hands, she wore a golden ring on her ring fingers. Joni paled when she noticed the ring on the right hand glowing dimly. Then the sudden change of energy struck Joni hard in the guts, and she grunted, turning queasy at once.

"Something isn't right," Slake growled.

Joni sucked in a shallow breath and let it out slowly then shook off Slake's grip. "Please, don't worry," she pleaded. "Bobby isn't in this class and Kipper's out of commission."

"That's not it."

"Are you three gonna keep blocking the door or what?" the teacher said dryly. "Make up your minds before the bell rings, will ya?"

Slake grunted and left Joni's side, walking away down the corridor. Signe shrugged then pulled Joni aside on the door's other side, keeping the path clear.

"Aren't we supposed to have a Geography quiz soon, Miss Finnian?" called a student from the middle row.

"Yeah, I'll let you know when we have a test," Finnian grumbled as she returned to her desk and sat on the edge. "I'm exhausted with you all. Get out!"

"What's the test about?" another student asked as the others prepared to file out of the class.

"It's going to be about the different countries that had name changes over the years," Finnian said, flashing a derisive smile. "Tonight's homework is all the little countries that make up Russia." She pulled out a copper cigarette case from her shirt pocket and snapped it open. "Keep pressing me and I might just grade on a scale this time around!"

"Man, what a hard ass!" a student grumbled as he collected his books.

"Then don't snore too loud in Detention for the make-up test, okay?" Finnian retorted.

The student paled and hurried out the room.

"*Always with the same old thing!*" a flat voice suddenly ranted.

"*Teach something new already! Ack, if I had half a mind, I'd lose it!*"

Joni stiffened and grasped Signe's sleeve. "*Where is it coming from?"* she thought as the mysterious voice continued.

"Come on, show a film or something and give this boring class a boost; give examples for everyone's sake!"

"Jeez, Joni!" Signe yelped, pulling away.

"Who is that complaining?" she demanded.

"What are you talking about?"

"Someone's fussing about the class."

"I didn't hear anything." Signe took her hand, looking down at her in concern. "Are you sure you're alright?"

"Yeah..." Joni pulled away, slightly abashed. "I just thought I heard someone complaining about how boring the class is!"

"Well, I can agree with them, but I don't hear anyone saying anything like that out loud."

"Maybe it's just my thoughts..."

Signe grinned and chuckled. "So tired that you can't tell which thoughts are yours, right?" he teased.

Joni nodded somberly. "Something like that," she replied wearily.

"Well, you know my thoughts..." He laughed once Joni flushed bright scarlet and struck his arm with her open hand.

"Get your head out the gutter, Signe!"

"I can't help it!" he replied, giggling.

Slake returned moments later with Joni's backpack after the last of the students filtered out of the classroom. Joni took her bag from Slake and entered with him and Signe, finding Finnian sitting at her desk with feet crossed at the edge, smoking a cigarette. The teacher glared at Signe as Slake left Joni's side, taking a seat in the rear.

"Who are you?" Finnian snapped, taking her feet off the edge. "Aren't you a little *old* to be in here?" She tapped the ashes in the nearby trash can.

Joni headed to an empty desk and set her backpack near the chair then motioned for Signe to take a seat.

"How old do I look?" Signe asked agitatedly as he stood before the desk. "I'm only seventeen."

Finnian narrowed her eyes. "You're lying."

"Is it because of the hair?" Joni asked nervously.

"Maybe," Finnian said, grinning darkly.

"Really?"

"I'm not a meat eater, so I guess that's why my hair's going white," Signe replied. "My dad's hair was completely white by the time he was twenty..."

"Completely white, yeah?" Finnian snapped and Signe nodded.

The teacher rose to her feet and Signe backed away when she approached. He glared back once she cornered him into another desk, standing defiantly as she blew smoke in his face.

"You really shouldn't be smoking in the building," Signe said caustically. "It's bad for the general health."

"You don't say?" Finnian licked her forefinger and her thumb. "Fine, I'll put it out." She pinched out the cigarette and Joni gasped when the smoke tapered and Finnian had no burns on her skin. Finnian handed the dead cigarette to Signe. "Care to save this for me?"

Signe took the butt and crushed it in his hand. The other students began entering the classroom and Finnian left Signe, heading to her desk. She picked up a silver lighter that had a pentacle etched onto the face and dropped it into her front pocket. Signe sank into the chair, his face unreadable.

Joni leaned over, tapping Signe's shoulder. "Why are you in my class?" she whispered. "I thought you were in Advanced Placement!"

"I'm flunking," Signe grumbled as Finnian announced the lesson of the period when the rest of the students entered the room.

"Stop daydreaming about me and maybe you'll pass!" Signe cracked a thin smile and Joni smiled faintly back.

"We've a new classmate if you all didn't notice," Finnian suddenly announced and pointed to Signe. "Pretty Boy here will tell us a little about why he's here now and not in fancy Advanced Placement classes."

Signe sat up rigidly, the color draining from his face. "Woman, why are you doing this to me?" he said through clenched teeth.

"Hell, why waste your smarts on some dumb redheaded girl, eh?" Signe grunted and sat back as the other students twittered. "Well?"

"*Hey!*" the flat voice cried. "*How would you like it if you were put on the spot like that?*"

Finnian glanced at the window sharply, then suddenly smiled, turning to face the rest of the class. "I guess we'll start the video lesson instead," she said, "since Pretty Boy seems to be under pressure."

Joni stiffened and cringed in her seat. "*She heard it too!*" she realized. "*There has to be a Legion in here...*"

Finnian headed to classroom's rear and grabbed a video from the nearby bookshelf, then loaded it into a cassette player resting on a rack underneath the television. "Somebody cut the lights," she ordered.

The lights were switched off and the video started. Joni watched Finnian approach Signe, placing her hand on the desk while leaning forward and the other hand rest on her hip. Signe turned away, not facing her.

"Miss Finnian..." Joni called.

"What is it, Kid?" snapped Finnian, not once looking away from Signe.

"Why are we watching videos today?"

"To learn more about the countries that's mentioned in the books," Finnian replied. "Hell, you might want to visit one day and get away from this dump." She knocked on the desk. "Look at me, Pretty Boy."

"Why are you bothering him?"

"Did you forget where you are, Pretty Boy?" Finnian said in a low tone.

"You don't know anything," Signe replied in a controlled voice. "I don't have to tell you one word."

Finnian pulled away, her expression stony. "So that's how it's going to be, eh?" she sneered.

Signe folded his arms against his chest, glaring icily in her direction. "Savvy," he snarled.

Finnian clenched her teeth and kicked at Signe's desk, bending forward as she adjusted the buckle on the side of her boot. "I have an errand for you to run for me," she growled, "So see me after class lets out for the day."

"Why should he?" Joni demanded and Finnian looked up, glaring at her.

"Why are you in my business?" the teacher snarled. "So, would *you* rather do it?"

Joni smiled sheepishly. "It's not too hard," she responded, "is it?"

"What would you call 'hard'?"

"*Don't do it!*" the flat voice called before Joni could answer. She turned in her seat, searching for the source. "*You'll be sorry if you did!*"

"Care to water the plants, Kid?" Finnian interjected.

"Huh? What?" Joni yelped, whirling around to face the teacher. "What did you say, Miss Finnian?"

"I know you wanna get your butt outta here," Finnian snapped in annoyance, "but it ain't happening!"

"I can't help but daydream about other countries mentioned in the books," Joni quipped.

"If you wanna pass, you gotta pay attention!"

"I'll water the plants, if that'll give me some points on my grade."

"Just water them," Finnian grumbled, rolling her eyes. "Getting up and moving that lazy butt of yours should keep you out of my hair longer."

Joni stood, clenching her hands. "What's that supposed to mean?" she protested.

"Water the damn plants," Finnian commanded.

Joni blew a hard sigh and scurried to other side of the room, grabbing a half-full bottle of water placed near the row of plants.

"*Yes! Sunlight!*" the flat voice cried in relief. "*About time!*"

Joni turned toward the window, spotting a mid-sized cactus that had red-framed glasses with rose-colored lenses resting on the plant's arms. A slight ray of sunshine filtered through the horizontal blinds attached to the window, streaming on the frames.

"*Now I'm really losing it,*" Joni considered as she watered the other plants. "*I need more sleep - I swear, the cactus is talking!*"

"*Hey, don't soak me!*" the flat voice protested when Joni approached the cactus and squirted the bottle, splashing water on the glasses.

"You need to be watered, you stupid dumb plant," Joni grumbled.

"*I'm not a plant, you stupid dumb human!*"

Joni dropped the water bottle, astonished. "Then what are you?" she hissed.

"*Take a wild guess!*" Joni picked up the water bottle and poked at the lenses. "*Owch!*" The pink lenses turned dark red. "*Hey, would you like me poking you in the eye like that?*"

Joni let out a cry and jumped back in fear.

"Did you prick your finger?" Signe asked in a strained tone.

"Um, yeah, I did," stammered Joni. "Stupid plant."

"Be careful next time!"

Joni snatched up the water bottle and poked at the cactus. "What do you know about Miss Finnian?" she whispered. "Answer me, or I won't miss!"

"*I can't tell you!*" the flat voice responded.

"I'll poke you in the eye until you tell me!" Joni jabbed the bottle's head into the rose-colored lenses, forcing them turning from dark red to black.

"*Owch! Stop it!*" the flat voice wailed. "*Stop hurting me!*"

Joni gasped when a firm grip locked around her arm and looked up, finding Finnian standing behind her.

"You'll need more water," Finnian said evenly. "I have other plants you missed." She gave a thin smile. "If you paid attention in Earth Science, you'd know that cacti don't need much to survive."

"I remember," Joni said faintly.

Finnian pulled her away and Joni stumbled backwards into a nearby desk. She frowned when the red glasses became silent as Finnian picked it up. Joni hurried into the hall, escaping the oppressive atmosphere.

Approaching the water fountain, Joni tensed when she sensed another presence. Looking down the empty corridors, Joni found no one around. After filling the bottle with water, she turned and gasped when she faced a tall golden-skinned man wearing all black: a three-piece suit contrasted by charcoal-gray shirt, leather boots and overcoat, draped by a long white cashmere scarf hanging around his neck. Around his eyes he wore smoky mirrored sunglasses and a black wool cap donned his head.

The man smiled, showing even white teeth. Joni backed away, shaking in fear and dropped the bottle she held. The plastic struck the floor with a clatter and Joni reached for the amethyst pendant she wore, grasping it with her fingers.

The man stepped on the bottle when it rolled near him then picked it up, handing it over toward Joni. Joni shook her head and he gestured again.

Reaching out with a shaking hand, Joni snatched it and took off for the classroom. She barreled inside and gasped, coming to a dead stop when Finnian gave her a sharp look.

"The hell's your problem?" Finnian snapped.

"Spider," Joni croaked and held out her hands. "This big!"

Some students laughed and Finnian shook her head. "Sit your ass down and shut up," she grumbled.

Joni watered the remaining plants then returned to her seat. Finnian sat at her desk with her hands folded atop the polished wood, staring intently at Signe. Signe continued to stare into space, not making eye contact.

Wondering what could be going on between them, Joni looked to Signe who avoided Finnian's steely stare, then glanced at the cactus, finding the red glasses missing. She swallowed hard, returning her gaze to Finnian. She blew a distressed sigh and held her chin in her hand, overwhelmed.

"May I be excused?" Signe finally said.

"Why, Pretty Boy?" Finnian retorted.

"I had some sushi and some greasy pizza and they're fighting each other."

Finnian kicked out the trash can near her desk. "Use that," she spat. Signe sighed and Finnian smirked. "I thought so."

Joni leaned over, tapping Signe's shoulder. "What's this weirdness between you two?" she whispered.

Signe grunted and gently pushed her away. "It's nothing," he hissed.

"Why is she acting like that to you?"

"It's a long story."

"Is it like with Labraccio's long stories?" Signe paled in response. "What's up with him and all these 'long stories' anyway?"

Signe shook his head. "Forget it," he muttered.

Suddenly a low whine droned in the room. Joni let out a surprised squeak and looked up and around.

"Dairine," a voice amid static called into the room.

"What?" Finnian called back in annoyance.

"This is Seamus from the office," the voice continued. Joni sighed in relief when she realized the source came from the public announcement system. "Is Joni Warren in this class?"

"Right here," Finnian answered, glaring at Joni.

"Have her report to Counselor Shorthand's office."

Joni stiffened in astonishment. "Shorthand?" she cried, incredulous.

Finnian snorted. "Oh, you know him, don't you?" she needled.

"I-I don't."

"You better get going, Kid," Finnian said and Joni stood indignantly to her feet.

"You can't–!"

"Maybe."

"Are you in trouble?" Signe asked worriedly.

Joni glanced at Signe and gave a faint smile. "Let's hope not," she said softly.

"I'll still be here," Signe murmured and reached up. Joni took his hand, giving a firm squeeze.

"Thanks," she said softly.

"Always."

Letting go, Joni scooped up her backpack and left the classroom, ignoring the hard thudding in her chest.

CHAPTER TWENTY-SIX

Entering the office, Joni spoke with the secretary and an office aide led her to the small room that had Greg's nameplate on the door. Joni opened the door and entered the space, overcome with nervous energy once she spotted Greg sitting behind a large walnut desk.

Greg, dressed in a navy suit with white buttons, had cuffed sleeves, showing off his heavily scarred arms. He casually turned pages in a paperback book and ignored Joni's presence.

"You wanted to see me?" Joni asked apprehensively.

"Shut the door," Greg ordered, not once looking up from his book. Joni shut the door behind her and set her backpack in a nearby chair. "Watch your step. Kieran's in a bad mood."

Joni looked down, spotting a stuffed tan nine-tailed fox with tiny yellow eyes on the floor across the room.

"What's wrong with Kieran?" she asked and pulled up the free chair adjacent to the door across from Greg's desk.

"I didn't tell you to sit down." Joni clenched her teeth and grasped the back of the chair. "He sensed Labraccio's presence on Tigris," Greg said simply.

"So, Kieran doesn't like Labraccio or something?"

"That's an understatement."

Joni glanced back at the small stuffed toy to see the beady yellow eyes glow dimly. "Why does Kieran hate Labraccio so much?" Greg didn't answer and she turned toward him. "It's a long story, right?" Greg nodded from behind his book. "Well, why did you call me down here? It's not to lecture me about something, is it?"

"I wanted an update," Greg answered casually.

"But why are you *here* when you're supposed to be in Records over *there*?"

"What does it matter?" Greg grumbled. "I'm more concerned about your link to two very evil Sorcerers that have no business practicing Magic."

"That's not my problem," Joni complained, "and it's not my fault they keep coming to me about stuff I don't understand!"

"You don't realize how important this is."

"You might as well explain it to me, since apparently I'm a Class-A dummy around here!"

Greg snorted and turned another page. "We can't get them arrested for mere infractions."

"So what do you want me to do about it?"

"The deal is thus: you train in order to keep them off your back and keep them at bay long enough so I can have officers arrest them for any crimes they commit."

"But it's for serious stuff only, right?" Joni put her hands on her hips. "So, what kind are we talking about? I thought injuring Aerians would be one of them!"

"Sadly, no." A paper appeared on the desk's edge, glowing in pale brown light. "That there is a list of possible crimes an Arcana Enforcer can arrest a Magician for."

Once the form fully materialized, Joni picked it up and scanned its contents. The tightness in her chest increased once she read that killing an Aerian was a crime.

"You think I can do something about this?" Joni groused.

"When are you going to include training sessions with the Legions?" Greg demanded.

Joni glanced up from the paper, glaring at him. "So *you can easily kill me*?" she thought, growing incensed.

"Well?"

"I don't know," answered Joni slowly.

"I can have someone assigned to you for that."

"It's okay." Joni tossed the paper back onto the desk. "I've got Labraccio for that."

Greg dropped his book and glowered at Joni. "What did you say?" he said through gritted teeth.

"You heard what I said," Joni spat, narrowing her eyes. "Labraccio's training me."

"How did he get assigned to your case?" Greg snapped irritably.

Joni gave a smug smirk. "You fill in the blanks."

Greg rose to his feet and clenched his hands, forcing corded veins traveling up his scarred arms. "When does it start?" he snarled.

"After Halloween."

Greg slowly blinked at her and suddenly grunted, shaking his head as a wry smile appeared on his face. "You liar!" he spat.

"Is that all you want to know?"

Greg snorted and dropped back into his chair, picking up his novel. "Don't try to skip out on this delicate assignment," he murmured and opened the book. "This is actually very important."

"Yeah, right," Joni grumbled and turned away, snatching up her backpack. "What good will this do me? I've got a life to live in the real world, last time I've checked!"

"You'll see once reality strikes you hard and fast."

Storming for the door, she tripped on a soft object, followed by a squeak. Looking down, she spotted Kieran underneath her shoe. "Oh, I'm so sorry!" she cried, picking up the stuffed fox. "What were you doing near the door like that?"

"He's trying to escape again," Greg grumbled.

"How can these toys move around like that?" Joni dusted off the animal. "He was across the room not too long ago!"

"They can move when no one is truly paying attention." Greg snorted. "What would you think if you saw a stuffed animal moving on its own?"

"I'd think I was losing my mind."

"Exactly."

The fox's body glowed dimly in pale white light and Joni gasped, sensing fear and confusion emanating from it. "*There's something seriously wrong*," she realized and shut her eyes. "*What are you trying to tell me?*"

Suddenly her vision shifted and her eyes fluttered open to a blur of bright white light. A shadowy haze surrounded Joni and she gasped when great heat blasted around her.

A heavy discomfort hung around her neck and she reached up to rub it away, only to find that she was unable to move her arms as pain thudded through her shoulders. Moving her head, Joni noticed a thick metal brace collared around her throat and her arms stretched above her head, fastened to strong iron posts in a blackened stone wall.

The swirling shadows appeared again, reaching out for her and through the thick gray fog her gaze fell onto a pair of hating glowing red eyes.

"Kieran," Greg's voice called, breaking Joni's thoughts. "To me."

Joni's her vision returned to normal, back in the florescent-washed pale beige office, with matching pale carpet and plain walnut desk. The stuffed fox vanished from her hand, reappearing on Greg's desk, facing him.

"What are you going to do to him?" Joni demanded as Greg opened a drawer and extracted a small wire mesh bin. He put it upside down over the stuffed fox with his free hand while keeping his book open with the other. Kieran glowed in red light and rocked slightly, bumping into wire's sides. "I thought that was for holding notepads or something."

"How perceptive," Greg replied as he shut the drawer then turned the page. "You see that it has another function." He glanced up at Joni with a steely gaze as the fox stopped glowing and became still, its yellow eyes turning dim. "It has a spell to keep the unruly ones from transforming and hence escaping."

"Is Kieran the only one?"

Greg returned to his book, ignoring Joni and Joni huffed, leaving the office. Entering the corridor, she shuddered when the eerie chill passed through her again.

"*Is Kieran trying to warn me?*" Joni wondered. "*Does he know about the plan?*" She clenched her teeth. "*Is he trying to tell me something else?*"

Approaching the Geography classroom, the doors opened and the students filed out. Joni waited until the other students left and entered, spotting Finnian sitting on the edge of Signe's desk with an unlit cigarette to her lips. Signe stared indignantly at her with his arms folded across his chest while Slake stood near his desk, his back tense and hands clutched at his sides.

"Hey, Kid," Finnian called to Joni, "so what you and Shorthand had to chat about?"

"None of your business," Joni replied coolly.

"Huh, so it's like that, yeah?"

"Yeah, like that."

"Maybe you oughta have different classes come next semester."

Joni's mouth dropped open in shock. "What are you talking about?" she cried. "You can't do that!"

"I very well can," Finnian said, grinning deviously. "I have influence 'round here that you don't even know anything about, Kid."

"I don't believe you!"

Finnian slid off the desk's edge and sauntered up to Joni, poking her in the chest with her fingers. "Better believe it, Kid," Finnian said darkly. "I can have you running on a different schedule come Spring and there's jack shit you can do about it!" Joni grunted once poked again. "So, how 'bout it? Why don't ya drop shit you don't need to spend more time with me, eh?"

"She's smiling," Joni realized, "*but her eyes are dead serious!*"

"Well?" Finnian pressed.

"Where are you going with this?" Joni asked anxiously.

"Come on, talk to me," Finnian longed. "We've got fifteen minutes before more of those dumb ass slackers file in here."

"I don't know what you're going on about," Joni said stiffly.

Finnian chortled and leaned forward. "I know you heard it," she whispered in her ear.

"Heard what?" Joni said softly.

"The voice." Joni swallowed hard and took a step away. "So what's your deal?"

"Nothing!"

Finnian's hand abruptly glowed in dark red light and Slake stormed over, grabbing her hand. Joni gasped and grasped her pendant as cold sweat broke out on her forehead and neck.

"You leave her be," Slake said evenly as he pulled Finnian away, "or deal with the likes of me!"

"Maybe that's what I want," Finnian snapped and yanked out of his grip then turned away, extracting the silver lighter from her shirt pocket. "You don't wanna test me, Kid." Finnian casually lit her cigarette, glaring hatefully back at Slake. "I won't hesitate to tear your scrawny ass apart!"

"Not in this place with so many innocents around," Slake retorted.

"Then you'd better back off if you know what's good for you!" Finnian turned back around, blowing smoke in Slake's face.

"Please, Slake," Joni pleaded. "She's got strong Magic!"

"Listen to the girl," Finnian said smugly. "She's right, you know."

"I can't sense her Power..."

"Is it because of what Bobby did?"

"Maybe," Slake muttered.

"Scary shit, huh?" Finnian retorted and let out a short laugh. "Don't start what you can't finish!"

Growing annoyed, Joni released her hold and clenched her hands at her sides. "Then what's with the glasses that were on the cactus plant?" she demanded. "I know you know!"

"Why, you want them?"

"Maybe."

"Then you know how to play the game, right?" Finnian walked around to her desk and plopped back in her chair.

"What do you mean?"

"If you're asking that stupid question, then I'm not telling you shit." Finnian chortled. "You'll figure it out in a bad way, real bad."

"Are you threatening me?"

"Look, Kid, do you need anything else?" Finnian took a heavy drag then blew the smoke through her nose. "'Cause if not, get the fuck outta my face."

"Why were you bothering Signe?"

"That's my business, like I said."

"So, what *is* your deal?"

"There's no homework assigned." Finnian waved her hand away, dismissing Joni. "I'll rap with you later. Just let me smoke in peace, okay?"

Slake took Joni by the arm and both left the classroom together. Signe followed them moments later, apparently shaken.

"Will you be...?" Joni started.

"Please..." Signe said faintly.

"Just leave him alone for now," Slake said softly.

"Signe..."

"Come on," Slake urged and they headed for their next class, leaving Signe at the lockers.

CHAPTER TWENTY-SEVEN

Once the last class ended for the day, Joni stood next to Slake's locker as he put books away.

"You have to talk to your brother," Joni complained, leaning against the open locker, "and convince him to train me."

"No," Slake snapped flatly. "I've nothing else to do with him. Ask him yourself!" He picked up his stack of notebooks at his feet and angrily threw them in.

"But he won't listen to me either!" Joni handed him her backpack and he put it in last, then kicked shut the door.

"That's not my problem!"

Joni grasped Slake by the arm before he stormed away and he blew a disgruntled sigh. "Slake, listen to me," she pleaded. "You know about earlier when I had to see that so-called Counselor Shorthand..." After explaining her encounter, Slake's face became unreadable. He broke away and she hurried after him as he took long strides.

"I can't help you and neither can Labraccio," Slake grumbled. "We're both stripped and we need some magical ability, even if it's only a fraction in order to train you effectively."

"How can I get your energy back then?"

Slake snorted. "Get it back from the one who stole it."

"You know I can't fight Bobby on my own!"

"Then you'll just have to figure out another way, Joni." Slake came to a sudden pause and Joni bumped into him.

"What is it?" Joni moved aside when Slake looked down at her with a hard gaze.

"Not every fight is won with pure brute force," he said sullenly.

"If you say so," Joni murmured.

"Sometimes defense can be the best offense, or letting the enemy wear itself down."

Joni rolled her eyes. "I see that Bobby's been employing that tactic," she grumbled.

"See what all your available options are, then choose the best one."

"I guess you're right." Joni glanced around when Slake appeared ill at ease and clenched his hands. "What's wrong?"

"There's something..." Slake muttered. "Come with me." He took her hand and led her through the corridors toward the school entrance.

"I thought you couldn't sense anything!" Joni protested.

"I feel energy that doesn't belong here... it's quite strong."

"I can't sense it... I hope it's not as powerful as Miss Finnian!"

"It seems to be."

Joni yanked her hand out of Slake's grasp and Slake whirled around, stunned. "What do you mean, 'it seems to be'?" she snapped. "So you're going to drag me over there and let me get killed?"

"Right now it's pointless to go after Bobby with the few Legionnaire you own at the moment," Slake said softly. "You currently don't have enough strength to sustain the Legions and they will need more power than you can ever provide in order to last a battle against him!"

"You're avoiding the question!" Joni protested. "What about the rest of you? Both you and Labraccio can't help me, even Randy's been stripped!"

"That's why I'm not leaving your side, Joni. They're trying to stack the odds against you."

Joni sensed the odd chill and whirled around, searching where it came from as other students passed by her heading for home. "I think I can sense what you felt," she said anxiously. "I've got a real bad feeling that something horrible might happen."

"We can only accept it as it comes," Slake responded.

Joni glared at Slake, appalled. "What if I get ambushed and lose the rest of my Legions to that crackpot crank?" She gestured toward the foyer's far end. "He's got too many and we're working with very little, you know!"

"It's not the number you have," Slake reprimanded, "it's your strength and your wits."

"But all I have left is nothing against something that can strip everything I own on contact!" Joni clenched her hands. "You've lost it if you think that we can defeat Bobby with just one stick!"

Slake sighed and ran a hand through his hair. "You need to trust yourself," he said evenly. "Believe that you can win this battle..."

"Bullshit malarkey!" Joni exploded.

"To think you've lost without trying is basically not trying at all and admitting defeat!"

Joni turned on her heel and stomped away. "You're just repeating yourself," she snapped, throwing up her hands in frustration.

"Maybe you'll understand!" Slake called after her.

"*Well, you're not the one that'll get your life erased if you mess up!*" Joni thought in annoyance. Approaching the main exit, she gasped when she sensed a warm tingling sensation course through her and turned around, finding Slake gone. "*It's impossible for him to be in two places at once!*" Joni backed away from the door. "*This is too freaky, even for me!*"

Searching for an alternate exit, she heard a shout and a loud crash. Racing down the corridor, Joni found Bobby exiting a classroom and immediately hid around the corner. Pressing herself against the wall, Joni watched Bobby storm past her down the hall, furious. She gasped, noticing he held the key-headed Legion.

"*He just stripped another magician!*" Joni realized in horror. "*I can't let him strip me next with Aecean!*"

Bobby came to a pause and whirled around, spotting Joni against the wall. "Hey!" he barked. "You're coming back for a piece of me?"

Joni shook her head. "I want nothing to do with you!" she retorted. "Forget it!"

"Then why aren't you back at home where you belong?"

"I can go wherever I want!"

"You must want me bad, Baby."

Joni stood her ground, glaring defiantly at Bobby rushing forward with his Legion held high. Striking down, Bobby let out a surprised yell when shocked by navy electricity and thrown back from the force.

Joni sucked in a shallow breath and stepped away in stunned silence as a tall, slender young man with short razor-cut black hair appeared out of thin air, wearing a white tailored suit with navy dress shirt and white loafers. He staggered forward, gripping his side in pain.

"Fuck..." the young man moaned and collapsed to his knees.

"Hey," Joni said tentatively and reached forward, touching him gently on the shoulder. "Are you okay?"

The young man recoiled, startled and Joni immediately pulled away. "I still have some fight left," he groaned and rose unsteadily to his feet. He turned toward Joni and Joni suddenly found her breath pulled from her body.

"Slake?" she cried. "What happened to you?"

The young man had narrow dark violet eyes and a slight array of freckles dotting his gaunt cheeks and across his sharply defined nose. The only distinctive mark he owned was a long thin scar across his nose and right cheek from the jaw line.

"Not my name," the young man said. "Are you alright?" Joni nodded, unable to answer. The stranger in white turned away and stomped up to Bobby, kicking him in the side. "Get the fuck up, man. I need to finish this."

Bobby growled and the young man dodged a mad swing from his intensely glimmering Legion as he sprang to his feet.

"I don't know who the hell you think you are," Bobby sneered, "but I'll strip you too, just like the others!"

"Keep dreaming!"

The young man whirled out of Bobby's fierce blow, delivering a cross hook across Bobby's face. The force threw Bobby back against the wall and he slumped to the floor, dazed as his glasses clattered at his feet. The stranger in white stood over Bobby with clenched hands, drawing dark violet light within them.

"You're strong..." Bobby spat blood at the stranger's feet. "I'm glad you dropped in..."

"I don't need this right now!" the young man muttered, generating a blackened long sword glowing brightly in navy light. He slammed the blade down into Bobby who quickly blocked with his Legion and pushed back, rising with an upward thrust. The stranger in white turned out of the attack and stomped down, thrusting the blade forward into Bobby, impaling him into the wall.

"Don't kill him!" Joni shrieked when Bobby hacked up blood.

"Just back off," the young man seethed as the energy from the blade surrounded Bobby's body, sending another charge through him. He withdrew the sword, forcing Bobby's slackened form falling as a crumpled heap at his feet. The Legion he held clattered from his hand, dull.

"You monster!" Joni cried as the young man sifted through Bobby's pockets and withdrew the red-tinted glasses. He placed them on his face and hoisted his sword over his shoulder, pushing past Joni.

"You're welcome," the young man in white called.

Joni shook in awe and fear, staring at Bobby's lifeless body then back at the mysterious stranger who walked away. "Wait!" she called after him.

Hurrying up to the young man, Joni grabbed his sleeve and he firmly grasped her shirtfront in return. She let out a mild cry when pushed against the wall and he leaned in, giving her a critical look.

"What do you want with me?" he sneered.

"Who are you?" Joni asked faintly.

"Why do you want to know?"

"I–!"

"I'm doing you a favor, so don't fuck things up by getting in my way!"

"I'm sorry!" The young man released his hold and Joni pushed him away. He smirked and continued the rest of the way down the hall. "Have you lost it?" Joni harped after him. "At least tell me your name!"

"If you really want to know," the young man called over his shoulder in annoyance, "then come on!"

Joni hurried to catch up as he rounded the corner and paused in step as the teacher Finnian exited a classroom, cigarette in hand. The mysterious fighter quickly dropped his blade, drawing dark energy around his body as the weapon struck the ground, sparking when it hit with a metallic clang.

"The fuck!" he squawked.

"What the hell?" Finnian snapped and gave the stranger in white a critical once-over. "I suggest you'd better get rid of that thing before it gets messy," she sneered, flicking her dead cigarette aside.

"Don't say shit to me!"

"Fine, I won't." Finnian leaned against the door, arms folded across her chest.

The young man heaved for breath and thrust out a hand, forcing the black long sword floating toward him.

"Are you really going to fight Miss Finnian?" Joni asked.

"She's not supposed to be here," the young man snarled as he caught the glowing blade and held it at ready.

"Same goes to you, Satei!" Finnian snapped. "I've got orders to send your scrawny ass back where you came from!"

"Come on!" Satei shrilled. "Show me how bad you want me gone, because I'm not going unless you're coming with me."

"Yeah?" Finnian left her place at the wall, withdrawing a silver chain from her rear pocket. "I can play that game too."

"Really, eh?" Satei changed his stance and the energy emanating from him charged the blazing long sword, turning the blackened metal into blue steel. He glanced back at Joni. "You'd better back up for this one." Satei warned and Joni stepped away, watching Satei shudder as he tightened the grip onto his sword.

"Are you shaking 'cause you're a scared little punk?" Finnian teased.

"I'm no punk," Satei replied and grinned shrewdly. "I'm actually pretty excited. Cutting your ass down is such a turn-on!"

"I'm giving you 'til the count of ten...!" Finnian's chain glowed dimly. "One..."

"You're not going through with that!"

"Two..." Finnian held the chain to her side, grinning sardonically. "Three..."

Satei charged forward and Finnian rapidly cycled through the remaining numbers then lashed the chain as it transformed into a knotted whip. Satei let out a yell and threw his blade forward as the whip struck him across the face. The glasses he wore cracked across the surface and his sword vanished as silver light flashed on impact. A sudden violent force threw Satei rearward, hurling him onto the floor. He groaned in pain, holding his head.

"Satei!" Joni cried and ran up to him. A barrier of blue light formed in the corridor, cutting her off.

"Stay back!" Satei thundered.

"You just fucking threw away the only weapon you had!" Finnian crowed, storming up to Satei. She snapped the knotted whip, striking him and heavy chains appeared, binding Satei's limbs.

"Yeah, I threw it away," Satei replied, "but that doesn't make me dumb."

"It leaves you open."

Satei's long sword reappeared, slamming into Finnian's back. She screamed in pain, staggering forward as a sudden charge zapped through her. Satei kicked her back with a swift boot to the groin, forcing her down to her knees. The chains holding him vanished and formed around Finnian, winding tight by invisible forces.

"Don't you feel great right now?" Satei asked sarcastically. "Because I sure do!"

"Once I get out of this," Finnian seethed, "I'm kicking your ass!"

"That's if you can get out of it, am I right?"

Satei rose to his feet and staggered rearwards as the barrier came down. Joni hurried to his side, grasping his arm to help keep his balance.

"Do you really want to end up back there?" Finnian exploded. "Lillian will fucking kill you for fucking around, boy!"

Satei bared his teeth, bristling. "I swear...!" he hissed.

"On what?" Finnian cackled. "Not a damn thing!"

"Burn!" Finnian wailed when the chains glowed brightly and she shuddered in pain. "You like that, huh?" Satei roared. "You want more?"

"Alright!" Finnian screeched. "Let me go this one time and we can forget about it; how's it sound, huh?"

"What about Lillian?"

Finnian struggled against her ties. "Get me out of this, you stupid fuck!" she bellowed. "Forget it!"

"I'm not helping you then." Satei grasped Joni firmly by the arm and pulled her away, storming down the corridor. "You're on your own."

"Damn it, you piece of shit," Finnian snapped as the long sword disappeared and formed in Satei's hand. He dropped it into a harness slung low around his hips. "Look," she cried, "here's a deal for you. Wanna cash in on it?"

"You really must be desperate," Satei grumbled, pausing in step.

"Listen to me, you stupid son of a bitch!" Finnian yowled.

"I don't have time for this." Violet light surrounded Satei's body and Finnian let out a distressed cry.

"Wait!" she howled. "I'll give you what you need to find those Remnants, alright?"

"What about it?" Satei snapped, turning to face her as the light faded as quickly as it developed.

"If you get me out of this, you'll get the two I have," Finnian pleaded. "I mean, how else are you gonna find the rest to keep your life intact, huh? You need something to fight with!"

Joni pulled against Satei's sleeve. "What is she talking about?" she asked.

Satei gently pushed her hand away. "Promise me *on your life* that you'll leave the girl out of this!" he growled.

"Let me out and I'll do it!" Finnian begged.

"You might be lying to me!"

"Damn it, you'd better hurry before *they* find out!" Finnian hollered. "Otherwise, you'll be the one up shit creek when those two come around!"

Satei blew an angry sigh. "How can I trust you?"

"I can't do anything to you right now, you dumb ass!"

Satei stomped up to Finnian and rammed his foot into her chest, forcing her groaning in pain. "Keep calling me names," he yelled, "and I'll crack your ribs!"

"Alright!" Finnian cried.

"Cian, Hedos, lend me your power," Satei commanded and a sleek black long-range rifle with white-gold bayonet attached to the end appeared in his hands.

"*What kind of weapon is that?*" Joni thought in shock, backing away as Satei held onto the narrow gunstock with faintly glowing hands. "*How can that be the evolved form of Hedos and Cian...?*" She gasped once a heavy arm held her back by the chest and a hand covered her mouth. Joni looked up, finding Slake holding her as he glared ahead at Satei.

"Are you alright?" Slake asked sternly and Joni nodded. "Did he hurt you?" She shook her head in response and Slake let go as Satei kicked at Finnian, screaming expletives.

"You give me what I want," Satei ordered, "or my little friends will shock you straight to Hell!" The black gun flared in bright violet light and Satei turned, baring his teeth at Slake. "What the fuck?" he said, alarmed.

"What are you doing here?" Slake demanded, pushing Joni behind him.

Satei narrowed his eyes. "You're weak," he hissed. "Cian, Hedos, get rid of him!"

Satei pulled the trigger and Joni rushed in front of Slake as a flash of indigo lightning released from the gun, striking her directly. She let out a cry and fell to her knees.

"Joni!" Slake yelped.

"I'm fine," Joni said weakly.

"She's not a part of this," Satei growled. "You're lucky she just got stunned, so you should just stay out of my way!"

"You leave her alone!" Slake bellowed and unleashed his glowing silver long sword as Joni struggled to her feet. Slake pulled her up with a firm hand then pushed her behind him, shielding her with his body.

"Do you want to die, man?" Satei exclaimed. "You're overdrawn!"

"I swore with my life to protect her!" Slake stated seriously. "If I die, then so be it!"

"Your dying isn't going to help matters, you stupid fuck!"

"Joni, get out of here! Now!"

Joni backed away and then turned around, bumping into Signe. Martel appeared at the corridor's end, armed with his oak staff.

"What are you doing here?" she cried, astonished.

"What does it matter?" Signe responded.

"Come on," Martel called. "It's too dangerous to stick around!"

"I agree," Signe murmured, taking Joni by the arm. "Let the experts handle it."

Leaving with them, Joni looked back over her shoulder at Slake glaring down Satei. She turned away, clenching her teeth as she hurried outside with her friends.

CHAPTER TWENTY-EIGHT

"*Why is that Satei guy here?*" Joni wondered as she raced for the exit. "*Why is he wearing the same outfit I saw Slake wear when he died in my vision?*"

Joni ran into another body and fell back, striking the ground. She looked up at Labraccio wearing his white coat with silver buttons and tan driving gloves standing over her. He grunted and held his side, seething in pain.

"Sorry," Labraccio muttered.

"What's the matter?" Joni asked as Martel held out a hand to Joni. She took it and he hauled her upright. "Are you fighting someone?"

"Why do you ask?" Labraccio narrowed his eyes. "Who are you running from?"

"What does it matter?" Joni snapped. "Why are you here?"

"I'm here to train your sorry butt. Don't give me attitude!"

Joni snorted. "What's with the change of heart?"

"Forget it." Labraccio turned away and waved at Joni to follow. She looked to Martel and Signe and they exchanged worried glances.

Joni shrugged and followed Labraccio outdoors with Signe and Martel in attendance. Exiting onto school grounds, they walked across the lot, approaching a large station wagon parked at the school's front lot. As they neared, muted rock music blared from inside.

Labraccio knocked on the passenger side window and the music turned down.

"It's open," a voice called from inside. "Get in."

Joni opened the door and let out a mild surprised cry when she recognized the curly sandy-haired driver wearing a heavy denim jacket and cargo pants.

"Kacey!" Joni said in astonishment. "When did you get back?"

"Not too long ago, Joan," Kacey replied, glancing back with a goofy smile. "Just finished moving stuff in Mom's house." She reached over and tousled Joni's hair. "Mom said it was okay for me to pick you up from school."

"I missed you!" Joni clamored inside and wrapped her arms around her sister's neck. "You don't know how glad I am that you're here!"

Kacey laughed and squeezed back. "Come on before you let all the heat out!"

Joni squeezed her hand, noticing a ring on her finger. She let go, looking at the silver band that had a diamond gem. "Get in, guys," Joni said and gave Kacey a firm squeeze then scoot over.

Martel opened the door and slipped into the back as Signe entered on the other side. Labraccio said nothing as he entered the front passenger.

"What a boat this is," Martel said as set his staff on the floor.

Kacey chortled and started the engine. "That's the way I like 'em," she said gaily. "Big and made of solid steel... You don't get no better than that!"

Signe snorted. "But you get horrible gas mileage in the long run!" he noted.

"That's what conversion kits are for - I'm putting batteries under the hood soon!"

"Then it'll weigh as much as a tank!" Joni protested and Kacey laughed out loud.

"Do you know Labraccio?" Signe cut in as Kacey pulled out the school lot and cruised down the road.

"Yeah, we go back some ways," Kacey answered. "Met him in school... good friends and whatever."

"Is that the same guy you talked about in your letters?" Joni pressed, looking to Labraccio who held his chin in his hand as he stared out the window at the passing scenery.

"How deep is it?" Martel asked.

"Seriously?" Kacey crowed and laughed harder. "Ya hear that, Shorty?" She gave him a friendly jab on his shoulder. "They think we're some kinda item!"

Labraccio grunted. "Spare me," he muttered.

"Then what's with the ring?" Joni prodded. "You're wearing it on your left, so did you get married or something?"

Kacey snorted. "Why bother with that?" she said. "Besides, Shorty ran off any boyfriends I tried to land."

Martel laughed as Labraccio's face lost color.

"I have nothing to do with that," Labraccio objected.

"I'm at the cottage," Joni reminded as Kacey turned off the road. "You don't have to go to Mom's."

"Are you there by yourself?" Kacey inquired.

"I can handle myself fine."

"No boyfriend or whatever?"

"Is that important?"

"This clown keeps scaring them off," Martel teased and Signe's face burned red.

"Man, so much happened since the last time I saw ya," Kacey went on. Joni showed interest, asking her questions, though her mind was preoccupied about Slake and the new stranger, especially concerning the teacher Finnian.

When they reached the cottage, Signe got out and Joni hurried past him, ascending the stoop.

"Where's the fire?" Kacey called as she stepped out the car.

"I'm expecting a phone call," Joni called.

"Without keys, you're sunk!"

"*I left my coat again!*" Joni realized and clenched her hands. "*I can't have them hear that message... I don't want them to worry!*"

"Got any food?" Kacey asked as she came up the walk with

Labraccio at her side and tossed Joni her keys. "Mom didn't feed me after I moved all that stuff."

Joni caught the ring and struggled getting the key into the lock. "I got noodles and beans probably," she answered, jimmying the handle. "I'm sure I can find something."

"Don't tell me you're a horrible cook!" Martel teased. "You'd die from starvation if the microwave was never invented, right?"

"Let's order pizza or whatever," Joni said once she got the door open. "Everyone likes pizza right?"

"I'm down for that," Signe said, grinning.

Joni scoffed and punched his shoulder while Martel laughed. "I'm surprised you didn't offer to cook," she chided and withdrew the keys, passing them to Kacey. "That's only so you can try to get in bed with me once I'm fully relaxed, right?" Signe chortled, blushing slightly. "You horn dog!"

"You said it, not me!"

Joni hurried indoors while Kacey entered after her, looking around.

"You didn't change anything," Kacey remarked, tossing her keys in her hand.

"I didn't want to," Joni replied and reached the phone behind the couch, finding it signaled a new message.

"Hey, Shorty, go on a beer run, will ya?" Kacey called as she took a spot on the couch and the others entered the parlor. "And get some coolers for the kids."

"I'm not your damn butler," Labraccio snapped.

Kacey threw him her keys, beaning him upside his head then clapped at him. "Get to it!" she barked.

Signe giggled and Labraccio grunted, scooping up the keys off the floor then stormed back outside.

Joni struck the 'erase' button, wiping out all the messages that remained, including the latest one. "What would you guys like?" she asked, picking up the receiver. "Kacey's buying obviously."

"Sausage," Signe called and Martel doubled over, howling in laughter.

After dinner over pizza and wine, Joni felt good, finding Kacey's stories about her various adventures entertaining. Labraccio rolled his eyes when Kacey pestered him for stories about their misadventures.

"I'm not telling her anything," Labraccio snapped. "That's a part of my life I'd rather not discuss."

"If I whoop you in a sparring match," Kacey threatened, "then you cough up the goods!"

"You're not stronger than me!"

"I want to see!" Joni goaded and Martel hooted at them as Kacey jumped up and hurried for the couch.

"Are you serious?" Labraccio said in annoyance while Kacey pushed the furniture against the wall and kicked back the carpet.

"Check it out, Joan," Kacey boasted. "I can beat Shorty no problem in my sleep!"

"Don't bet on it!" Labraccio spat.

"Here's Five!" Signe called and dug through his jeans pocket. He slammed the bill on the table and Joni doubled over, giggling.

"You're such a short-ass dude!" Kacey said brightly as she slipped out of her jacket and tossed it aside on the couch. "I can whoop you with my arms tied *and* hopping on one foot!"

"It doesn't necessarily take strength to defeat someone!" Labraccio protested.

"You think you have the advantage 'cause you're so tiny?" Kacey teased.

Labraccio huffed and grabbed his can of beer, downing it. "You know what they say," he warned, setting down his beer with a firm bang, "the bigger they are, the harder they fall!"

"Let's do this!"

"Yeah, Kacey," Joni cheered, "beat him down!"

"I'm betting on Kacey," Signe declared.

"Hey!" Labraccio spat, standing.

"You're only betting on Joni's sister to get on her good side," Martel teased and Signe blushed bright red.

"C'mon Shorty, let's try out your skills!" Kacey goaded as Labraccio left the table and stood at ready. "Let's see those kick-ass moves!"

"You'll regret me humiliating you," Labraccio warned.

"Stop talking Shorty, and bring it!" Kacey beckoned at Labraccio. "Come out of that coat already!"

"I feel cold."

"It ain't that cold in here!"

Labraccio blew a disgruntled sigh and peeled out of his coat, revealing his open red blazer and tight white jeans held up by navy suspenders. He tossed the coat aside on the floor as Kacey circled him, bouncing from side to side on her feet.

"He's pretty strong and fast," Joni said, "despite the stupid clothes he wears."

"I know he is, but don't worry - I'll try not to hurt him too bad."

Kacey threw a punch and Labraccio caught it with his hand. He shook slightly as Kacey struggled against his hand, then turned out, slamming his elbow into Kacey. Labraccio grasped her arms, grappling with her as they struggled for control.

Throwing Kacey over his head, Kacey landed on her back and kicked up her foot, striking Labraccio against his chest. Labraccio grunted and stumbled backwards as she jumped to her feet, dropping low for a tackle.

Labraccio stepped out of her rush, hurling a punch and Kacey swiftly turned, taking his fist and yanked him forward. She jumped on his back, wrapping her arm around his neck.

"Gotcha!" Kacey teased and tickled under his arms. Labraccio yowled and turned her over down onto the floor. Kacey locked her

arm around his leg, flipping him head over heels on his back. She turned over, straddling Labraccio's hips, grinning.

"I win!" Kacey declared, poking Labraccio's nose.

"Boo!" Joni jeered. "You lost on purpose!"

"Who knew he was ticklish?" Signe called and he and Martel convulsed in laugher.

Kacey stood, holding out a hand to Labraccio and he took it, getting pulled to his feet. She yanked him close and reached around, unsnapping his suspenders. Labraccio cried out in surprise and grasped his jeans before they fell, pulling away as Kacey held a hand to her mouth, suppressing her laughter.

"You still go commando?" she accused as Labraccio's face burned scarlet.

"I swear!" Labraccio huffed and stormed down the hall.

"On your right," Joni called and the bathroom door slammed shut moments later.

Kacey broke out laughing and Joni grinned once she returned to the dining table.

"That was so mean of you," Martel needled.

"He let me win on purpose, but whatever," Kacey said and took up her beer. "So what you got up for the rest of the day?"

"I'm thinking of visiting Ryan again," Joni replied.

"Isn't he your best friend? Doesn't he like to party or whatever?"

"He's in the hospital," Signe filled in.

"Wanna ride?" Kacey offered. "I ain't got nothin' in my schedule but sleep!"

"Are you okay to drive?" Joni asked.

"I've been nursing this one." Kacey withdrew her keys from her pocket, swinging them around on her finger. "I had to get my stuff from him somehow."

Martel snorted and broke down again.

Joni jumped to her feet. "Let's go!" she said brightly.

Once at the hospital, Joni entered Ryan's room and sat at his bedside, taking his hand. She closed her eyes, sensing warmth course through her.

"You're back again," Ryan called to her.

Joni opened her eyes, finding him sitting across from her on the bed. "Are you doing better?" she asked.

Ryan gave a sad smile. "I'll make it," he said softly.

"What's the matter?"

"Those shadows won't let up... I keep fighting, but I don't know how much longer I can hold out."

Joni paled. "Please don't tell me you're dying!" she moaned.

"I'm not!" Ryan reached forward and Joni mewed when his hands passed through her hair. "They keep wanting this ring I have..."

"What ring?"

"I don't know why they want it, because I don't have it on me. I take it off when I play."

"Do you think it's cursed or something?"

"Like demons or whatever?" Ryan scoffed. "Demons aren't real!"

"But shadows that are looking to snack on your soul are?"

Ryan smirked. "Good point."

"Where is it? Maybe I can help make them go away."

"It's at home. It looks like any other ring with a sapphire in it."

"I don't see how that could cause weird dreams."

"But that's the thing!" Ryan pulled away, then stood beside her. "Ever since I bought it, it's been nothing but freaky dreams all night, even if I haven't been wearing it!"

"Is it like the shadows trying to eat you?"

"No. Lately it's been that, but all the other times..." Ryan appeared embarrassed and turned his back to Joni. "It's always this cute red-headed girl who comes to me. She's always asking me about it, wanting me to give it to her. I tell her I can't, that it's mine, and I don't plan to give it to anyone."

"Do you think your dreams are because you're conflicted about giving it to me?"

Ryan let out a nervous laugh and ran his hands through his hair. "We're just friends, Joni!" he protested. "I never thought about us going steady or anything!" Joni clasped a hand over her mouth as her face burned bright red. Ryan turned to her and smiled brightly. "I'm sorry," he murmured, "I don't mean to..."

"No, it's okay." Joni clasped her hands around Ryan's. "Look, let me check it out for you and see if there's anything weird with it."

"It can't be any more weird than now." Ryan approached and leaned forward, smiling gently. "Promise me you won't steal my underwear as a token, okay?"

Joni gave Ryan a horrified look as he broke out grinning. "Ah, you freak!" Joni squealed and he laughed. She let go, watching him fade as his laughter rung in her ears.

Joni smiled, shaking her head and left his bedside, only to pause and frown when she faced Kipper standing at the door.

"So," he sneered, "he's got something special that he doesn't understand..." Kipper grinned, pushing his oily hair out of his eyes. "I knew if I hung around long enough, you'd lead me to it!"

"Stay out of this," Joni yelled, "and leave him alone!"

"Make me!" Kipper vanished in a puff of yellow smoke, his cackling laughter echoing in the room.

Joni raced away, rushing for the waiting area. "Come on, guys," she cried. "We need to get to the Arcendos, like right now!"

"What's going on?" Kacey protested, dropping the magazine she held.

"No time to explain... Let's hustle!" Joni barreled outdoors, hurrying for the car.

CHAPTER TWENTY-NINE

Kacey's left foot tapped nervously on the floor and her hands clutched firmly at the steering wheel while she sped through the city streets. Joni grasped Signe's hand tightly and he squeezed her hand in response.

"It'll be okay," Signe said in assurance.

"Do you think you'll have to fight?" Martel asked nervously. "We'll be there to help if you need it!"

"Thanks guys, I'll need it," Joni said gratefully, "especially since we're dealing with that crazy nutjob."

"You'll handle your business," Signe responded, "and we'll cut him down a bit."

"Why are you so bitter?" Joni asked in surprise and Signe shook his head in return, silent.

Looking out the window as Kacey pulled into the driveway of the Arcendo residence, Joni struck the door in anger when she caught sight of Kipper standing at the front door, conversing with Ryan's mother.

"Damn everything," Joni growled once Kacey parked. She pulled out of Signe's grip and bounded out the car.

"Missus Arcendo!" Joni called and hustled up the walk with Signe and Martel in close pursuit.

Ryan's mother looked up as Kipper stepped indoors and waved to Joni. "Hello!" she said brightly. "Care for some tea and cake?"

"Sure, Missus Arcendo," Joni said nervously.

"Are you here to pick up some books for Ryan as well?"

"Sure, right," Joni answered upon entry. She grasped Signe's arm, pulling him close before he went after Martel who pushed past him, taking his place in the parlor. "Entertain her," Joni said softly. "Or I won't even let you kiss me!"

Signe flushed and grinned wolfishly. "Sure thing!" he said brightly.

"I'll be back," Joni announced and waved at Martel. "Come on." Martel nodded and hurried along her side as they headed for Ryan's room.

"Where is it?" Kipper grumbled, sifting through the bureau. "I can't find it!"

"Maybe it's not meant for you!" Joni snapped at the doorway.

Kipper turned around, baring his teeth. "Get the fuck out of here!" he snapped.

"Make me, you slime!" Joni yelled back.

"Here, take this!" Martel said, palming Joni a vial full of dark brown powder.

"Shit!" Kipper growled and unleashed his black steel saber as Joni thumbed the cork, pouring the powder inside at her feet. The granules glowed brightly as it formed into a solid oak staff floating before her.

"You leave Ryan alone!" Joni demanded, taking the staff.

"Make me, you bitch!" Kipper snarled. "I'll cut you to ribbons!"

He rushed forward with a horizontal slash and Joni swiftly blocked, throwing him back. She quickly followed through with a riposte, whacking Kipper in the face with an upward thrust, before kicking him down and hooking the young man onto the staff, hurling him across the room. Kipper let out a shout as he crashed onto the bed.

"Try that again!" Joni vaunted.

"What the fuck?" Kipper screeched. "You're not that good!"

The staff pulsed brightly. "*She's good enough to fight for!*" a high shrill voice spat in return.

"Yeah, I'll make you come back," Kipper sneered, "even if I have to wear you down!" The black saber transformed into heavy dark blue broadsword, flaring in violet energy.

"*Not that again,*" Joni thought in terror. "*That's how he drained Slake!*"

"You know what I can do to you," Kipper warned as he rose to his feet, holding the broadsword at ready.

"Martel, make sure he doesn't find that ring!" Joni commanded, quickly switching her stance for the defensive.

"Right away!" Martel called and began rummaging through Ryan's articles.

"You're fighting with almost nothing!" Kipper spat. "So give up while you still have a chance!"

"I'm not backing down," Joni declared, "no matter the odds!"

"Then you'll regret it."

Kipper came at her with a forward attack and Joni blocked, struggling against his strength when he brought down the blade. The dark energy coursed through him and she shook intensely, using all her might to stave him off.

"He's too strong!" Joni realized as her arms weakened. "*Maybe I don't have what it takes...*"

The staff pulsed dimly in her hands. "*Don't doubt yourself,*" the shrill voice cried as Joni stepped back from the force, shuddering. "*When you doubt, you weaken your resolve... your true strength comes from within, no matter what you hold!*"

"She's right," Joni told herself as she took another step back. "*Dad always told me to believe in myself, no matter what I do... so if I believe I can kick this greasy blond's butt, then I will!*"

The staff's glow became brighter and Joni let out a shout, pushing Kipper back onto the bed. She rapped him over the head, knocking him dazed.

"Found it!" Martel whooped.

Joni turned to Martel and he tossed her the ring. She caught it, overwhelmed by forceful energy coursing through her body and gasped as her vision flashed, washing in gray tint inside a hollow world.

Joni dropped the staff, watching in stunned silence as her father's spirit appeared, pointing a silver revolver at Kipper's head before vanishing. Her world turned back to normal and Joni slipped the ring on her hand.

"*What's going on?*" she wondered and the ring glittered brightly as a silver revolver formed in her palm. Kipper shook his head, coming out of his stupor and Joni pointed the gun in his face.

"The fuck!" Kipper shrieked, eyes widened in fright.

"Don't make me use this!" Joni yelled.

"You don't have the guts!" Kipper pushed her hand aside and jumped to his feet. "Moon Staff," he called, "reveal to me!"

Joni pulled back the hammer with her thumb and squeezed the trigger, releasing a silver bullet. She fell back from the forceful kick and Kipper let out a cry as the bullet perforated his shoulder, throwing him down on the bed. The staff forming in his hand exploded in particles of blue light.

"I'm not letting you hurt my friends!" Joni cried as Kipper crawled back only to fall off the bed. She advanced and Kipper pointed his broadsword at her chest.

"Back off!" Kipper shouted.

"I've got five more in here!" Joni pulled the hammer again. "You must like lead for dinner!"

"It doesn't matter!"

"I don't care if you're down!" Joni fired at him again, falling against Martel who caught her from behind. Kipper screamed when she blasted into his arm and his broadsword shattered. "Don't push me!"

Kipper grasped his shoulder, stunned. "How the hell you drain me?" He staggered to his feet and reached into his jacket, pulling out the small yellow sachet. "I'm gone!"

"No, you're not!"

Joni shot three rounds, piercing his hand, chest, and leg. Kipper struck against the closet as the small bag and his leather jacket vanished. Joni pulled away from Martel, stalking toward Kipper. She held the revolver with both hands, heaving for breath.

"I have one more left in here!" Joni growled as she thumbed down the hammer for the remaining bullet. "You want to eat that too?"

"Joni, that's enough," Martel called. "He's already powered down - one more may kill him!"

Tears streamed down Joni's face. "He seriously hurt Ryan!" she wailed. "Why can't I hurt him back?"

"Then you'll be no better than he is!"

Joni kicked Kipper in the groin and he crumpled forward to his knees, groaning in pain. "You'd better be glad I'm not a badass like you think you are!" The revolver faded from her hand and the staff on the floor behind her glowed dimly in gold light.

"*Don't worry*," the shrill voice said softly. "*I would've probably done the same...*" Joni turned, watching it vanish into golden light.

"Are you alright?" Signe called from outside and entered the room moments later. "I heard you two arguing."

"It's settled now..." Joni murmured and wiped at her eyes with the back of her hands.

"Can he get up?"

"Barely," Kipper snarled. "You win for now, bitch." He struggled upright and leaned against the wall, glaring at Joni. "I don't know how long I'll be out, but once my Power comes back, I'm coming after you with no holds barred!" He shoved past them and shuffled out the room in obvious pain.

"His Magic's stripped," Signe murmured. "How did *that* happen?"

"This ring did it," Joni said softly, showing Signe. "It changed into a gun..." Signe gave a wry smile and Joni grabbed his sleeve, burying her head into his shoulder. "What am I saying?" she cried. "You don't believe me!"

"Why wouldn't I?" Signe replied and rubbed at her back.

"Because you'll think I'm crazy!"

"I'm still here, aren't I?"

Joni pulled away, sniffling. "You're just trying to entertain me!"

"Try me then." Joni explained the details and his face shadowed in worrisome concern. "That's different... why would your father show up as a spirit?"

"But I don't feel his energy or anything on it to tell me he's a ghost!" Joni complained. "I... I just don't get it!"

"Let's talk to Slake about it. He's the more knowledgeable one."

"How... How would you know?"

Signe took Joni's hand and led her back into the parlor. She frowned when she found Labraccio dressed in his white coat sitting with Kacey while she talked animatedly to Ryan's parents.

"Find the books you needed?" Missus Arcendo asked.

"Sure!" Martel said brightly, coming in with an armful of books before Joni could make up an answer.

She clenched her teeth, utterly at a loss. "We *didn't take any*," Joni thought, glancing at the titles Martel held. "*They're all classics... stuff I know Ryan could care less about!*"

"That's good," Ryan's father said warmly.

"Come on, Kacey," Joni said, feinting cheerfulness. "Let's get going before you eat all their cake." She pulled away from Signe and headed outdoors ahead of everyone else.

"Nice meeting ya," Kacey said brightly.

Joni returned to the car and slipped into the rear passenger seat, looking down at the ring she wore. "*This feels like a Legion, but also doesn't*," she mused. "*What gives?*"

"What's that you have there?" Labraccio asked once he entered the car. Joni leaned forward in her seat, showing him the enchanted jewelry and he pursed his lips, grunting. "I don't like the feel of it."

"Why is that?"

"It's got powerful Magic, much more than mine."

"Really?"

"Take it off."

Joni sat back and pulled against the ring. Her eyes widened in fright when the ring glowed in pale silver light, tightening around her finger. The ring transformed into a solid silver band with small blue stones around the circumference.

"I can't!" Joni mewed. "It's stuck!"

Signe opened the door and Joni scoot over, letting him in. "What's the matter?" he asked in concern, noticing Joni's frightened expression.

"I don't get it," Joni protested. "Ryan wore it, but it didn't do anything like this!"

"Maybe he doesn't have any Magic?" Labraccio insisted.

"He has some ability..."

"Maybe you're strong enough to wear it then?"

"Do you think it's cursed?" Joni grasped her pendant with trembling hands. "Please don't let it be cursed! I don't know how to break them!"

Labraccio shook his head. "I doubt it," he assured. "From the looks of it, it seems you're the new owner."

"What should I do?"

"Once I track down my brother, we'll figure something out."

Martel returned with his books and Joni leaned over, opening the door for him. He stepped inside and dumped the books at his feet, only to have them vanish in particles of light. In its place were several slips of paper drawn with the same cryptic symbols Joni saw in her thick black hardbound.

"What was that?" Joni asked, intrigued.

Martel grinned. "An illusion," he chirped.

Later, Kacey pulled into the cottage estate's driveway and Joni clamored over Signe to hurry out, racing indoors. Finding the door unlocked, she threw it open, catching sight of Slake standing before Satei in the parlor.

Slake clutched his profusely bleeding side, holding his dimly glowing silver long sword while Satei stood across from him, holding his blackened long sword at his side. He gripped his cut arm that bled through his hand and stained his suit.

"Slake!" Joni cried. "What are you doing?"

"Joni, get out of here!" Slake yelled. "This madman's a monster; he's going to kill you!"

"No, *you* are going to kill her!" Satei screeched. "I'm trying to *prevent* that!"

"You two need to quit!" Joni complained.

"No!"

Joni took a step inside and Satei screamed as silver electricity coursed through his body. He struck the sword into the floor, falling to his knees as he panted hard for breath, struggling to support himself with his good hand.

"What's going on?" Joni wailed, taking a fearful step away. "Slake, please don't hurt him!"

"I had nothing to do with it!" Slake protested.

"It's your fault," Satei hissed. "You've got a Force Remnant..."

"Force Remnant...?" Slake spat in disbelief. "What are you talking about?"

"A different type of spirit weapon similar to the Legions supposedly formed of pure element," Labraccio answered from behind.

Joni stepped aside as he entered the house. "I thought there was only one kind of spirit weapon," she argued.

"Hey, wait up!" Kacey called and entered with Martel and Signe. Satei howled in anguish as silver lightning charged through his body again.

"I'm sorry!" Joni cried and rushed up to his side.

"Stand back!" Satei yelled and a sphere of blue light surrounded his body.

Joni dropped to her knees beside him. "Please let me help you," she pleaded. "I don't want you to die!"

"I think there's another one of those Force Remnants nearby…" Labraccio murmured, unsheathing his silver long sword.

"Where is it coming from?" Slake demanded as his sword flared in golden light.

"I sense it from three different sources…" Satei moaned. "In the back somewhere is the strongest."

"Same here," Labraccio grumbled.

"Hey, Shorty," Kacey said, grabbing onto Labraccio's arm as her silver ring glittered brightly. "This ring's shining like crazy!"

Labraccio pushed Kacey away as an elegant saber formed in her hand with a gilded roped hand guard and ivies etched onto the flat of the blade.

"Don't touch me!" Labraccio cried, pointing his long sword at Kacey.

Kacey put up her hands and stepped away, stunned. "Hey man," she protested, "I didn't call it!"

"Why did it appear?" Joni asked nervously.

"I seriously don't know!"

Kacey dropped the saber and Joni gasped as her vision flashed in gray once again. She watched the wounded spirit of her father Terrell appear in a bloodstained suit, leaning against his silver saber. He struggled to stand, only to collapse forward on his knees. Slicing his wrist with the blade, Terrell vanished and Joni's vision returned to normal.

"Did you see that?" Joni cried, putting a hand to her mouth in shock.

"See what?" Kacey asked, raising an eyebrow. "What's your deal?"

"I saw Dad cut himself on that thing!"

"Yeah right, Joan!"

"I don't understand... He was hurt, yet he cut himself with it!" Joni clenched her hands. "It's the same as I saw him use the Magic Gun my ring came with that stripped Kipper!"

"You're talking crazy, Joan."

Joni crouched down before the glowing saber. "It suddenly appeared for some reason." She grasped Kacey's hand and the ring around her hand also brightened. "They're similar in design - I think they're the same origin!"

"So what?" Kacey complained, shaking out of Joni's grip. "That's not explaining why that thing showed up!"

Joni picked up the sword and pointed it in Labraccio's direction. The sword flared brightly and he backed away.

"Hey," Labraccio squawked, "don't point that at me!"

"I'm testing a theory," Joni said, pointing the saber at Slake, then to Kacey. The blade's light grew faint in response.

"Hey man, you're creeping me out," Kacey complained. "What are you thinking?"

"I'm thinking it appeared because Labraccio's hurt," Joni said and turned the sword around, handing it to her sister by the handle. "Kacey, cut him," she ordered.

"Are you nuts?" Kacey cried.

"I mean it; cut him with it!"

"Why?"

"Yes, why?" Labraccio demanded.

"I think that thing heals!"

"Yeah, right!" Kacey complained.

"Try it!" Joni insisted. "You don't have to carve him a new one, Kacey. Just cut him a little!"

"Ugh, this grosses me out big time..."

Kacey quickly made a small jab, piercing Labraccio in the shoulder. He staggered back, stunned as bright white light surrounded his body. After the light vanished, the sword he held cackled in bright gold energy.

"Amazing..." Labraccio said in awe. "I don't believe it... you were right!"

"That's too far out!" Kacey said, dumbfounded as she stared down at the blade in admiration.

Labraccio turned around as the energy increased around his sword. "Kacey, heal my brother and that new guy," he ordered. "Come on, Joni."

"What are you planning?" Joni asked as Labraccio stormed for the rear entrance, leading out the back door. She looked to Slake and he shook his head.

"I'll catch up," he murmured.

"Please hurry," Joni pleaded. "This is getting to be too much."

Slake nodded and Joni clamored away, following Labraccio outside into the woods.

CHAPTER THIRTY

Joni met Labraccio on the back porch where he paced in agitation.

"I still sense that other Force Remnant," he responded.

"Then what are you going to do about it?" Joni asked.

"What else?" Labraccio twirled his sword in his hand. "Try to find it..."

"Do you think that's the reason why Bobby and Kipper have been bothering me?"

"It could be..."

Labraccio stiffened and whirled around, then sprinted off into the woods.

"Wait!" Joni cried and raced after him. She ignored the branches tearing at her sweater as she doggedly pursued him, trying to keep his pace.

Going deeper into the forested area, Labraccio's silver long sword's energy increased, sparking wildly. Slake appeared by Joni's side as Labraccio came to a sudden stop. Joni coughed and put her hands on her knees, huffing and wheezing for breath. Suddenly, the black wand with the violet orb formed before Joni without calling, pulsing brightly.

"Hedos! Cian!" Joni said, surprised. "You're back... But why? I thought you were stripped!"

The golden broadsword appeared in Slake's free hand, just as the lightning short sword formed in Labraccio's, also glowing intensely.

"They're freaking out," Labraccio murmured. "This Magic is too strong..."

"I can't sense this Magic you say is here," Joni said worriedly and grasped the bladed scepter. A caustic charge coursed through her hands, traveling up her arms. "I've never been in this area before."

Labraccio pointed the flaring short sword ahead. "There," he called, "straight on." He raced off into a sprint, then vanished in a flash of light.

Slake took Joni's arm and her world abruptly washed out in white. Reappearing at a base of a large mound surrounded by roots and rocks, at the top was a towering willow tree with light green leaves.

"Are we still on earth?" Joni said in shock as she looked up in awe. "That huge tree is so old!"

"About five-hundred years, you think?" Labraccio replied as he came around, circling the base.

"But the leaves!" Joni contested. "They're the only ones still green out here - they should've changed or at least fallen off by now like the others!"

"It's possibly enchanted," Slake demurred.

"If so," Labraccio remarked, "then it's hidden here."

"Cian, Hedos, find that Force Remnant for me!" Joni ordered and raised the staff. A spark of violet light zapped from the orb, striking the trunk. A dim red glow surrounded the plant as part of the wood splinted slightly.

"It *is* hidden in there!" Labraccio confirmed. "See if you can capture it."

"Capture?" Joni blustered. "How do I do that?"

"The sealing spell varies from person to person," Slake explained. "The one Terrell Warren used is the one we have on record: *'return to the form you were bound to occupy'*."

"I'll try it." Joni recited the spell and thrust forward the staff, throwing another lightning attack at the tree. The ruby glow brightened and the tree's pale green leaves darkened.

"She's not strong enough..."

"Here," Labraccio said, tossing her the electric short sword.

"Combine Contis and Liang with them!"

"What for?" Joni probed, catching it.

"To enhance Hedos and Cian's lightning ability!"

"That's right!" Joni looked down at both glowing weapons. "Ready guys?" The two weapons pulsed dimly. "Liang, Contis, Hedos and Cian, evolve and get that Remnant!"

The two combined weapons vanished in separate orbs of light, changing from blue and violet. The lights merged, reforming as an indigo wand with a clear base. Joni struck the tree with the staff, unleashing a chain of cyan lightning. The dark red light around the tree darkened almost to black.

"I think it's weakening..." Labraccio murmured.

"Add Lysisner to them," Slake suggested, handing her the golden broadsword. "It might break the spell once and for all!"

"Lysisner," Joni said, "evolve with the others, okay?"

The broadsword pulsed frantically and vanished into yellow light as the indigo staff disappeared. The two orbs combined, returning as the indigo staff once more, with a topaz crystal on the head. Joni struck the tree, unleashing a blast of golden lightning. The charge released a pulsing wave of force, hurling everyone onto the ground.

"Damn it," Labraccio moaned as he staggered to his feet and unleashed his gray wings.

"Why isn't this working?" Joni groaned, sitting up.

Slake stood and lent Joni a hand, pulling her upright. "I'm not sure," he answered.

Labraccio hovered near the tree, watching it tremble as the black light sparked around its core.

"Tiranus, help Joni," Labraccio called and the gloves left his hands, forming as a brown sphere near Joni.

Joni touched the light with the wand's orb and her weapon glowed brightly, reforming with a golden claw encasing the topaz gem. The bladed scepter shone brilliantly in white light and Slake nodded to

Labraccio, holding his long sword at ready. Labraccio did the same.

"Joni, we're going to weaken it," Slake warned. "So try the sealing spell again."

They both slashed at the tree, unleashing a blast of light forming a cross cut through it. The tree blackened and its leaves wilted as deep cracks appeared in rivulets across its trunk. Black sap seeped out the deep crevices, pooling down the sides.

"Now!" Labraccio shouted.

"Return to the form you were bound to occupy!" Joni shouted and jerked the staff forward as Slake and Labraccio followed through with another attack.

The weapon Joni held let loose a bright gold volt, striking the base and blasted away the rocks the roots gnarled around its center. The tree shook violently and the willow's long hanging branches animated, changing into vines that stretched and whipped forward.

Labraccio swooped out the way, slashing the vegetation coming at him, while Slake jumped and turned away, hacking the plants going for his limbs.

Joni screamed when a vine grasped itself around her ankle and threw her in the air, swinging wildly.

"Joni!" Slake wailed as more vines surged forward, tying her down. Joni struck the leaves, shocking them and scorching them black, only to have more dark green vines appear and tie her down, taking hold of her legs and feet.

"It's not working!" Joni wailed.

"The lightning's being diffused," Labraccio yelled, chopping at vines spiraling near him while Slake continued darting away, avoiding contact with the possessed weed. "It's only making it stronger!"

"But Wood absorbs Lightning!" Slake shouted.

"Switch hands!"

Joni did as told then gave the tightening plants another whack with the indigo scepter. The released bolt immediately sparked and died out on contact. She let out a horrified cry as the vines wrapped around the staff and crept up around her arm and hand.

"Do something!" Joni cried.

"It senses the water ring!" Labraccio said in horror. "Give me the Legionnaire!" Joni ripped the scepter free and tossed it down to Labraccio who caught it. "Disengage!" All the spirit weapons separated, falling to the ground.

"It's trying to kill me," Joni yowled as the tangled mass of leaves and branches curled tighter around her chest and neck, threatening to choke out her breath.

"Voldec, Hedos, Tiranus, Lysisner, Liang!" Labraccio called, "evolve and subdue this Remnant!"

The flaring copper fan, the red scepter, the tan enchanted gloves, the golden broadsword and the blue electric saber disappeared into various orbs of light, coming together and formed a pair of large green punching daggers.

Labraccio sheathed his long sword over his back, making it disappear and put forward his hands as the punching daggers floated over to him. Latching onto his hands, the blades blazed in golden flame.

Joni wailed in fear, weakening from the crushing force threatening to steal away her life. Labraccio raced forward, striking the tree with a combination of vicious lashes, blackening its leaves and vines with each successful hit.

Fire surged through the greenery, burning their hold on Joni and her breath slowly came back as she pulled free. The vines weighing down Joni turned brittle and shattered, releasing her body.

Joni screamed as she fell and Slake easily caught her before she struck the ground. He gently set her down and Joni let out a horrified cry when the vines battered Labraccio as he twisted and turned from the leaves, only to get surrounded by wooden spikes thrusting from the ground, impaling him.

"Labraccio!" Joni screeched when he fell forward and a mass of heavy thorny roots enveloped his body, shredding his wings. Slake grabbed Joni's arm, pulling her away as the tree's monstrous leaves grew, winding around his body.

"Wood Force Remnant," Labraccio's voice faintly called, "return to your place restrained!"

A blast of crimson flame erupted from the center and the plant exploded, raining white ash around them as Labraccio fell to his knees, gasping for breath.

"*He's not bleeding!*" Joni thought in astonishment as a copper ring with emerald stones set around the circumference floated before Labraccio. "*But that coat he always wears... Why didn't it protect him?*"

"That was tough," Labraccio wheezed as the white coat and flaming punching daggers faded. He reached out, taking the ring and the other remaining weapons scattered on the ground vanished in a flash of red light.

"Brother!" Slake wailed as Labraccio fell forward unconscious onto the cold ground. He let Joni go, running up to Labraccio's side, alarmed when dark violet blood pooled beneath his weakened body and stained the earth underneath him.

"How could he get hurt?" Joni cried. "Was the coat too weak?"

"Sykalias only protects from *physical* attacks," Slake explained and Joni gasped in horror.

"He used up all his strength," she moaned, "just to take in all that punishment!" Tears ran down her face. "Please don't die. I can't handle it if someone else dies..."

Hearing footsteps fast approaching, Joni whirled around, shaking in distress.

"Joan!" Kacey's voice called. "Hey!"

"Joni!" Signe's voice shouted. "Where are you?"

"Over here!" Joni called back.

Satei appeared hacking through the thicket's overgrowth of limbs and dead vegetation with his sword, accompanied by Kacey. Bringing up the rear was Signe, armed with the sharpened oversized ring and his brother Martel, armed with his staff.

Joni ran over to Kacey and hugged her sister firmly, breaking down in choking sobs.

"Asking you if you're okay is a stupid question," Kacey murmured, embracing her sister tightly.

"We couldn't get through," Martel said as he leaned against his oak staff for support.

"A really strong barrier came up," Signe explained. "Nothing we did could break it."

Joni pulled away once her pained crying ceased and she wiped at her eyes with the back of her hands. "I'm sorry," she muttered.

"It's fine, Joan," Kacey said warmly.

"Who do you think made that barrier? I thought any spell could be broken."

"The original creator of that Force Remnant made it," Satei grumbled. "The power behind it... It's pure evil."

Slake immediately rose to his feet, pointing his cackling blade in his direction. "You caused this!" he screeched.

"No, I didn't!" Satei shouted back, glaring at Slake.

"You monster, if you hadn't come here...!"

"Do you really want to die?" Navy energy drew around Satei's blade. "I can make you disappear for good!"

"Please!" Joni cried and ran over to Satei, pulling against his sleeve. "That's enough! Kacey might be able to revive him, remember?"

"That's right!" Kacey said and approached Labraccio's burned and mutilated body as the silver saber appeared in her hand. "Yo, Shorty," she called, poking his side. "Wake up, man!"

A brilliant charge surged through Labraccio and he stirred, groaning. His eyes snapped open and he looked up at Kacey standing over him.

"What are you doing here?" Labraccio mumbled.

Kacey grinned. "Welcome back."

"You'd better not be here once I return!" Slake sneered and vanished in gold light.

Joni backed away from Satei as he shook in rage. He let out a roar and bashed his flaring dark sword into the ground. She hurried over to Signe and he draped an arm around her waist, pulling her close to him.

"What's going on?" Joni whimpered.

"I'm not sure," Signe murmured. "Your guess is as good as mine."

Labraccio sat up and ran his hands through his hair, appearing slightly vexed.

"So, will you explain something for me?" Joni called to him.

"What is it?" Labraccio called back.

"Why'd you fight that Force Remnant when Martel simply gave me the other one?"

"Really?" Labraccio waved at Joni to come over.

Joni peeled away from Signe's hold and approached, holding out her hand for him to examine the ring.

"It's true," Martel filled in. "It was in her friend's room."

"How did you get this?" Labraccio demanded.

"Ryan said some cute redheaded girl gave it to him in a dream," Joni answered and Satei growled, shaking in fury. "What's wrong...?"

"Never mind," Satei hissed and vanished in black light.

"Something's not quite right here..." Labraccio said curtly, gently pushing Joni aside as he rose to his feet.

"What do you mean?" Joni asked nervously.

"I'll have to ask Slake." Labraccio also vanished and Kacey shrugged her shoulders.

"Don't know what to tell ya," she murmured.

"I guess we should get back," Joni said and approached Signe. "Any idea where my house might be?"

Signe grinned. "What makes you think I can find it from here?" he gently teased.

"Because the way you like to stalk me, I figured you might have a clue!"

Signe chortled and Martel frowned, looking into the distance. He grabbed Signe's sleeve, tugging against him.

"What the matter?" Signe asked, raising an eyebrow.

"There's another one..." Martel said softly.

"There's no use getting it now," Slake's voice declared as he reappeared next to Joni. "It's much stronger than the one we just fought." He sheathed his silver sword and started walking ahead. "Come with me, Joni. Your training starts now."

"What kind of training?" Joni asked apprehensively and left Signe's side, hurrying to catch up. Kacey, Martel, and Signe came along, matching the man's strides.

"It's getting much more serious than we thought..."

Returning to the cottage, Joni found Labraccio standing at the house's rear, surrounded by a large circle of blue light. Floating before him were the combined form of Cian and Hedos.

"Labraccio," Joni said anxiously, "what's this all about?"

"I think an ordination is called for," Labraccio answered. "Since you're a hot property at the moment and somehow you're tied to these Force Remnants, it'll be only a matter of time before someone of greater power will appear to challenge you."

"I don't need this!"

"Joni, step forward," Labraccio ordered.

"Why me?" Joni complained, standing her ground. "Why not anyone else? I didn't ask for this!"

"It's because your father left you the weapons and the Legionnaire themselves made a conscious decision to fight for you," Slake explained. The glowing dark violet scepter dimmed slightly in response. "You have the power within you to use them effectively."

"But Kipper had Hedos and Cian!"

"His hold on them's too weak now to be much influence," Labraccio said.

"I guess so, being shot to pieces," Martel piped and Signe guffawed.

Labraccio shot them a dirty look, then turned his attention to Joni. "Take the staff," he commanded.

"What if I don't?" Joni protested.

"Then you're dead!"

Joni swallowed hard and reluctantly did as told. She reached out, releasing a bolt of lightning once she touched the wand. Violet flames flared from the blue circle of light, changing to white as the circle turned gold. The staff transformed colors, becoming white-gold with a clear crystal orb on top, a golden blade on the bottom and a brass handle in the center, losing its previous violet body with black orb, dark blue blade, and indigo handle.

"Now," Labraccio announced as the flames died and the circle of light vanished, "you are the new ordained master."

"I am the new ordained master," Joni murmured, holding the newly evolved Legion close. "That was simple enough."

"Hey, we don't have time for long, drawn out rituals anyway," Labraccio said in annoyance. "Ever heard of *kotodama*?"

"Koto-what?" The orb pulsed wildly in gold light and Joni cracked a smile. "Thanks for cheering for me, I guess..."

" *We have a lot to look ahead for,*" said the calm, cool voice.

" *This is only the beginning,*" replied the harsh voice.

"*The beginning for what exactly...?*" Joni wondered and blew a distressed sigh when she received no reply.

"Now, Joni, get ready to leave your old life behind," Labraccio asserted. "You're going to train until you feel like dying. You're going to sleep, eat, breathe, and dream about nothing but Magic." He pointed his thumb in her direction. "I'll train you so hard that you'll puke your guts and *like* it!"

"What the hell?" Joni squawked.

"You will start tomorrow night. Prepare for then." Labraccio vanished in silver light and Joni stood there, dumbfounded.

"Don't worry, Joni," Signe said gently. "I'll be here to support you."

"And revive me when that nut job kills me!"

Signe chortled. "That too."

Joni groaned and stomped back indoors.

CONTINUED IN VOLUME 2:

DETERMINATION

Joni Warren has skills few other 17-year-olds have: she can cast simple spells, heal minor injuries and see (somewhat) into the future.

When a mysterious fighter from another realm arrives in town, he also brings a dire warning: *the impulsive use of magic can lead to corruption and break the rules of existence.*

In order to protect her friends from attacks by sorcerer assassins, summoned demons, and dimensional battle mages fighting for powerful mystic artifacts, Joni must use her supernatural powers at her command and risk her life training with spirit weapons called Remnants.

Unwilling to accept the threat of death, mastering dangerous magic may cost more than she ever imagined... Will Joni have enough power to prove herself as a magician and combat life-stealing dark forces?